OUT OF MY HEAD

THE SAGE CREEK SERIES - BOOK TWO

DILLON BANCROFT

This book is a work of fiction. Names, characters, businesses, organizations, places, events, and incidents either are the product of the author's imagination or are used fictitiously. Any resemblance to actual persons, living or dead, events, or locales, is entirely coincidental.

For information, contact:

Dillon Bancroft

PO Box 1181

Wimauma, FL 33598

http://www.dillonbancroft.com

Book and cover design by © The Pretty Little Design Co.

Editing by: Kimberly Steinke, Parker Mayne Editorial.

Ebook ISBN: 978-1-7369012-4-3

Paperback ISBN: 978-1-7369012-5-0

First Edition: June 2022

10 9 8 7 6 5 4 3 2 1

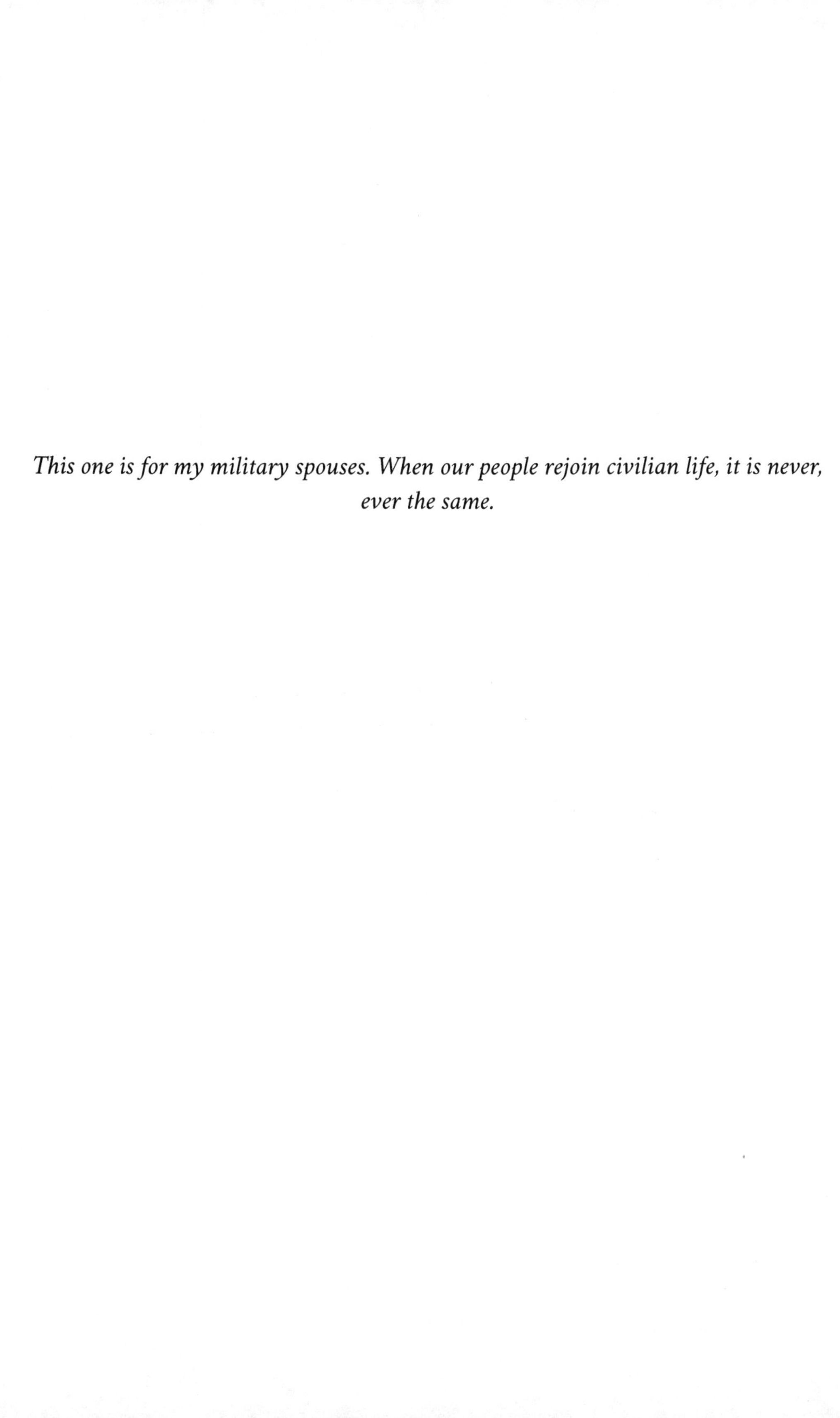

This one is for my military spouses. When our people rejoin civilian life, it is never, ever the same.

LOOKING TO CONNECT?

Do you want to stay in the know and receive behind the scenes musings, deleted scenes, and upcoming project updates? Signing up for my newsletter is the best way to do that!

Email: dillon@dillonbancroft.com

Social Media Profiles: https://linktr.ee/dillon.bancroft

Website: www.dillonbancroft.com

Bancroft Boulevard Facebook Group: https://www.facebook.com/groups/bancroftblvd

TRIGGER WARNINGS

Out of My Head is a military romance. It follows Jay Parker, a former victim of domestic abuse, who suffers major PTSD from both the horrors of his childhood and the gut-wrenching reality he witnessed from his time overseas.

This story contains graphic violence, domestic violence, explicit sexual scenes, and other mature situations. For a more detailed list of triggers, please visit www.dillonbancroft.com/oomh-trigger-warnings

If any of these situations trigger you, I urge you not to read this book.

Out of My Head is a standalone. Reading Book One of the Sage Creek Series, Make Me Dream, will only enhance your reading experience. There will be plot points and side stories that are not immediately resolved—that run through the entire series. As this is PART ONE of the Jay and Annie Duet, **please be advised that this story ends on a cliffhanger.**

I truly hope you fall in love with Jay and Annie as much as I have!

1

JAY

The whistle of a mortar has us ducking for cover. Graves shouts for everyone to find cover while the insurgents throw one more. As soon as the explosion hits, we're out of our spots and moving in on the targets.

"Suppressing fire!" I shout.

The fight goes on for what seems like hours. There are people cowering in buildings that house insurgents who fire at us ruthlessly. The innocents become casualties, but not on purpose.

A child wanders out to the middle of the dirt street, tears streaming down his face. He doesn't want to do this, but he doesn't have a choice. The bomb is strapped to his chest as he cries for his mother.

My heart leaps into my throat. There's no hope. There's no chance of us approaching and disarming the bomb without one of us getting hit. Much to my horror, Jones approaches the little boy.

"Jones! Do not engage!" My voice is hoarse from shouting orders for the last hour. He's only a corporal. He knows better.

His eyes find me. I'm standing in the open, a prime target for anyone watching. He's like a son to me. His sad eyes narrow, as if to tell me he has this under control.

"Jones!" I shout again.

He shakes his head and crouches beside the little boy, fiddling with the wires.

"Jones! If you don't remove yourself right fucking now, I will have you court-martialed!"

It doesn't matter.

The second he touches the wires, the bomb detonates.

I AWAKE WITH A JOLT.

Fuck!

I'm no longer in Afghanistan. This happened years ago, but it's always *right there.* Jones saw a child in distress and felt compelled to help. It's what any good person would do. I gave him a direct order to not engage. Instead, he left us all behind. We're all still angry at him. So is his wife, who was eight months pregnant at the time and ready to pop any second.

Raking a hand through my short, sweaty hair, I gasp for air. *You're in North Carolina. You go home today for good. Get a grip!*

I'm drenched in sweat, but I don't have time to be hung up on this. My flight leaves in five hours, and it'll take me one hour to get to the airport. Time be damned. I'm taking my last run at Camp Lejeune. This will be the last time my shoes slap the pavement here. It'll be the last time I take in the scenery. Only this time, I won't have to worry about when they'll next ship me off to protect the country I serve.

My time in the Marine Corps is up.

I stretch, pull on my PT shorts, and lace up the same ratty tennis shoes I've had since boot camp.

When I step outside, I'm greeted by darkness. At just four o'clock in the morning, the sun hasn't yet risen above the horizon. But I know I won't be alone. It's our ritual. Every morning, we're up at the ass crack of dawn, treating our bodies like a temple. I trot down the stairs from the barracks and stretch in the grass before I embark on my last hurrah. I jog out of the parking lot and start down C Street.

Jones is still on my mind, but it doesn't take long for a certain blonde to push him out of the way.

Annabelle Martha McKenzie.

The love of my life.

The woman I've loved since I was an asshole teenager.

Her bluebell-colored eyes emblazon themselves on my brain. It's much more peaceful when I can focus on her rather than how I'm out of breath.

God, I've fucking won the jackpot.

And today, I go home to her. I get to hold her in my arms, kiss her pillowy, pink lips, and claim every inch of her like it's our first time.

That is, if her younger sister, Aria, hasn't told the whole world about us yet.

My legs stretch with each lunge. Every stride is one stride closer to her. One stride closer to inhaling her floral scent and tasting her sweet lips.

Shoes thunder behind me. It doesn't take long for my whole unit to rally behind me. Their eyes are ahead of them, focusing on the run. Graves briefly glances at me and smirks. He *thinks* I'm regretting this choice already.

We run all over the place. We run past the Post Exchange and Commissary, past the seven-day store, and down a side street for my last gander at Servemart.

I'm going to miss the fuck out of Camp Lejeune. But in order for me to live life *properly,* I have to leave. The USMC has been my home for the last thirteen and a half years. They've stripped the asshole teenager away from me and made me into a man—one that clings to honor, integrity, and justice. I've been made into a perfect man who is worthy of a woman like Annabelle.

When we eventually circle back to the barracks, we stretch out in the grass as we catch our breath.

"Nervous?" Graves asks with a smile.

"You know how they say they teach you how to be a marine, but they don't teach you how to become a civilian again?"

Graves nods. "You afraid of getting lost?"

"I know who I am, buddy. The Marine Corps didn't completely strip me of everything."

With his hands on his hips, Graves summons a deep breath and exhales slowly, deep in thought. "Don't get cocky, Gunny. The world isn't the same as you knew it."

I chuckle and shrug. "You don't think I can hack it?"

He grimaces. "I'm not about to shit on your parade, Parker. But I'm happy for you. And for Annie too. You deserve a good life away from this bullshit. Away from Jones, for once."

There's a sharp pain in my stomach at the mention of his name. "That doesn't bother me anymore."

He gives me that "Yeah, sure" look and rolls his eyes. "You're not foolin' me, buddy. But the sentiment remains. Any idea what you're going to do yet?"

"I have an interview set up with Sage Creek PD next Monday. So that should be a good way to reacclimate to being a civilian again."

Graves stretches out his thighs. "Not a college boy, huh?"

I chuckle. "It's not for me. It's for assholes like you who think they know everything."

"Don't tempt me with a good time. Anyway, I think your movers are here." He points behind me to the U-Haul pulling up into the parking lot. A smile spreads across my lips. They're here, and I get to go *home.*

"You're still good to take me to the airport?" I ask.

He nods once. "Let me shower first. Then I'll help you get the rest of your shit, and we can start heading to Wilmington."

I nod in acknowledgment and give him a two-finger salute.

"Gunny!"

I stop in my tracks and wait for Sergeant Smith to catch up. "What's up, Smith?"

"I know you don't like the mushy shit, but we all chipped in." He hands me a yellow envelope with my name sloppily written across the front. "Look, man. For some of us, you were our first taste in leadership. For the rest of us who have dealt with other NCOs, you're the greatest we've ever had." It was a great day when I became an NCO, or noncommissioned officer. I wanted to be someone my guys could look up to.

I slide my pinky through the opening and open the envelope to find fifteen hundred dollars neatly stacked in a card they all signed. I refuse to cry like a little bitch, especially in front of all of them. But they each wrote something under their names. *Fuckers!*

"Thank you."

Smith gently smiles, something that isn't like him since he's always so serious.

"You're a great marine, Smith. Don't think I haven't seen how much effort you put into the guys below you. They look up to you too. You're gonna go places. I have no doubt about that."

Of course, this exchange turns into a swarm of my juniors wishing me well. Part of me wonders if I'm making a mistake by leaving, not when all of these . . . *kids* are looking up to me.

Shaking the thought, I say my final goodbyes and race upstairs. I take my final shower and collect the rest of my stuff. Graves comes back and helps me move my footlocker down to the U-Haul along with the other shit I've picked up along the way.

When he's downstairs, I open the drawer of my nightstand and pick up the thick stack of letters from my best gal. She's written to me every single day of my deployment. A letter postmarked for today lies unopened on top of the stack. I place the stack in my lap and open this new unread letter, terrified of what it could say.

GOOD MORNING, handsome,

COULD I have written this in a text message? You bet your ass I could've. But I feel like special occasions deserve a full-blown letter. This is probably the most special occasion, don't you think?

I'm so proud of you, Jay. You're a good man. I know this transition won't be easy. Things have changed here, especially now that Aria is getting married. But I want you to know, when it comes to me, I'm still Annabelle. Your Annabelle. I'll be with you through all of it—because that's what we promised each other, right?

I hope you're excited about coming home. Because having you home under my nose, where I can hug you any time I want, makes me feel safe. It's been so long since the last time you were here. I want the world to know you're my everything.

You're so loved, Jacob. I want you to know that. I wish I could be there to help you through this, but I know you needed your moment to say goodbye.

Just know I'll see you soon.

And if you're dreading this, or wondering if you're making a mistake, I promise you you're not. We'll get to spend our whole life together. Out loud. In the open. What's better than that?

I'll see you soon.

I love you so much.

Annabelle

My stomach plummets at the thought of telling her father. He's the only real father figure I've ever known, and when he finds out about the relationship we've kept under wraps for the last two and a half years, I'm afraid of what the consequences might be. But her words bring a smile to my face. She's the calm in the storm. She's the rock garden in a therapist's office.

"Dude! Move your ass! I'm not your little bitch, you know!" Graves snaps when he walks back inside.

Chuckling, I fold up her letter and stuff it into my pocket. "I outrank you, motherfucker," I quip.

He grumbles as we take the last of my crates downstairs.

It's time to say goodbye to the life I once knew to start the life I always wanted: a life with a McKenzie by my side—with *Annabelle* McKenzie by my side.

2

ANNIE

The ceiling looks so menacing in the dark.

It's like a smooth, black sea of nothingness. It's oddly soothing. Especially since I've been staring at it for the last eight hours.

Lavender oil in my diffuser didn't do anything for me. Neither did a hot bath or melatonin gummies.

Jay is coming home.

In a matter of hours, the home we've secretly shared for the last two and a half years will be full again. No more sneaking in at two o'clock in the morning to throw the family off or waking up at four for him to scurry back to my brother's house, acting like he's been there the whole time. His military memorabilia will dec the walls. He'll cook in my kitchen because he's the only one skilled to. We'll have wild, animalistic sex on every surface of the dwelling because we won't be hiding anymore.

My smile can't be fought.

I'm anticipating a bit of resistance when we tell my family later today. They'll butt in where they're not welcome. They'll try to tell me that he might not be blood, but he's still my brother.

But he wasn't a brother to me.

Not when I was four and he was seven.

Not when I was ten and he was thirteen.

Not even when I was fifteen and he was eighteen.

He has always been the boy holding my heart in the palm of his hands, even when he didn't want to. You don't get to choose *who* you fall in love with. It's written in the stars by fate. We learned that the hard way.

Needless to say, it took a lot of coaxing. Jay has always been the one who's refused to become his father. With that came this uncanny and unrealistic responsibility that automatically took me out of the running for him to ever pursue me.

Fortunately for him, I'm not a quitter.

Perhaps our destiny is written the stars. The universe. Some pyramid walls in the middle of Egypt or something. Or maybe, it's because our hearts have been intertwined for lifetimes. Contrary to my momma's belief, I don't believe in God. But I *do* believe in destiny.

When the alarm shrieks into the darkness, I bound out of bed, determined to get the day rolling. It's four thirty in the morning. I have four barns of horses to feed, not to mention the other twenty or so living in the pastures.

I wore my barn clothes to bed, eager to get up and get going so I can lock eyes with the guy who stole my heart for the first time since the Marine Corps scooped him up. I carelessly throw my hair into a messy bun and a hoodie over my head so I don't have to bother with putting on a bra. I grab a Nutri-Grain bar on my way out the door, only to find my little sister, Aria, emerging from her house with her fiancé in tow.

The couple has me smiling despite my jitters. I catch up with them and get an amused smile from Derek. His dark hair is still messy, as if he didn't comb it and rolled right out of bed.

Aria, on the other hand, looks like she's been awake for two weeks straight. Her hazel eyes are heavy with sleep. She leans into Derek as they walk, and he practically drags her along for a few extra minutes of shut-eye, not that it will help. She yawns obnoxiously with her mouth wide open, giving the nearby flies a place to land.

"Good morning, Peanut," I greet happily.

"It's not a good morning, so I'd appreciate it if you kept your cheerfulness to a minimum."

Derek chuckles. "Don't mind her. Troy has had a sleep regression the last few nights and hasn't been kind to Aria."

Aria grimaces. Her son, Troy, the eight-month butterball I love so much, has been an easy baby for the most part. Of course, we always thought the traits of his father would come to bite us in the ass at some point. As it turns out, Charlie, Aria's baby daddy, didn't like to sleep. No, he'd use the wee hours of the morning to torture my sister and make her pray for death. Unlike his biological father, Troy likes to use the wee hours of the morning for the sole purpose of disrupting a quiet house because he enjoys the sound of his own voice.

"Aw, I'm sorry. I could keep him for a night if you want some uninterrupted sleep . . ."

Aria snorts. "Fat chance. Jay's coming home in, like, eight hours, and I fully expect the entire neighborhood to hear your . . . excitement."

I roll my eyes at her loaded statement. She's the only one besides Jay's mother who knows we're together. And now I suppose Derek does too, but I'm not too worried about them blabbing.

"Fine. Keep your insomniac baby. I'll just enjoy the sex."

Derek barks out a laugh when Aria groans.

"Keep it to yourself. That's my extra brother, and I don't want to hear about it."

I gently pull her into a side hug and breathe in her coconut scent.

She's been home a year. But I will *never* take advantage of her presence ever again. Those two years of her being locked away with a madman were the loneliest two years I ever encountered. I'm grateful she found Derek and that he loved her despite her being pregnant with another man's baby.

"What time does his plane land?" Derek asks genuinely.

"Noon. So we should probably leave here around ten thirty," I say, letting go of my sister.

My eyes are heavy, and the dryness stings. I'm operating on adrenaline and zero sleep. Luckily, it's nothing a little makeup and color-correcting concealer can't fix. And coffee. *All* the coffee.

Like most mornings, our older brother, Chris, is the first one in the barns. For a guy who claims he doesn't want to take on the farming mantle, he sure acts like he wants to. At the sight of Aria, his face lights up. At the sight of me . . . Well, he's not as happy to see me. Sibling rivalry and all that.

"Good morning, Christopher," I greet with a smile.

"Mornin'. I've already set up pasture horses. If we can split up, this will go a lot faster, which means we'll have plenty of time to shower and eat a *real* breakfast."

If the three of us stood next to each other, you'd never know Aria was our sister. Where Chris and I take after our Momma with our blond hair and blue eyes, she takes after Daddy with her black hair and amber eyes—not to mention her strong-willed personality.

"Right, well, let's get going. Maybe we can get a few stalls in before we head up—"

"Absolutely not," Aria interrupts Derek. "After we feed, we're going to take a shower, go up to the main house for breakfast, and then I'm passing out on the couch while the rest of you jerks watch my kid so I can catch at least an hour more of sleep."

Derek snickers while Chris watches her in bewilderment. Had this been a year ago, she would have obliged to not rock the boat.

"Okay . . . Well, Peanut has spoken. I'll do barn number one and the pasture horses; Peanut, you get barn number two; Annie, barn number three; and Derek, you can handle the rescue barn. I don't want to waste too much time down here because I'd like to be on the road by ten," Chris announces.

Derek and Aria stifle their laughter as they shift their gazes to me. *Assholes.*

Without another word, we push on.

Unlocking the feed room door, I praise Jesus when I find that past me was looking out for future me and already set up feed for this morning. The horses, still sleepy, wake up once they hear the grain rustling in the buckets. I feed in record time. Once grain is delivered to hungry bellies, hay comes next. While the other three take their sweet time feeding, I sweep down the aisle and lock up again. Derek and Aria finish up a few minutes later and walk with me back to the houses.

"So . . . have you thought about telling everyone?" Aria asks slyly.

"Not yet. Besides. It's hot sneaking around."

She rolls her eyes. "The longer you wait, the harder it's going to be to break to everyone else."

Maybe so. But if there's anything I've learned from this relationship, it's that we *like* sneaking around. "Even if that's the case, why are *you* so worried about it?"

"Because you've forced me to be an accomplice, and I don't like lying." She wraps her arm around Derek's bicep, holding on tightly as we climb the hill to the cul-de-sac. Even after eight months of Charlie's attempted kidnapping and murder of her, she still worries about what's on the other side of that hill.

I heave an exasperated sigh. "We'll talk about it, okay? But I expect you to be on my side and not throw me to the wolves *when* the shit hits the fan."

Aria giggles. "Fine. Go shower. You stink."

"Back atcha, Peanut."

We go our separate ways once we hit the paved road and disappear into our respective houses to get ready for the day. As for me, my heart hammers in my chest. *How do I greet him? I forgot what it's like to be around him when my family is around. Do I hug him? No, that's stupid.*

My phone vibrates with a text message, and instantly, my heart steadies when I see it's him.

Jay Parker: Breathe, Blondie. I'll be there soon. I love you.

Breathe. In. Out. Repeat.

Time to get my ass in gear.

The hot shower is a welcome reprieve. Rivulets of water stream down my body, taking sweat and dirt along with them. I stand with my eyes closed, my face directly in the shower spray. It does nothing for my nerves, no matter how much I lie to myself about it.

After I get out, I apply makeup that is slightly sexy, but underhanded. An "every day" look, if you will. I carefully curated the perfect outfit for today a week ago. Every day, it hung in the closet, taunting me with each passing day.

The short-sleeved, button-up blouse clings to my curves. The shirt he bought for me last Valentine's Day is one of the most beautiful pieces of clothing I own. It's his favorite, and I definitely don't mind the sexy feel of the red silk against my skin. I hobble as I pull on a pair of skinny jeans, then slide on my sandals and start the trek to my momma's house.

Four acres of distance between us and my parents' house is just enough that they have to think about walking up this way to see us. Not that it matters to my mother. In fact, when she gets into a nostalgic mood—which is often—she'll pop in and cook.

Not that I'm complaining.

I'm fortunate to live on my parents' four-hundred-acre property. In a way, I think my parents enjoy it too. That way, we're not out of sight where my protective father can't jump in to save the day.

He built four houses—our houses—as an incentive for us to stick around in case he kicked the bucket early. Not to mention he had hopes one of us kids will take over the family business. I live next door to Aria on the left side of the street. Derek's old house is next door to hers on the right. And because my brother is obnoxious in every sense of the word, his excessively large log cabin is on the right side of the street. We're an entire four acres away from Momma and Daddy's house, but at least we're still together.

When I enter the front door of my parents' house, I'm hit with the smell of bacon and maple syrup. My stomach growls with anticipation. I find my soon-to-be niece, Zoey, in the recliner in her natural position: her nose in a book.

"Good morning, sweet pea," I greet softly, placing a gentle kiss on top of her mousy brown hair that is *definitely* not brushed. *I'll help Aria with that later.*

"Good morning, Auntie Annie," she replies sleepily and preoccupied.

I crouch down next to her, eager to see what she's reading today. "*Holes* again?"

She shrugs. "I'm running out of things to read. And . . . I'm a little nervous about today. Reading something familiar helps."

She's so sweet. "What's got you so nervous, Zo?"

"I only saw Jay like three years ago. What if he doesn't remember me?"

"I can promise you with a thousand percent certainty that Jay doesn't forget anything."

She chews on her bottom lip as she lets my words sink in.

"How about we brush your hair?"

She groans. "I knew you were going to say something. I got lazy. I just wanted to get here and read."

Chuckling, I shrug. "Sorry about your luck. I notice everything. Let me go say good morning to Nana and Poppa, and I'll be back."

I straighten and walk into the dining room to find my father sitting at the table with my nephew in the high chair, making airplane noises and feeding him cereal. It's unsettling, but in a good way, to see my serious father who hardly ever cracks a smile be so . . . jolly with a baby that wasn't wanted only a few months ago.

"Good morning, Daddy," I greet as I kiss my nephew's chubby cheeks.

"Annabelle," he greets in his typical gruffness.

From my spot in the dining room, I catch sight of my mother rushing around in the kitchen, slamming every cabinet door.

"Good morning, Momma. Can I help with anything?"

"You can set the table, baby. Jo should be here at any moment."

Meandering into the kitchen, I place a swift kiss on my momma's cheek and grab the plates and silverware from their respective places. I'm in just as much a hurry, so I race back into the dining room where I now find my nephew finger painting with the pureed banana.

Awesome.

As I set the table, voices filter in from the living room. Jo, in her whimsical and cheerful way, sweeps in with warm greetings. When she enters the dining room, she winks as she greets me with a kiss on the cheek.

Chris arrives a few minutes later and helps move the food onto the table. Aria and Derek arrive with Aria promptly stretching out on the living room couch while Derek takes over for Daddy.

I have a minute before the food gets blessed and it turns into a family-style eating contest, so I sit down at the foot of the table and whip out my phone. I wish Jay safe travels and that I'll see him soon, but then I go back to my travel notes, jotting down a few ideas that float in my head. It keeps my mind from running away with itself.

"You know how I feel about that thing at the table," Momma scolds when she steps into the dining room with a stick of butter for her famous biscuits.

"I'm just getting a few more words in."

She scrunches her nose in disapproval and continues rushing around.

I get a picture in reply from Jay. He's seated near the window at the gate. His tanned skin is as smooth as ever. His strong jawline clenches, making his smile seem just a little more intimidating. His jade eyes shine with muted excitement. A black NFL ball cap worn backward shows just how "free" he's feeling.

Jay Parker: I hope you're ready for me. I've got over a month and a half of pent-up sexual deprivation that I'm ready to take out on you.

My cheeks heat, and I quickly lock my phone so nobody reads over my shoulder.

"What's wrong with you?"

I glance up to find Chris standing at the island in the kitchen, staring me down suspiciously. "Nothing. Mind your business."

He steps away, muttering something unkind, and helps Momma with whatever.

Oh, God. How the hell am I going to keep a straight face all day?

"Come to the table, y'all. Soup's on," Momma calls.

Tired adults and children amble into the dining room and groggily sit at the table, barely able to keep their eyes open. It's six thirty now. We'll eat and help clean up the breakfast dishes, but until ten o'clock, I'm a bundle of high-strung nerves that will unravel at the slightest prod.

"Stephen, I think God can forgive us this once for not saying grace since we're in a hurry."

"Yep. He might not even smite us down on the way to the airport," I smart.

Aria and Chris snort as Momma shoots daggers at me as she sits down.

"On second hand, better not tempt fate," she snaps in annoyance.

Leave it to the middle child to rob her of her peace when it isn't even seven o'clock in the morning.

After Daddy says grace, it's like everyone has forgotten their manners and turned into Neanderthals overnight. I'm lucky to get a biscuit and a slice of French toast before my brother takes four slices for himself. *Pig.*

"Has anyone heard from him?" Momma asks.

I have. But you won't find me offering that information up. Luckily, Jo comes to my rescue.

"He's boarding now. He went for a run this morning and was able to spend time with the rest of his unit before he left."

Everyone murmurs their approval. Meanwhile, Derek smirks when he realizes I'm keeping my trap shut.

"So does this mean he'll be moving in with you?" Chris asks Jo.

Jo's gaze briefly meets mine, silently warning me she's done keeping this secret, and shrugs.

"I don't know, baby. We haven't really talked about it. I assume so. Unless he's found an apartment in town."

He'll be living with me.

"And what is he going to do about a job?" Chris asks.

"The guy just got out of the Corps. Give him some time to breathe," I scold.

He shrugs carelessly. "He didn't retire. He'll need money to survive. I'm just curious, shit."

"Language," Momma growls.

Snorting, I reach for a cinnamon roll on the table.

Zoey barely touches her food and, instead, closet reads her book under the table while Troy babbles from his high chair, occasionally accepting torn-up pieces of food from Aria.

I'm desperate to do anything with my hands when breakfast is over, which is how I got stuck with dish duty. Jo brings the food in from the dining room and places the leftovers in containers while I wash.

"Baby," Jo scolds softly.

I close my eyes in frustration. I already know what she's going to say. It's what she has been saying for the last two and a half years. I reluctantly turn around and narrow my eyes. We're alone for now, but it won't take long for someone to come traipsing in here for something.

"Yes?"

Sensing my nerves, she softens. "Don't be so nervous," she reminds me softly. "He's excited to start life with you."

My hardened heart softens just the tiniest bit. "What if it isn't what he thinks it's going to be like?"

She shrugs. "I've known you since birth. If I know *anything,* I know the two of you are destined to be together. I mean, you've made it this far without any resistance."

I snort and return my attention to the dishwater. "Yeah, well, distance will make you appreciate the relationship for what it is."

She hums as she thinks. "And what's that?"

"That it's *right.*"

She grins and squeezes my shoulder in reassurance.

We work together in silence, our minds a million miles away.

"Are you coming with me?" Chris asks as he saunters into the kitchen, stuffing another biscuit into his ginormous trap.

"Sure," I answer easily.

Jo goes with Momma and Daddy while Derek and Aria take their own vehicle. I ride along with Chris and ponder his reaction to the news I've yet to give. I'd bet my house Chris is going to be the first one to explode. He's had his claim on Jay as the brother he never had since the moment they met. When he finds out I've been secretly dating his best friend for the last two and a half years, he'll be pissed. But what will send him over the edge is that he was none the wiser.

Well, at least I'll get a free show out of it.

WE'RE at the airport at eleven thirty on the dot. Our whole posse takes over a large chunk of the baggage claim. While they wait impatiently in chairs for his arrival, I sneak off into the bathroom for a breather.

Disappearing into a stall, I take a deep breath, desperately trying to ignore the smell of human waste. I pop open a few of the top buttons and readjust my blouse so that my breasts are on full display and properly embraced by the red lacy bra that barely contains me. I snap a picture and send it to him.

Me: I'm ready.

Fixing myself up to present myself as the angel my parents think I am, I flush the toilet and walk back to the sink. I fix my smudged eyeliner and refresh my lipstick.

Returning to my family, my anxiety ebbs. I seat myself in between Aria and Jo, praying to whatever god is out there to allow his flight to land early.

"You look like you've seen a ghost," Aria comments with a knowing grin.

"I'm fine," I assure her, even though I'm certain she can see my heart beating outside my chest.

"Are you? Because your chest is all flushed—"

"I don't remember teasing you relentlessly when you were sneaking off with Derek behind everyone's backs."

My clipped words have the opposite effect I wanted them to. Instead of shying away, Aria squares her shoulders and laughs. "Sticks and stones, Annie. I tease because I care."

"You tease because you don't have any other entertainment."

Troy crawls over and asks to be picked up. I swoop him up and place him in my lap, peppering him with kisses while he whines in disapproval.

To fill the time, she drones on and on about motherhood, but I'm hyper-aware of everything around me. He's here. I don't see him, but I *feel* him. I stand up along with Aria and Jo as a bunch of people flood the baggage carousels.

I look for that black ball cap on one of the tallest human beings I know. The escalator is packed like sardines. *Is everyone else picking up on my nervous energy?*

He steps on the escalator, and suddenly, my world is kicked right side up on its axis. Everything is right again because he's *home.*

It isn't long before I lock eyes with his pools of jade. I've always been a sucker for his crooked smile. It's probably the first thing I ever fell in love with.

When he steps off the escalator, he breaks into a jog toward us. I know he won't come to me first, not when we're going to *delicately* break our relationship to the family later. He scoops his mother in a hug first. Jo sobs into his chest as he whispers that he's home now and she can rest. He moves on to Momma and Daddy, then to Chris. I see the anticipation rolling off his broad shoulders and large biceps.

He locks eyes with Aria, who is probably more emotional than I am. The two of them share a bond of abused souls. They found comfort within each other as brother and sister.

He wraps her in a tight hug while she murmurs her apologies. She has nothing to be sorry for, and he lets her know just that. He greets Troy and Zoey with big bear hugs. He shakes hands with Derek, though he's half listening to what Derek is saying to him because he's looking for me.

And finally—*finally*—it's my turn. That arrogant smile spreads across his plump lips. His eyes darken, promising me a night I won't forget.

"Annabelle." His gravelly voice is the heaven my dreams are built upon. It's the little voice inside my head reminding me I'm the center of his universe. It's the devil on my shoulder saying that our life together in secret is *hot.*

"Jay," I greet.

So many pairs of eyes are on us. But I wrap my arms around him anyway because I'll die if I don't. He faces away from everyone, and as much as I want to close my eyes to savor this moment, I keep them open.

When he crushes me against his chest, his lips graze the shell of my ear and whisper, "I love you, Blondie. Forever."

3

JAY

Annabelle in my arms is the most natural thing in the universe. The fact I can't kiss her and claim her in front of all these people is physically painful. I breathe in her jasmine-scented hair and whisper that I love her. Reluctantly, I part from her and paint on a smile for everyone else.

"Good to have you home, son," Steve says, clapping my shoulder.

"Good to be back," I reply easily.

"Did you check any bags, baby?" Betty Lou asks.

"No, all of my stuff should be here tonight."

I'm thankful nobody asks where I'll be putting my stuff. I'm sure they all assume it will be with my mom. For the public's sake, I need them to *think* I'll be living with my mom.

Annabelle stands beside me, keeping her gaze trained on the floor. Can she feel the sexual tension in the air like I do? She lifts her eyes to mine, her bluebell eyes darkening into something more sinister, begging me to take her now.

I need a minute alone with her.

I can't wait to come clean to everyone else. The secrecy added a sexy heat to our relationship, but it's been two years. I'm done hiding.

"I have something for you," I say quickly, unfolding the letter from my pocket and handing it over to Annabelle.

Her grin reaches her eyes, and when she meets my gaze, her eyes soften. "From Tom?"

I nod. "He says he misses you."

"I miss him too."

Aria rolls her eyes impatiently when I wink at her.

Tom was engineered to throw her family off our scent. We lied and said he was someone in my unit. For two and a half years, it worked. But I don't want to be the dirty little secret anymore. Like Graves said, I deserve to live my life.

"Well, why don't we head out?" Chris suggests.

We walk together to the garage. Annie stays a few paces behind, though I can *feel* her nervous energy. Troy babbles as we walk, and Zoey walks in step with me, glancing up at me curiously.

"How come you left the marines?"

I grin. "Because I wanted to come home."

She nods with furrowed brows. When she meets my gaze, her cheeks redden. "Is it because you love A—"

"Aria? You bet your ass, kid," Derek quickly cuts in, looking around to make sure nobody is listening too closely.

She stares at Derek in bewilderment. "Kid?"

"It wasn't meant as an insult, babe. It's sort of like a nickname. Like 'Zo' or 'kiddo.' "

She nods in acknowledgment and scowls at her father.

"Aria's my sister. It's been years since I saw her last," I explain as delicately as I can to her.

"Are you happy to be home then?" she asks.

Annie glances over her shoulder and winks at Zoey before meeting my gaze.

"Without a doubt, Zoey, I'm *elated* to be home."

THERE'S COMING HOME on leave, and there's coming home for good. Personally, coming home for good is more satisfying. It's a weight off my shoulders to see my mother relieved that I'm not running into the next battle. It's relieving to know I don't need to shave my face anymore or wake up at the ass crack of dawn to run until I puke. Though, I don't expect to give up running any time soon. *That* I can still control.

While Momma and Betty Lou cook dinner, I stand outside the front porch and stare up at the house that became my safe haven. There's a window in front that is just a little bit smaller than the two surrounding it. When Chris was a teenager, he fixed the window so it wouldn't screech every time it was opened. Soon enough, Annabelle figured out what he was doing, and inevitably, she started pulling the same stunts.

"How many boys did you beat up for climbing up there?" her sweet voice says from behind me.

"Too many. They were told not to come back."

Annabelle's giggles are music to my ears. "That was me getting your attention, Parker."

Annabelle has always been as subtle as a gun when it came to her feelings for me. At eighteen, loving your best friend's sister—who is only three years younger than you—is considered predatory. I wasn't looking for jail time. Especially when I was going straight into the Corps once I graduated.

"You already had it, McKenzie."

She grins and nervously peels the label off the bottle. "Jay . . ."

"We need to come clean, Annabelle. We can't keep sneaking around."

She chews on her bottom lip and glances up at me with her big, blue doe eyes. A smile spreads across her lips, and her chest inflates with an inhale.

"They're not going to take this well."

Honestly, I don't care. I'll get my ass kicked. But that smile on her face is worth the pain I'll endure.

"Your grandparents didn't take kindly to your daddy either. I think we'll be okay."

"Yeah . . ." Her voice trails off with uncertainty. She sidles up next to me, our arms touching in a juvenile display of affection. "But it'll be okay. They'll get used to the idea of us being together."

I turn to face her, my hands itching to push her golden locks out her face.

Soon.

"It's killing me to not kiss you right now."

She sighs. "Me too. I've missed you so much."

"Soon, baby."

With a mischievous gleam in her eye, she grabs my wrist and pulls me to the side of the house. She leans up against the siding and pulls my head in, pressing her plump lips to mine. All of the blood in my body rushes to my dick when she wraps her leg around my torso, grinding her molten core against me.

"Annabelle," I growl in her ear.

She shudders against me, her breath exploding when my fingers dip below her waistband.

"We can't do this now," I murmur.

"Shh. I can be quiet. I've waited too long for this," she whimpers.

I pop the button on her skinny jeans and spin her around. I'm about to unzip my pants when I hear a sharp, "Parker!"

Derek stalks over to us while Annabelle shimmies her pants back on, pouting at the incessant cock-block. He approaches with a shit-eating grin. He's not even sorry for interrupting this moment.

"Hey, Dr. I-Think-I'm-So-Pretty. What do you want?"

He chuckles and shoulder checks me. "Are you doing all right? You look scared."

"Don't even pretend you weren't shitting your pants when Steve found out about you and Peanut."

A mischievous grin spreads on his cheeks. "And you'll never know about it, either."

Annabelle rolls her eyes and playfully shoves Derek. "Don't you have somewhere to be?" she asks pointedly.

"I do. I've got to relieve that baby off of Aria. Maybe put a new one in her."

I internally groan, ready to rip him to shreds. I don't want to know *that.*

Derek saunters off and I causally wrap my arm around her waist. She rests her head on my pec and sighs contentedly.

"It won't be like this forever," I remind her.

"Remember this moment," she warns with a smile. "This is the calm before the storm. I'll also take bets on who explodes first. Do you think it will be Daddy or Chris?"

"My money's on your dad."

"I hate to break it to you, handsome, but your best friend is a drama queen." She pauses, her bluebell eyes searching mine. "Jay . . . we have to tell them the other thing too."

My stomach twists.

"That day is not today," I remind her with a crooked smile.

There is no way I'm dropping *two* bombs on them. I made it out of Afghanistan in one piece. I'm not about to die at the hand of Stephen McKenzie in my own home.

She grins and squeezes my hand. "Let's get this over with. I'm not sure when you're expecting your moving truck to be coming down the road, but I'd rather tell them before they realize what's happening."

We traipse inside to find Derek spooning Aria on the couch, with him nearly falling off since it's so narrow. Zoey reads her book in the recliner while Troy gets into things he shouldn't. Without a word, Annie scoops him up as he cries in annoyance.

"Hi, baby," Momma greets me warmly.

"Hi, Momma. What's for lunch?"

"I don't know, but I'm *starving.* Are you settling in okay?"

"Do you think they're going to be upset?" I whisper, so I don't give it away to Betty Lou, who is just a few feet away from us.

"Probably," she replies with a giggle. "Don't worry about it too much. You're family."

I glance over at my blonde beauty who's nuzzling Troy's nose with her own. They both giggle, and it makes my heart race. She'd be such a good mom if we had kids of our own. She doesn't seem to think so. I can see a whole brood of the perfect McKenzie/Parker mixes. They'd be perfect.

Jackie, Aria's best friend, arrives fashionably late with a hesitant smile. She avoids Chris like the plague and mingles with everyone else.

"It's so good to see you, Jay. I'm so glad you're home." She wraps me in a tight hug and kisses my cheek.

She's another "honorary McKenzie." With her mother being a teen mom and ostracized by the town, it was natural she fell into the comforting grace of the McKenzies.

"All right, y'all. Come to the table," Betty Lou announces.

We've gathered at this table my entire life. And while it doesn't matter where I sit, I still sit in between Annie and my mother. I can count on Annie to jump in the middle of a physical fight between me and her father. And Momma . . . Well, I don't expect anyone to try anything when she's around.

Steve says grace, and while he prays, I study the spread. All of my favorites are on the table. From Betty Lou's roast beef to green bean casserole. Mac and cheese to mashed potatoes. I'm not a McKenzie by blood, but damn it, they make me feel like one of their own.

When Steve finishes, plates are passed around in a frenzy. This crowd loves food—they won't let one morsel go to waste.

"So what are your plans?" Chris asks abruptly.

"I have an interview with SCPD on Monday."

I don't miss the way everyone freezes. This is news to them, but not to Annabelle. We've been talking about this for months. It's time to get the damn thing in motion. It's time to get this town on the right path. It's time to take the Parkers out of power.

"You're going to be a cop?" Steve asks with bewilderment.

"I'm trying to circumvent the inevitable identity crisis. The police are the closest thing to the military. I'll have the camaraderie until I can start turning things around."

Nobody wants to bring up the fact that the cop shop is staffed full of Parkers. Uncle Jeremy, the chief, will no doubt be glad to have another Parker on the force. In his mind, it's one more person to boss around and hide his prejudice that everyone who doesn't hold our last name is the scum of the earth.

Though I'm a Parker by blood, my true family is the one right here. The ones who picked us up when my father beat the living daylights out of us. Though I suppose, at times, they wonder if I'll succumb to the influence of my biological family. I won't. Not after the kindness they've shown me all these years. The Parkers are all in for a big surprise. I'm bringing order and fair trial back to Sage Creek, whether they like it or not.

"What about college?" Chris butts in again.

"Not for me. I already wasn't a good student in high school. I don't see that changing."

Anything would've been better than law enforcement in his eyes. He's the golden boy. He found a job where he's safe and gets extended breaks throughout the year. I'm not ready to be trapped within four walls.

"I think it's a great idea," Derek pipes up. He gives me a reassuring nod and continues eating. "Not all of us have an easy time transitioning into civilian life. The police force isn't the military, but it's the next best thing."

Exactly.

"I'd say you can move into your old house, but I don't know what you plan on doing. Do you need a reference for an apartment in town? Are you going home with your mother?" Steve asks.

I meet Annabelle's gaze and steel myself for the backlash.

"He's going to live with me," she pipes up, her eyes never leaving mine.

The silence is deafening, almost like she was speaking a different language.

Steve's eyes snap in my direction. Briefly, I drop Annabelle's gaze to face him like a man. I don't know what to expect. Is he happy? Sad? Homicidal?

For the other half of the table, meaning Chris, the confession hasn't fully sunk in yet.

"You're not serious," Chris scrambles. "Dude, you could always move in with me. I have the extra room. Annie's house is small—"

"Jay and I have been together for two and a half years now."

"Jesus Christ, Blondie," I scold with a hint of laughter. There's no such thing as sugar coating the truth.

I stand corrected. *This* silence is deafening. I study everyone's reactions. Zoey pays us no mind, Derek and Aria are trying to hide their shit-eating grins, Chris gapes as his face reddens, Betty Lou stares at me in disbelief, and Momma hides her grin behind her hand.

"What?" Betty Lou asks in surprise.

"We've been together for two and a half years," Annabelle repeats cautiously, scanning the table for a threat.

"What happened to Tom?" Betty Lou asks.

This time, Annie's face falls. "See, here's the thing . . . Jay *is* Tom."

"Are you fucking serious?" Chris erupts.

Great. I knew he was going to be livid, but I didn't expect him to resort to cursing in front of his mother.

"We wanted time to ourselves to figure out—"

"Dude, she's your *sister!"* Chris interrupts me.

"Not by blood," Annabelle states.

"Like that matters!" he shouts.

From my peripherals, Aria scoots closer to Derek for comfort. The shouting makes her uncomfortable.

"Two and a half years is a long time to lie to your family," Steve clips.

"Before Christopher interrupted me, we weren't sure if it would work out. We wanted time to figure *us* out. Time sort of slipped away from us, and it got harder to tell you."

"You lied, then. Kept us in the dark because you were too afraid to tell us," Steve admonishes. He turns his cutting gaze to me. "And what about you?"

"How many guys have you snuck in through that window?" Chris demands, interrupting Steve before turning to me. "Dude, she's not who you think she is."

I stand from my chair as his words poison my adrenaline. *How dare he talk about her like that!* "And who is that, brother? Because *I* know who she is."

He flounders, his gaze bouncing from me to Annabelle. "She had a line of boys coming through that window—"

"I know you're not talking about the window between your rooms," Steve interrupts. "Again, *why* didn't you tell us? You're a willing participant in this relationship, are you not?" he asks me.

"Because Annabelle wanted to be the one to break the news to you."

"Did you ever stop to think I was doing that to get his attention?" Annie snaps at Chris, standing up from her chair. "I've loved him since we were kids, but he never made a move because of *you.* Step off your high horse, Christopher. It's unbecoming."

"To get his attention?" he booms.

"He chased out all of those boys. He knew what I was doing. He knew I was just trying to goad him into being with me. But he respected your friendship too much to do anything about it!"

"You snuck boys into our home?" Steve directs at Annabelle. She ignores him completely. This isn't going to end well. "Secrets are what destroys the family," he snaps. He grips the table and rises slowly.

He's going to hit me. Steve McKenzie is going to fucking hit me.

"Respecting *our* friendship," Chris spits poisonously. "If he respected our friendship so much, he would've steered clear of you!"

"Now there is no reason to be raising your voices like this," Betty Lou scolds. Unfortunately, Chris ignores her.

"I don't know why you're getting so up in arms about this!" Annabelle smarts, leaping out of her chair. She stares her brother down, daring him to say anything else. "Nothing has changed, Christopher. We've been together under your nose, and you didn't even know about it. *Nothing* has changed!"

"*Everything* has changed!" he roars.

My anger leeches into my muscles. I clench my fists, not that I'll use them. But I hate this. This is exactly why I didn't want to say anything in the first place. Not today, anyway.

"You've had your pick of guys all around town. I know we don't get along, but this is a low blow, Annie. You've always been selfish, but this really takes the cake."

"Better the devil you know," Aria teases unhelpfully.

Everyone glares daggers at her.

"Too soon, Ace," Derek chides.

"It isn't any different than your *thing* with Jackie," I spit poisonously.

Yep. I went there.

Except, when Jackie's face blanches, I immediately regret it. All eyes snap to her and then to Chris.

"What is he talking about?" Aria demands, now standing up while Derek wraps his burly arms around her waist to stop her from pouncing.

Chris's face falls, but only for a moment. "It was *nothing—"*

"Nothing?" Aria shrieks. "Are you the reason she refuses to come here anymore?"

"I'm sitting right here," Jackie reminds everyone harshly. Not that it matters.

He shrinks back. Before this gets any more out of control, I quickly get us back on topic.

"Dude, I love her, okay? I'm not going to hurt her—"

"Do you honestly think it's *her* I'm worried about? No, idiot. I'm worried about *you!"*

"What the hell is that supposed to mean?" Annabelle demands.

Here we go.

Chris dangerously shifts his gaze and narrows his eyes at her.

"I don't care that this whole fucking town thinks you're so damn charming. You're going to do what you do best. You're going to 'be with him,' get bored, and dump him. You'll ruin the whole fucking dynamic."

This time, Steve storms over and turns his quiet rage to Chris.

"Now that's enough of that. Take a walk, Christopher. You *will not* talk about your sister like that."

I expect Chris to square up to him. For a moment, he straightens, his muscles tense, and he narrows his eyes at him. *He's going to pounce.* Instead, he takes a deep breath and storms out of the dining room, his boots thundering against the hardwood floors, and slams the door behind him.

"I think the two of you need to reevaluate if you want to be a part of this family or not." He turns to us, narrows his eyes at Annabelle, and stares her down. "There is a time and place for everything, Annabelle. Learn some grace, won't you?"

"That's a little dramatic, don't you think?" Annabelle asks with an edge.

"You tell me, kid. Families share things with each other no matter how painful it is." He shifts his gaze to me. "Trust is earned, Jacob."

And now I've been called out by my full name.

Great.

Aria turns to me with a frown. "Jay, is it true? Or were you just trying to piss him off?"

I didn't want to have to use that card, but I'm no pushover. I won't have anyone questioning my choices when their shit doesn't smell like roses, either.

"Aria, I don't think now is the time to discuss this," Betty Lou groans.

She's absolutely right. I don't want to talk about it. And now, telling them the other thing is completely off the table.

We eat in silence, and Chris doesn't come back at all. After dinner, I help Betty Lou clean up while the girls do the dishes. Betty Lou hangs by close to Annie, and it's only now that I realize I might have just started World War III.

4

ANNIE

Momma is my shadow. We're the same person when it comes to looks and personality. The only difference is she's fearless. No matter how dire the situation is, she's going to tell you like it is whether it puts her in the doghouse or not.

When it comes to me, I'm slightly more . . . diplomatic.

"If you're gonna say something, Momma, just say it. I won't bite your head off, I promise."

She approaches the sink as Jo walks away, taking Jay with her.

"Why didn't you tell me?" she whispers, the hurt in her voice chipping away at my conscience.

"Because it would have turned into a big deal when it didn't have to be."

"Annabelle, I wouldn't have said anything if it meant that much to you."

I shut the tap off and turn to face her, narrowing my eyes.

"You don't keep *anything* from Daddy. He would have blown it out of proportion."

Tears well up in her bright eyes, the same eyes we share.

"But he didn't," Momma unhelpfully reminds me.

"I knew you guys wouldn't approve of us, and I didn't want that to be an excuse to end us before it even began.

Momma's hand reaches for my cheeks and caresses them with her thumb. "I'm sorry we made you feel that way. And that you felt like you couldn't tell me," She murmurs.

Tears fill my own eyes. So far, this secret has hurt everyone we love. Are we the bad guys here?

"Your happiness is what matters to us, baby."

"He's a good man, Momma. He loves me."

"I'm southern, not stupid, Annabelle." I snort despite the rivers of tears that pour out of my eyes. "I know you've loved him since you were little. And I know he loved you too. I thought maybe once you graduated the two of you would start something, but nothing ever came of it. All I ever wanted for you is to find a love that catered to *you* specifically." She drops her hand and takes a deep breath.

"No more secrets, Momma. I promise."

Her waning smile has my stomach churning. There is one more secret, but that's one I'll take to the grave. It's not worth losing my family over.

It's been the longest day of my life. The U-Haul got here half an hour ago, and the small number of belongings Jay owned have all been put in their place. For the first time ever, I'm walking into a house that isn't only mine, but one I share with the love of my life. While I finish my article, he relaxes on the big ugly green sofa and I silently thank whoever is looking out for me. The dust hasn't settled yet, but tomorrow is a new day.

We're nearing nine o'clock, and I'm three-quarters of the way done with this article before I can send it to my insufferable boss. The sun has since disappeared below the horizon, and the battery-operated twinkle lights in the decorative mason jars hanging on my walls flicker on, bathing our living room in a warm glow. Jay nurses a beer while he watches highlights from the baseball game from earlier today.

A smile spreads across my cheeks. *This* is what I imagined when I thought of our life together. He's never demanded I quit my job. In fact, we've been apart for so long that it's natural for us both to be away from each other.

"Who are you smiling at like that, Blondie?" he asks, wriggling his eyebrows suggestively.

I rise from my chair and cross the room, straddling his lap and bending over to gently kiss his lips. "I'm happy you're home."

"Me too, baby. Though, you're going to get tired of me."

I laugh as his hands grasp my hips tightly, my stomach swooping with anticipation. *God, how long has it been?*

"Your brother will come around."

I scrunch my nose in disapproval. "Gross. Don't talk about him when I'm trying to seduce you."

He barks out a laugh. His cock hardens beneath me. The air suddenly changes. His jade eyes darken, and his rough hands skim my jean-clad thighs.

"It's hot in here, Jay."

"I can help with that," he says in his low, gravelly, baritone voice. He slowly undoes the buttons on my blouse. He sits up and buries his nose in my cleavage, gently nipping and kissing the exposed skin. "Fucking hell, Blondie. I love the way you taste."

My head dips back as he pulls the blouse off and swiftly unhooks my bra, allowing my breasts to hang free. He stares at me with a satisfied grin, taking me all in.

My hand rakes through his short, dark hair. He picks me up and brings me into the master bathroom and turns on the shower. I help him undress, taking in the corded muscles on his arms. It's like I'm trying to memorize every single inch of him in case I wake up in the morning and it was all a dream.

"Tell me what you want, Blondie."

I groan in frustration when he picks me up and enters the shower, pulling the shower curtain closed. I don't want to talk.

"Jay," I growl impatiently.

He smirks and challenges me with his narrowed eyes.

"Annabelle." He pins me against the subway tile, the freezing tile behind me is a mind-blowing contrast to the heat from the shower spray . . . and the heat between my legs. He nips at my neck. "Tell me."

His lips crash into mine, and he swallows my moans. He reaches in between my legs and rubs my swollen clit. It should be relaxing, but the anticipation builds in my belly, and my legs contract around him.

"I've been away for too long." His long fingers probe me, tracing my slit and coating his fingers with my desire. "I want to know how my baby wants me to take care of her."

"I want you," I murmur breathlessly. "Please," I beg. "I love when you fuck me hard. Don't make me wait."

Smirking arrogantly, he dives into my lips again, his tongue swirling with mine. Every nerve ending is on high alert. His skin blazes against mine with every movement.

"Beautiful," he whispers as he lines up with my entrance. The first one will be fast. I've waited for this for months. I've been walking on eggshells all day waiting for this moment.

He slams into me with no apologies. A moan escapes me. My head hits the tile behind me, and his fingers dig into my hips.

"Please, Jay," I whimper. "Please don't make me wait."

On a growl, he lowers me to the tub and spins me around. My back arches in anticipation, my hands steady on either side of the tub.

His cock enters slowly at first as he hisses. His hips piston faster when my walls relax around him.

"Oh my god," I whine.

"Don't hold back, Annabelle. I want to hear you come."

His thrusts are the right kind of painful. My screams reach higher decibels. He could plow me however he wanted and I'd be okay with it.

My walls squeeze him in a vicelike grip.

"Fuck, fuck, fuck," he chants as he loses control.

I take off before he does. Black dots swirl in my vision; my ears pop in satisfaction. When Jay finishes, he drapes himself on top of me, kissing a trail down my spine as he straightens.

"I'm going to love you forever, you know that?" he murmurs.

"Remind me," I reply, out of breath.

I straighten, and he sits at the bottom of the tub. I straddle his lap and press my forehead to his.

"No matter who's against us, Annabelle, I will love you forever. When you're irrational and hangry. When you're sick and it's coming out of both ends—"

My giggle interrupts him. He kisses the tip of my nose.

"No matter what, Blondie. I'm with you for the long haul."

"You better not go back on your promise. I'll cut you if you ever leave."

He chuckles and pulls me into a tight embrace. "I'd let you."

5

JAY

When living on a farm, the day starts early. It doesn't matter if you're hungover or if you're sick. It doesn't even matter if you've recently gotten out of the Marine Corps after being in for thirteen years. You're always well enough for the bare minimum. When Annie's alarm shrieks into the silence of the early morning, I pull her close to me and kiss her temple.

"Good morning, gorgeous."

She sleepily reaches for her phone, disabling the alarm and slamming her phone back onto the nightstand. "I'm not in the mood for your bullshit, Jay. Go back to sleep."

I chuckle. She's not getting out of this.

The streetlight from outside just barely illuminates her silhouette. Her naked back curves so elegantly. The sheet clings to those curves like a second skin.

"You're always in the mood for my bullshit. Wake up, Blondie. I want to gaze at your pretty face."

She groans and turns to face me. She isn't a morning person. It would be endearing if I didn't want to eat her alive right now. Now that we're out in the open, we can truly let go of everything that was holding us back before.

"I'm giving you a free pass since it's day two. But don't get used to this, Parker."

I push her wild hair out of her eyes and gently trace her bottom lip with my thumb. Her tongue darts out, licking the pad of my thumb, making my cock rev to life.

"You don't mean that," I murmur, pulling her leg over my hip. She's hot and ready to go.

"We have shit to do, Jay."

"Mm-hmm," I breathe into her ear. "Your pussy is *begging* for me."

I tease her pussy with the tip of my cock. She throws her head back in ecstasy.

"We have four barns to feed," she whines.

Her leg hikes up over my hip, contradicting her words.

"You better get moving then," I whisper.

She dives in for my lips, but I move my head back.

"Jacob," she warns. Her bark is worse than her bite. I'm having a lot of fun teasing her.

"Annie," I counter. She growls at the careless nickname her parents gave her.

"We should incite a new rule. Morning sex for Annabelle, twenty-four seven. Regardless of if you're mad at me or not."

I chuckle and suckle the crook of her neck. She purrs with approval and grinds against my dick. "Yeah? And what about me?"

She giggles. "You get something out of it too."

Without warning, I enter her, her long nails scoring my shoulder blades.

"Fuck," she hisses.

"I love you," I whisper.

"I love you too."

My libido has never slept around Annabelle. Two and a half years ago, when she showed up at the front gate of Camp Lejeune demanding the military police to get a hold of me, I lost my resolve.

Just like now when she swings on top, riding me like she's done this her entire life.

"Fuck, baby. Ride my cock."

A Cheshire smile spreads across her pillowy lips. I grab hold of her hips and slam her down onto me. She cries out and grabs handfuls of my skin, her fingernails digging into me. Grabbing hold of the headboard, she picks up the pace. I tease her nipples, suckling on her left while teasing the right. Her walls clench me tight, refusing to give me any room to breathe.

"God," she growls.

"No, baby. He isn't here."

I lie back, bringing her with me. I piston my hips as she moans and screams into my ear.

"Fuck, Jay! I'm going to come," she whimpers.

"Come all over my cock. It's all yours, baby."

Seconds later, her body slacks on top of mine. I erupt inside of her, ribbons of hot cum coating her on the inside and writing my name all over her.

I could get used to this. Having her on top of me, gasping for air, sweating profusely with a sated smile.

"You're the most beautiful woman alive," I whisper into her ear.

She sighs and shakes her head. "No, I'm not. But I'm *yours.* And that's what matters."

AFTER MORNING FEED, we attack the empty stalls side by side. Chris still isn't happy with the both of us, and he's avoiding Aria like the plague. Fortunately for him, she has a job that will take her off the property until about six o'clock tonight. As for Derek, he works exclusively in the rescue barn, rehabilitating his patients before either turning them out to pasture or selling them to vetted horse owners.

When the sun rises, and we're deep into mucking stalls, Annabelle's phone starts ringing off the hook. From her annoyed and angry expression, I know it's work, just like I know she requested the week off so she could spend time with me.

"You should answer it," I quietly encourage her.

"Trust me, nothing good can come out of that phone call while I'm on vacation. Autumn can either leave a message or email me. But right now, I'm on your time."

With her wearing my Marine Corps T-shirt and her daisy duke cutoffs, I can't help but stare at the creamy, white, long legs that plunge into her boots. She's a sight for sore eyes. When she catches me staring at her, her cheeks blush a vibrant red.

"Do you remember that rodeo where that schmuck asked you to the winter formal at school?"

She scoffs and rolls her eyes. "Of course I do. I was humiliated, and I canceled my run so I wouldn't have to answer him."

She was *livid.* He made a big show of it, coloring on poster board and having the announcer stop everything so he could ask her out in front of an audience. She threw her father's keys at me once she got Archie into the trailer and told me to drive.

"You know what sounds good?" I ask slyly.

"Hmm?"

"Frosties in front of town hall."

It's what we did that night. I was old enough to drive. I'd just gotten my license, and Steve and Betty Lou gave me permission to take Annie home. Instead, we stopped at a Wendy's close by and ate our treats in front of town hall while everyone was watching bull riding and barrel racing. We were alone, and it was perfect.

Little does she know, I barely had five dollars to my name. But she was upset and needed a minute to cool off. Even then, I would've burned the world down for her if it made her happy.

"You're right. That does sound good."

"What do you say, then? Is it a date?"

Her bluebell eyes meet mine. Her smile nearly brings me to my knees.

"Tonight, for sure. I'm sure the parentals won't miss us."

"Stop it." Chris's voice cuts through our lighthearted moment, and suddenly, I feel I need to protect her from him.

"Dude . . ."

"You can't do this around me. I'm not okay with it."

Annabelle goes from concerned to angry in point two seconds. "There's an exit on either side of the barn. If you'd like, I can release the goats so you have an extra push to get the hell out."

"Oh, fuck off, Annie," he spits poisonously.

"Hey, your fight is with me. Not with her. Don't be an asshole," I warn.

"My fight is with both of you. This is the shittiest thing either of you could do to me. I came over here to tell you I have a meeting at school. I'll need you to cover for me until I get back."

"News flash, Christopher, it has nothing to do with you. We didn't just sit around, shrug, and say, 'What's the best way to piss Christopher off?' Grow up. This isn't the end of the world," Annie snaps.

"You've done that your entire life," he snaps.

"We'll talk later, okay? I've got your chores. Just leave her alone."

He's looking at me like he's ready to pounce. It's funny because he shares the same eyes with Annie, but while she's always happy and bubbly, he's angry and . . . unsettled.

He nods once and strolls out of the barn. Annie stands with her pitchfork, glaring daggers at me.

"*Do not* encourage his bullshit behavior."

"I beg of you to walk a mile in his shoes for once. I'm not on his side, Blondie. I'm on *ours.* I know if the situation was reversed and he dated my sister in secret for two and a half years, I'd be pissed too."

She purses her lips and turns around slowly. I can brave her cold shoulder, though I'm not looking for a fight.

My phone vibrates off the hook. Text messages from Graves and my other guys asking me how I'm doing. My heart aches for the life I left behind. But when I look to my right and watch the love of my life angrily muck a stall with me, I know I made the right choice.

"When were you going to tell me about Jackie?" she asks softly.

Shit. I shouldn't have let that slip. I swooped to Chris's level.

"It wasn't my secret to tell, and I didn't want to embarrass her."

"He's a hypocrite," she seethes. "God, I thought when Peanut came home, he'd turn some of that angst down. He switched gears for like five minutes, and suddenly, I'm the bad guy again."

"He loves you, baby. He almost lost Aria. He doesn't want to lose another sister."

She scoffs and continues to muck the stall while I watch. "He's never been good about sharing. Everything was automatically his growing up, and I'm tired of it. It's not like you were only *his* friend. You were ours too."

"I'm not fighting you on that." I lean my pitchfork against the wall and close the distance between us, wrapping my arms around her waist. "I love you both. You know that?"

"You love me more than him, right?"

I snort in her ear and kiss the side of her head. "Remember when I told you that it didn't matter who protested? It would always be us?"

She nods sadly, her grip on the pitchfork handle loosening. It eventually drops to the ground.

"I promised you forever. There's no way I'm backing out of that promise now just because your brother is throwing a bitch fit." I kiss her forehead. "Forever, baby."

She sighs. "Forever," she agrees softly.

"I'm going to attack his shit now. Maybe we'll get up to the house at a decent hour for lunch." Shrugging, she escapes my grasp and bends over for the pitchfork.

I race out of the barn and catch up to him before he angrily throws himself in the truck. "Chris, wait!"

He stops in his tracks and turns around, his eyes boring a hole into my skull.

"What?" he spits.

"I'm sorry I didn't tell you."

"I didn't know what to expect when you got home. I hoped we could pick up right where we left off, but then I hear you've been fucking my sister behind my back. Not only that, you fucking run your mouth to Aria about Jackie."

"I'm sorry for ratting you out about her. But you were attacking *my* integrity. That's not something I take lightly."

His nostrils flare like he's getting ready to knock me the fuck out.

"You're my brother, and I love you. But I love Annabelle with everything I have, and I'm not letting go just because you don't like it."

His eyes narrow to slits. It's about now I know he wants to hit me. I even gear myself up for it. "We'll see." He gets into the truck and peels out of the driveway, kicking up loose gravel.

Fucker!

For the next two hours, I get each barn up to snuff. Annie takes care of the group lesson that arrives around ten thirty, and by noon, I'm not even hungry anymore. I leave to bring Tippy back inside when a silver car drives close to the fencing and heads onto the property.

"Are you expecting anybody?" I ask Annie from the feed room.

"They were my only lessons for the day. Why?"

The car turns into our makeshift neighborhood, drives the circle, and leaves the property. We don't get visitors out here unless they sign up for lessons. Maybe he just got lost.

"And set. We have dinner reservations at Rico's, and then we can do frosties in front of the town hall." She jumps off the stack of hay and gently pecks my lips.

"Rico's does reservations now?"

"What can I say? Sage Creek is hopping. Lots to do and see." She grins and wraps her arms around my neck. "Tacos sound good, don't they?"

She wriggles her eyebrows. I promptly ignore the double meaning and laugh it off.

"Tacos sound amazing," I agree. "Let's go home and cool off for a bit."

I pull my phone off the dock and find a whole slew of text messages from the guys, one from Texas Roadhouse, and one from my mom.

Momma: Would you and Annie like to come over for dinner tomorrow night? I can make your favorite.

I can't say no to my momma.

Me: Sure thing. I'll see you tomorrow after you get home from work. Sound good?

Shoving my phone in my pocket, I lock up the rest of the barn and lace my fingers with Annie's as we start the trek home.

This life of farming and cleaning stalls is what I know. It's what I was trained to do. But I can't help but give that hollow feeling in my stomach attention. I can't be a farmer for the rest of my life. Not when I have too much work to do here.

When we get home, she pulls out some premade sandwiches from the grocery store and grabs a bag of salt and vinegar potato chips out of the pantry. We sit around the island as we unwrap our lunch. Around this time, I'd disappear into my room at the barracks and contemplate life until it was time to return to work.

Now it's just a fuel stop on the way back to the farming way of life. I'm sure Steve needs help with the crop. The thought of him asking me to help with that makes me want to jump off a bridge.

"So we're on day two. What do you think?" she asks slyly with a raised eyebrow, reminding me of a younger version of her mother.

"About what?"

"Is it everything you remembered it to be? Three McKenzies and a Parker doing barn chores like the old days."

No. It's nothing like the old days. "Last time I checked, it was one McKenzie and one Parker. The other McKenzie ditched so he wouldn't have to hear me whisper sweet nothings in your ear."

Snorting, she takes a bite of her sandwich and pours herself a glass of sweet tea. "But . . . ?"

"I enjoy getting to spend the day with you, Annabelle."

But it's not the same working on the McKenzie farm doing exactly what I was doing as a teenager. I'm older, more established. I have a vendetta with the people who share my name. It's my job to take them down a few pegs, to remind them that looking the other way is just as damning.

"What other trips do you have planned for the rest of the year?" I'm asking because I need to start mentally preparing for her absence. Not that it would be an issue. We've been apart before. But there's a niggling feeling deep in my gut . . . one that cautions the notion of being alone.

I've been alone before. Not like this.

"I'm not sure. I have one more domestic trip for this year, and I think I'll be going to Germany around Christmas." Her face falls, and she closes her eyes in frustration. "I hate that they send me away for the holidays. I don't like celebrating days after."

She has the FOMO, just like I do. I couldn't come home last year. I was stuck on duty while my guys enjoyed time with their own families.

"You could leave, you know."

She rolls her eyes and scoffs. "They've got me by the balls, unfortunately. Autumn isn't budging when it comes to the web series idea, and Geoffrey and Nick won't let me go." She sighs. "I don't like being boxed in. I was an idiot for signing that contract."

"In a bar, no less."

Her smile grows. My girl is a free spirit. She does shady business dealings with the owners of an online magazine in a wine bar. To be fair, it wasn't that shady. She met Nick and Geoffrey and became instant friends. That's what happens when you meet her. To know her is to love her—and her way with words.

"Leave me alone. It got my foot in the door."

I press a kiss on her cheek and finish my sandwich.

"So . . . I know we haven't talked about this for a while, but I'm only going to ask you once. Are you sure you want to get in with SCPD? Your family doesn't treat people well, and after everything that happened with you and your mom . . . I worry they'll take hazing to a new level."

I turn to face her, leveling with her eyes. "I depended on the police when I was a kid. When my father was beating the shit out of us, I depended on the 'good guys' to save us. And since they didn't, I expected them to step in as my family. They didn't do that either, Annabelle. I can only imagine how many other people in town are suffering the same shit we did and the police are covering it up. I won't stand for it."

Jackie's family is one of those families that comes to mind. Her mother dated a lot of duds back in the day. Nora was young and a little on the naïve side, but I remember a lot of times when Jackie would recount the stories of calling the police on her mother's boyfriends who got a little too fresh with Nora, only for Jeremy to tell her to mind her business and go to sleep. Luckily, nothing ever spiraled out of control when Jackie was the one getting knocked around.

It's because of those incidents that I *know* a new Parker needs to step up and atone for the sins of their family. And that Parker is *me.*

She reaches over and strokes my cheek with her thumb.

"You're a good man, Jay. The *best* Parker that ever lived. I'm proud of you. I know you're going to do great things. But I hope you know you can bring your shit home if you feel like you're not handling it well."

Absolutely not. "I love you. But I'm going to be just fine."

6

ANNIE

"Next week, Annie. Vacation's over, and it's time to get back in the saddle. The bosses didn't like the other articles you had on deck for the next few weeks."

Meaning *she,* Autumn, hated them and wanted to bring me back early so she wouldn't have to write something in my place.

"I'm pretty sure there are laws about this."

"You gave shit material, Annie!" she shrieks.

I give Aria a telepathic look for her to pause her death metal from the stall across from me.

"Are you trying to fire me?" I challenge. I'm done being the rag doll in this power trip she has going. I'm not interested anymore. I think I'd rather muck stalls for a living than keep the abusive relationship between the two of us.

"You're being dramatic."

"No, I don't think I am." I lean my pitchfork against the wall and poke my head out the open window. "I know you and I have had our differences from the time I started here, but ever since you were given a promotion, you have been singling me out, and I have half a mind to go to Nick and Geoffrey about you."

That part's not true. I don't do drama. Besides, my worst fear would be for them to promote me to her position if they fired her.

The silence on the other end is deafening. I hope she fires me. Go ahead! Once our contract is broken, I can do literally anything else.

"I'd like to schedule a meeting with HR," she finally grumbles.

"Fantastic. Send me the Zoom link, and I'll be happy to join in."

I end the call and shove my phone back into my back pocket. My good day has gone down the drain. All that's left are articles I'll shuffle around to give her on another day when she's too busy to remember any of them. They're good articles I've slaved over. I'm not about to trash them just because Autumn is having a bad day.

"So . . . I know this has been assumed since birth, but I was wondering . . . would you want to be my maid of honor?" My sister hangs on the stall door, an amused grin on her porcelain face.

"Of course I want to be your maid of honor! Do you *want* me to be your maid of honor?"

She hesitates. "I feel a little guilty. Derek wants every one of his brothers to stand up with him, and all I have are you, Jackie, and Zoey."

"There are no rules. The wedding party can be uneven if you want it to."

"Well, I'm not inviting Bethany Hunt, so that solves that problem."

"Good. She'd be live-tweeting a beautiful ceremony and ruin it with her poison. Fuck her."

Aria giggles and sighs. "I don't want to get married at church."

Ah. Can you hear that? That's the sound of my mother's heart dropping out of her chest.

"I'm not a Christian like Momma. I don't want to be married by some stuffy priest who doesn't know us. I don't want an organ. I just want something that's . . . *us*."

"Momma will get over it," I assure her. Though I know for a fact this will be a dagger through her heart. "Besides, it's *your* day. Where would you want to have it anyway?"

She shrugs. "The property is nice, isn't it? We can set up tents by the creek . . ."

My mind wanders to the many stolen moments at that creek. The back pasture is three miles long, and right in the middle, there is a creek that runs through our property. We spent summers swimming in it. Later, when we were teenagers, that was where I went to clear my head. Almost every single time, Jay found me. A small smile spreads across my lips when the memory of the night he first kissed me enters my mind.

"They sell those laminate tiles that can be put down for a dance floor. We'd have to figure out a power thing, though. Maybe we can get a couple of generators?"

Ugh, shit. I'm not the best person to talk to about this. "I'm sure getting married at home is just as good, if not better, than getting married at church in Daddy's eyes. Plus, if you're worried about the bridal party being uneven, maybe you can have one of them officiate."

Her face lights up, her amber eyes take flight. "Nate would be a good officiant, don't you think?"

"Sure."

She sighs impatiently.

"I mean it. Anyway, are you doing anything this weekend? I was hoping to go into town and browse wedding dresses. If I can't find anything I like here, I'll go another time to Richmond. I was just hoping to find something unique to Sage Creek."

"Have you picked a date yet, Peanut?"

This time, her cheeks heat. After the events of eight months ago, she still battles with the thought of not being worthy of her future. She's always looking over her shoulder. I wonder if she's constantly surprised that she makes it this far with every passing day.

"Well, it'll be summer of next year. So we've agreed on June fourteenth," she replies.

I can picture it now. Aria is a simple woman who puts sentimental value in everything. I can see wood pieces and vine-y flowers. I see fairy lights and floating candles . . . "That sounds like a good day."

She smiles. "I didn't think I would get married. Not after everything—"

"Excuse me?" a new voice echoes through the barn.

I step outside of the stall and meet the man in the middle of the barn. He's not from around here. Not with black hair slicked back with what I assume is motor oil. His face is scarred with pockmarks, and a studded diamond earring reflects the sunlight from his left earlobe.

"Hi, I'm Annie. How can I help you?"

"I was looking for Aria McKenzie?"

Immediately, the hairs on the back of my neck stick straight up. The guy reeks of danger. "Oh? Can I ask what for?"

He reaches for something in his pocket. My heart hammers in my chest as I pray it's not some knife he's pulling out. Instead, he pulls out a white business card and hands it over to me.

"My name is Dominic Reese. I'm the new CEO for Dodge Enterprises in Chicago. The board has caught me up to speed on the incident with Mr. Dodge. I was hoping you'd agree to sit down with me so we can talk about the trial."

Aria licks her lips nervously. Even dead, Charlie Dodge continues to stick his ugly nose where it doesn't belong.

"Thank you, Mr. Reese, but I have an attorney, and I would be more comfortable if you directed your questions to him."

"There are at least a hundred other women he's traumatized. You're entitled to a massive payout—"

"Sir, she said she doesn't want your help. Please leave the property."

Aria isn't a coward, but this whole situation has her on edge. She's ready to say something rude out of fear, and I can't let it happen. Not when we don't know this guy's motive. As he takes a reflexive step back, his jacket moves to show the silver gun in his suit pocket. Collectively, Aria and I gasp, and I yank her behind me. A sinister smile spreads on his chapped lips.

"Is there a problem here?" Jay's booming voice comes from the middle of the barn.

At the sound of his voice, my muscles relax. Jay will help us.

"I was just talking to Annie here about setting up some time with Aria McKenzie about the Dodge trial."

"Get in touch with her lawyer, then," he barks.

Dominic takes a reflexive step back and narrows his eyes.

"And who are you, sir, to Aria?"

"None of your business. But you've been asked to leave the property by one of the owners. You're trespassing, and I promise you I can have the cops here within minutes."

It's a bluff, but we have someone better than a cop here, just in the barn across the way.

His gaze shifts from Jay to Aria.

"Again, Ms. McKenzie. Think about what I said. I'd be happy to set aside some time to meet with you *anywhere—"*

"That's enough. I trust you know your way back to town. Don't come back."

Jay follows Dominic all the way outside. I turn to Aria who furrows her brows, her anger pooling on the surface.

"You okay?" I ask.

"He doesn't seem like the CEO type, does he? Not with that gun."

"You're asking the wrong person, Peanut. I'm a country bumpkin. But I think you're right. He's sketchy."

She sighs. "I think I'm going to go home for a bit. Don't worry about my stalls. I'll come back later."

My stomach drops at her retreating form. Charlie keeps popping up beyond the grave, and I'm sick of it. I'm sick of him stealing all the progress she's made.

"Is she okay?" Jay asks from behind me.

"I don't know," I answer honestly, turning around.

"I've seen that guy before."

I raise my eyebrows. I think I would remember that guy anywhere. I haven't seen him around town. I didn't even think any city slicker would know how to navigate these back roads.

"Where?"

"Here."

"Here?"

He shrugs. "I thought he was lost. He turned around the cul-de-sac and left right after."

My stomach knots. That doesn't make me feel any better. In fact, it makes me want to throw up.

"Well, I think we've seen the last of him. She said no, and her pit bull attorney won't let her go—not when he's Derek's brother," I assure him.

Logan, one of Derek's "brothers" from the Marine Corps, was here a year ago to help keep her safe from Charlie. It just so happens he's a lawyer too. It stays in the family that way. There isn't a soul in the world who could corrupt Logan.

But as I say that, Jay doesn't look so sure. The doubt creeps in.

7

ANNIE

When we arrive at Jo's house in the early afternoon the next day, Jay starts dinner without delay. He's making some fancy pot roast that will take hours on the stove. I hoist myself onto the counter while Jay opens a package of meat and gets busy.

With his back toward me, I can admire his fit physique—and how his ass looks in his jeans.

He glances over his shoulder and smirks. He puts on some music, something Aria would listen to, and sways his hips along to the music.

"Take a picture, McKenzie."

"Why would I do that when I'm getting a free show? Besides, you said no flash photography."

He chuckles and places the hunk of meat into the pot. The meat sizzles as he turns around and quickly washes his hands. He moves closer to me, wrenching my legs open and settling between them. He presses an urgent kiss to my lips, and my heart races when his tongue taps my bottom lip for entrance.

My mouth willingly falls open, his tongue dancing with mine. My hands trace his pecs. He reluctantly parts from me, quickly pecking me on the lips and returning his attention to the meat.

"You're a temptress, Annabelle."

I shrug carelessly, a mischievous smile playing on my lips. "Give into it."

He chuckles. "Later."

Pouting, I hop off the counter and stretch. "When she finds out you broke in, she won't be happy."

"She's come to expect this from me," he explains. "Besides, when was the last time somebody prepared something for her after work? She deserves a break."

I agree wholeheartedly. Even when things were unbearably horrible for her, she remained positive and pushed the cynicism aside. I don't think I've ever seen her take a break before.

"Well, it *is* a bit dusty here. I'll go ahead and start tidying up."

As I turn, his hand flies down hard on my ass, a resounding *crack* echoing in the small galley kitchen. My sharp inhale has him snickering. My cheeks heat as the implication has me wanting to drop the cleaning and have my way with him right here and now.

Not when you just rejected me, ass!

The linen-closet-turned-cleaning-closet near the bathroom has everything I need. Grabbing a dangerous mixture of spray bottles, wipes, and a duster, I make my way around the house.

The entertainment center was the worst offender. The picture frames were carefully placed around a gross film of dust and grime on the glass shelf. Once I was done with that, I moved to the office to start tidying and cleaning the windows.

The smell hits me before I see where it's coming from. The mustiness makes my stomach swirl with nausea. It smells like someone left a bowl of milk out for days on end before finally pouring it down the drain.

I wrench the closet open, hunting for the smell. I move boxes upon boxes out of the way. I'm half expecting to find a dead raccoon in the back of the closet. But once again, my imagination fails me, as the closet is empty save for the line of dust from pulling the boxes out.

Standing up, I scour the office to no avail. I approach the window behind her wood laminate desk. I pull the blinds up, and the scent wafts into my nose as the dust blinds me. I launch into a coughing fit, nearly peeing my pants at the ferocity of my coughing.

The window is closed, but it looks like the top of the window has become unsealed. Mold grows on the sides of the window and the windowsill.

"I think we're going to need to call someone to reseal the window," I call out to Jay.

Waving the dust out of my line of vision, I tidy up the desk and sort the wild stack of papers on top of her keyboard when I see something that makes my stomach drop.

Tumor . . . right breast . . . malignant.

My throat constricts, though I'm not sure whether it's from the dust and mold or the fact that Jo has cancer and hasn't told anyone.

Why wouldn't she tell us?

It's like a train wreck I can't look away from. I reread the form over and over in gross denial. This can't be Jo. This has to be someone from the shelter she's helping out.

But it's not. Her name is at the top of this paper.

Jay is going to lose it.

"What was that?" Jay asks, appearing in the doorway. Once the stench hits him, his own cough attack sends him into the hallway.

I quickly flip the letter over and turn on my heel.

"The window isn't sealed anymore," I explain, the sweat pouring out of my head. God, he's going to find me out. "I can clean up the mold, but that needs to be fixed."

"I think there might be some caulk in the garage. I'll be right back."

I turn the paper over and exit the office with my heart racing. She has to tell us, right? There's no way she was just going to a hide away a life-altering situation without telling us . . .

My stomach churns with unease.

I love Jo. But when things get uncomfortable, she hides. It's obvious she's on this crusade that nobody can help her but *her.*

Is it wrong of me to not want to break the news to Jay?

This isn't my secret to tell.

And . . . I'm hoping he gets curious enough to find the results himself.

While Jay reseals the window, I make myself scarce in the living room, finally taking my time by cleaning up the picture frames I left on the sofa. By the time he's done, he sits next to me and helps me finish up the rest. Jay talks about whatever's on his mind while my mind wanders.

Has she told Momma at least?

What is her treatment plan? Should I offer to take her?

Do I even offer up that I know?

" . . . totally get Graves in on it. I heard he has a big dick."

I snap my head in his direction, my eyes wide. *What the hell?* "What?"

"I was just saying. A threesome. Could be kinky."

He laughs at my deadpanned face and playfully pushes me.

"Lighten up, Blondie. You've been ignoring me for the last fifteen minutes. I was getting bored talking to myself."

"I always knew you had a thing for him," I tease, grateful for that distracting image.

"BDE, baby. BDE."

Big dick energy, my ass. Graves doesn't even have a sense of humor.

"What are you thinking about so hard, anyway? You're on vacation. You should be thinking about trail rides and my bangin' bod."

I roll my eyes as my stomach drops.

"A little bit of this, a little bit of that," I reply, refusing to meet his gaze.

He stares at me for a long moment. He can read me like an open book. I know this. And the fact he didn't at least rifle through the paperwork on the desk is concerning. He doesn't know, and now I'm an accomplice.

I grab the first frame in the stack and take the pictures out so I can give the whole frame a cleaning. When I go to set the pictures down, I notice a few more pictures. I flip through them and grin like a fool when I see Jay through the ages.

At fifteen, he was the biggest guy on the football field. With a forehead of acne and a smile full of metal. At ten, when he was *so* into *Pokémon* and dressed up like Ash Ketchum for Halloween. Then there's the infamous picture of the five of us kids at the lake house: me, Jay, Chris, Aria, and Jackie.

And the last one has us both freezing: William Parker, Jay's father, has been a sore subject from the get-go. He was a marine, just like Jay. I can't imagine the horrors he saw, but he took that residual anger out on Jo and Jay, beating them daily.

It's impossible to count all the times Jay showed up at our house out of breath because he ran away from home, or he was beaten so badly he could hardly walk. It took a long time for Jo to get out. It wasn't easy, especially with Jay's uncle as the chief of police.

The picture I'm holding shows William holding Jay as a toddler. When I look at Jay now, I see more features of his mother: beautiful jade eyes that hold kindness and amusement, a smile that disarms you from the moment you meet him, and a laugh that is beyond contagious. But looking at this picture, it's like Jay could be his twin from all those years ago. William is grinning from ear to ear with Jay in his arms as Jay looks off into the distance with a toy phone up to his ear.

Jay quickly grabs the picture from me and studies it with narrowed eyes.

"I can't believe she kept this," he murmurs.

"It's weird to see he wasn't always a monster."

He scoffs, shoving the picture under the sofa and continuing on with the task at hand. "A monster hurts for pleasure, Annabelle. Just because there's a moment frozen in time where he's looking at me like I'm the golden boy, it doesn't mean jack shit." He turns his head so that he's looking me dead in the eye. Intense. "He doesn't deserve your sympathy, baby. He's a waste of life, and he doesn't deserve another moment of your thoughts."

Licking my lips nervously, I hesitate just for a moment. "Look, I'll only say this once, and we can move on. But he hasn't made contact with you since the night you came to live with us forever. Maybe he changed. Maybe he's sobered up and sorry for his actions."

He ponders this for a beat, holding the rest of the pictures in his hands. "We were going to leave that night," he says softly. "Momma made sure he was going off to the bar for the night. I packed a suitcase, and we were almost out the door." He swallows, his Adam's apple bobbing with emotion.

He doesn't need to finish because I already know the rest of this story.

They tried to leave, but William was tipped off. He beat Jo so badly she had to go to the ER. She received a few rounds of facial reconstruction surgery. Jay wasn't as bad off. He had a broken collar bone and cuts all over his body. His eyes were black and blue, and he spent the night in the ER as the doctors patched him up.

I don't think Jeremy could hide it any longer. There were too many witnesses. Something needed to be done about William, and throwing him in the drunk tank for a night wasn't going to cut it. They almost *died.* Try to hide a double murder!

"Okay," I murmur, rubbing his arm soothingly. "I want you to be happy, Jay. I know you don't like talking about it, but maybe forgiveness will give you that closure to move on."

He sighs deeply, the tension leaving with his exhale. "I appreciate what you're trying to do, but I can't forgive him for what he did to us. People like that don't change. They just get worse."

He pecks me on the cheek, abandoning the conversation altogether, which only brings me back to worrying about Jo.

"You're back to looking weird," he points out unhelpfully.

Jo saves me by walking in the door. We're the first thing she sees, and I'm expecting her to get huffy because we're cleaning her house for her, but she surprises me with a tired smile.

She slumps her purse off her shoulder at the entryway table and walks our way. She places a tender kiss on the crown of my head and does the same for Jay, right before crashing on the couch.

"You look beat, Momma. How was your day?"

"It smells lovely in here, you two. Thank you for cooking." She exhales dreamily, allowing her eyes to droop closed for a moment. We stare at her expectantly, waiting for her to elaborate.

Cautiously, Jay reaches out and pokes her bicep. "Momma?"

"Oh, sorry. It's been a long day," she replies without opening her eyes.

Jay glances at me with worry. "Can I get you anything? Some tea? Or water? A 5-hour ENERGY?"

Jo cracks a smile. "Thank you, but I just need to lie here a minute."

Oh, God. Just tell him. Put me out of my misery.

Jay leaps out of the seat and meanders into the kitchen. Jo cracks an eye open, making sure he's out of earshot.

"You don't have to do that," she whispers, referring to the picture frames.

"I don't mind," I reply absentmindedly.

As I sit here, occupying myself with mundane chores, my mind takes off. How do you tell somebody you rifled through their shit and you know what they're hiding from everyone without sounding like a jerk? Will she say something now that we're here so I don't have to be the asshole who breaks the news?

"Oh, look at this one," she says wistfully, taking a framed picture of her and Jay at Disney World forever ago. He had to be eight years old. "Our first and only trip to Florida. I didn't understand when everyone told me how hot it would be over there. I regretted not bringing a pack of scrunchies with me."

I laugh through my nose and slowly put the frame I was working on back together.

"I found this one too," I say, pulling the Halloween picture out of the frame and showing it to her. Her crow's feet deepen as her smile grows wider. She lets out a small chuckle.

"Oh boy, I haven't seen this one in a while. That was the year we went trick-or-treating in Jackie's neighborhood, isn't it?"

We'd always trick-or-treat in Jackie's neighborhood because she lived in a traditional neighborhood, whereas we lived in the middle of nowhere. Jackie's mom was only twenty-two and living with her parents. I remember meeting up with them—Aria and Jackie in their witch costumes at six years old, running ahead of us and eating their candy on the curb while the rest of us had our eyes on the prize. Jay and Chris eventually snuck off to egg one of their teachers' houses, and I tagged along because I wanted to be a part of it.

"That was fun, wasn't it? Daddy took us out for ice cream afterward."

"It was already cold," Jo giggles. "But we couldn't talk you and the boys out of it."

That still rings true. We've inherited my father's stubbornness. Or maybe it's my mother's. Regardless, we're as stubborn as they come. When we set our minds to something, it takes an act of Congress to stop us.

Jay reenters the living room with a mug of tea, gingerly setting it on the coffee table and reoccupying his seat next to me on the floor.

"You know, I have a whole box of old photos from the nineties in the closet of my bedroom. I could go get them . . ."

Jay grimaces. "Let's not."

I bark out a laugh because I know most of his adolescent pictures are *super* embarrassing, but now that I think of it, there may be more pictures of William he doesn't want to see.

Jo stretches before curling her legs under her. Jay covers her with a blanket and heads back to the kitchen to finish up dinner.

All the while, I stare at my second mother because *I don't know what to fucking do.*

"Baby, why are you looking at me like that?" Jo asks. I finally realize she's caught me staring at her.

"Jo . . ."

"Just spit it out, sweetheart. You keep whatever's bottling up inside of you for too long, you're bound to explode."

Okay. We're doing this, I guess. "Look, it wasn't like I went in there to snoop . . ."

She sits up, her eyebrows knitted with concern. "You're scaring me, Annabelle."

I lift my gaze and meet her eyes. "I was *trying* to figure out where the smell was coming from. And I saw that the window in your office isn't sealed anymore—"

"Oh, *god,*" she whimpers, burying her face in her hands.

Oh no. She's crying . . . "I'm sorry—"

"Does Jay know?" she asks urgently, cutting me off.

"I don't know if he saw it too, but I haven't said anything."

She leaps out of her seat and paces the length of the room. When she comes into eyeshot of the kitchen, she peeps in to find Jay working, oblivious to the world around him.

"Okay," she breathes as she continues to pace. "Okay. We can get ahead of it."

Thank God! "Good. Because we can't sit on this—"

"That's *exactly* what we're going to do," she interrupts, finally sitting down on the floor with me. She takes my hands in hers and squeezes tight.

I'm not equipped with the right emotional tools to sit on this, Jo!

"He just got home. He's going to that awful police station on Monday, and I don't want this to ruin it."

No. Absolutely fucking not! "This isn't my secret, Jo! I can't keep it. It's too much!" I whisper-shout.

"I know, and I know it isn't fair of me to ask you to keep this under wraps." Her chest rises and falls rapidly, like she's just run a mile down the road. "Wait until after the interview, okay? And then I promise I'll come clean."

Jay calls us all to the table a few minutes later, and Jo is acting like nothing's happened. Monday is a few days away, but let's be honest. The cop shop is full of Parkers, and what have the Parkers ever done for these two?

My stomach growls as the smell of Jay's pot roast wafts into the small dining room. He carries the red Dutch oven to the table with a proud smile and places it in the middle.

"I don't know about y'all, but I'm *starving,*" Jo announces, piling her plate with mashed potatoes and a roll from the basket in between us.

"It's so nice to have a kitchen again," Jay says, placing a thick slice of meat on her plate.

How the hell can she be so calm and collected? How hasn't he realized she's keeping a monster truck of a secret?

"Baby, can I fill your plate up?" Jay asks me with his hand out.

I glance over at Jo, who watches me expectantly.

Be cool. Act cool.

I hand it over and try to smile, though I suppose it probably looks like I'm using the bathroom or something.

Not that Jay notices. The two of them chat and laugh like old friends. I sort of feel like the outsider who isn't in on all the inside jokes.

Jo spends the evening in denial. They make plans for a vacation for the three of us next year that I'm only half listening to. All evening long, she avoids my gaze.

"You all right, babe? You've hardly eaten," Jay points out.

Yeah, because I'm guilty! "Sorry, I'm not feeling well. If you don't mind, I'm going to lie down on the couch."

I don't give them the opportunity to say anything to me. My chair scrapes against the linoleum floor, and I race out of the dining room. Jay and Jo talk in hushed whispers about me, but I don't care.

How the hell did I keep my relationship with him a secret for so long?

I occupy Jo's seat on the sofa and cover up with the same plaid blanket to where I only see red-tinged darkness.

The chairs in the dining room scrape against the floor and the rushing water from the sink can be heard all the way out here, clueing me in that we're a few minutes from leaving.

"I'm going to check on her," he says softly to Jo.

Great.

I hear him approach, and it isn't until he pulls the blanket off of my head that I see him. He grins and crouches down, pressing a sweet kiss to my forehead.

"Are you ready to go home?"

Yes! God, yes!

I swing my legs over and nod. Jo turns off the kitchen sink and wanders out into the living room.

"Thanks for inviting us over, Momma. I'm going to get Annabelle home before she passes out on the couch."

She turns to me and offers me a hesitant smile.

"Of course. I love having the two of you over." She moves toward the front door and rests her hand on the knob.

"You know what? Why don't I meet you in the truck? I just need to use the bathroom." I'm lying straight through my teeth. If I were Pinocchio, my nose would be as long as the empire state building.

Jay nods, pecks Jo on the cheek, and lets himself out. The door slams a little too hard, a resounding *thunk* echoing in the small living room.

We stare each other down. It's less like a showdown and more like a silent plea from both of us. We're begging different things, and I'm not sure any of us will back down. For the sake of my sanity this evening, I will.

"Annabelle—"

"I can wait until Monday," I say softly. "He won't like that you've kept it from him."

She nods. "Okay. Monday night. I'll tell him then."

Jay is living in his ignorance-is-bliss world, and at the moment, I envy him for it. This secret gnaws at my stomach, threatening to allow the word vomit to take over. I *need* to tell somebody.

He pulls into the driveway and stretches.

"I'm going to go for a run if you don't mind," he announces.

"Okay. I have to get this article going, so perfect timing." *Another lie. Another inch of my nose grows.*

He leans over and pecks me on the lips. I slowly follow him inside, taking residence at the head of my dining room table. I crack open my laptop, silently begging for the space to scream. Jay sticks his earbuds in his ears and starts down the paved road.

Before I know it, my legs move for me. I'm bounding out of the house and across the street to the person I typically never seek comfort from: right now, I need my big brother.

I knock three times on his red oak door and hold my breath. His footsteps cross the hardwood floors inside, and he wrenches the door open. He glares when he realizes it's me but softens when he notices the distress.

"What's going on?"

"Can I come in? I have to tell you something, and I'm not allowed to tell anyone else."

Reluctantly, he steps aside and allows me entry. His living room is something out of a Colorado wilderness lodge magazine. We all had free rein when our father decided to build the houses. I wanted a craftsman, Aria wanted a colonial, and Chris wanted to be a mountain man and live in a log cabin. I'm not entirely sure how it holds up in the rain, but then again, I'm not willingly hanging out with my brother on a regular basis.

I take a seat on his brown leather sofa and take a deep breath. His denim eyes search minc.

"Annie . . . what happened?"

"I was sworn to secrecy, Chris. You can't tell anyone that you know, okay?"

"I can't—"

"Chris, *please,*" I cry, the tears leaking out of my eyes.

He sits in the recliner next to me. My chest aches as if this secret is literally trying to burst out of me. "I promise. I won't say anything."

"Jo has breast cancer."

His blond eyebrows raise so high they practically get lost in his hair. His chiseled jaw ticks, and the anger in his eyes from earlier completely dissipates. He feels what I feel: *pain.* She's our second mother. She's family. This can't be happening. We don't lose family.

"What?"

"We went to her house tonight for dinner. Jay was being his normal, sweet, protective self and asked if I could see if the office needed a cleaning. It was right there in the open. I swear I didn't go looking for it . . ."

"What was out in the open?"

"Her test results," I cry. "Tumor. Right breast. Malignant." I meet his gaze and sob. "Jay doesn't know. She doesn't want to tell him yet."

Chris leans against his forearms on his lap. He can't form the words. The C-word is taboo in this family. Pappy, Daddy's father, died of lung cancer. Soon after, Nana died of breast cancer, leaving my father an orphan. He was grown, and I don't remember them that much, but still . . . the ache is there.

"Shit," he breathes.

"I feel *horrible.* This is going to kill him."

Silence leeches into the air. What could one possibly say to this news? There isn't a way to make it better, not when there's literally nothing you can do.

"How long has she known? Do you know what stage?"

I shake my head wildly. "I don't know. I didn't read any further, and she didn't offer it up."

He finally meets my gaze.

"What do I do?"

He sighs and scrubs his hand over his face. "I don't know," he admits quietly. "Honestly, it's up to her, not us. She doesn't like help, and she'll be embarrassed to ask for it." He opens his mouth to continue but immediately shuts it. "People beat breast cancer all the time . . ."

"Yeah, they do. But even if it was stage one or something just precautionary . . . Don't you think she would've told Momma by now?"

"You think it's worse than she's letting on?"

I don't know. I don't want to think about the alternative reality. Not when he's excited to start his life out of the Marine Corps. "I don't know."

He leans back in the recliner and stares at the wood ceiling in disbelief. Jo has been a pivotal person in our life. Where Momma was the disciplinarian or the hard-ass, Jo was the one sneaking us chocolate and candy or calling us out of school when we needed a mental health day.

"I'm sorry you're dealing with this on your own," he says softly.

"When does she catch a break?" I ask, not necessarily to Chris, but to anyone who's listening.

"She's lived a hard life. And Jay . . . Well . . . The best we can do is support him through it."

"He'll be devastated when he finds out that I knew."

My brother narrows his eyes and swallows his stupid pride. "Yeah, he will. But you were honoring her promise, Annie. He can't fight you on that."

But he can still hold it against me. "Will you tell me when she tells you more?"

I nod slowly. I'm in the thick of it now. I'll need all the support I can get. "Yeah. I don't know when that will be. But Chris . . . I don't think I can keep this in forever. I can't be that person."

"You have to be who you *need* to be. She's scared. She's going through this alone, and I'm sure she's embarrassed. She confided in you because she trusts you."

And I went behind her back to tell my brother.

"I won't say anything to anyone, I promise."

I sniffle and wipe my snot on the sleeve of my hoodie. "I know you're mad at me right now. I really am sorry, Chris. That might not mean anything to you, but I love him with every fiber of my being."

He scrunches his nose. "I don't want to know that. But . . . I forgive you. I don't like the two of you together. If you're asking me, this is a disaster waiting to happen. But if this will help you deal with this a little better, I'll learn to get on board."

We stand at the same time. We're not huggers by a long shot, but hugging him makes my brain hurt a little less. I can't do this by myself.

8

JAY

Graves slaps his cards on the table and everyone around us groans. "Pay up, you little bitches."

"Isn't there a rule that NCOs can't bother us on off time?" Hilderbrand whines. Technically, there aren't any rules about your noncommissioned officers hanging out with the lower ranks, but it's frowned upon.

"This is Afghanistan, dipshit. There's no such thing as off time," Graves retorts, pocketing the cigarettes they all push his way.

"What do you think she's having?" Jones asks, staring at the cloth lining of the tent.

"I don't know, Jones. We're not around to check your wife out," Smith teases.

Jones flips him off and turns to me.

"You're southern and superstitious. What do you think, Staff Sergeant?" Jones asks.

I give him a pointed glance. "They're called 'Old Wives Tales,' idiot," I snap, laying my cards down and taking the cigarettes away from Graves. I pocket them as he growls in disappointment. "And Smith is right. You won't tell us what she's saying about it. You're not showing us any pictures, so there's no way I could put in my two cents, even if you wanted it."

Jones smirks and twirls the toothpick in his mouth.

"Do you ever think you're doing the right thing?" Jones asks quietly.

The men in our small circle suddenly turn serious. The laughter and playful jabs come to a complete halt. This is where I have to become the papa bear. We joined the Marine Corps to make a difference in the world. I haven't regretted my decision to join. Ever.

"Is this really a conversation you want to have with us or the chaplain?" Graves answers for me.

"I don't mean with the Marine Corps." He turns to us, his denim blue eyes narrowing with intensity. "I mean, do you think I'm doing the right thing by having kids so early?"

Graves sighs with relief and chuckles.

"I'd say you're on par with everyone else, Jones. You're behind the eight ball, if I'm being honest."

Most men go into boot camp engaged to their high school sweethearts and have a kid by the time they get to the fleet. Jones is almost done with his first contract.

"Dude, I can't believe you're bitching about this," Smith snaps, shuffling the cards and dealing them out. "There are some of us who would kill *to have the extra BAH in our checks." BAH, or basic allowance for housing.*

I glare at Smith with an unspoken warning. "That shit's illegal, so don't go putting ideas into everyone's heads," I smart. I turn to Jones and offer him some reassurance. "Look, Jones. Whether you're in the military or not, fate already has your story written up. You love your wife, don't you? You see a whole future with her with the picket fence and shit?"

"Of course I do."

"Well then. It sounds like you're doing the right thing."

The tent enters an awkward silence as they let my words marinade.

"So . . . does that mean you'll start showing pictures of her?" Hilderbrand pipes up.

The boys erupt into hoots of laughter, with Graves being the loudest. For a moment, I feel like I'm at home again, playing cards in the middle of one of the pastures, everyone having a good time.

I glance up to the top of the tent, wishing Annabelle was here. She's always quick-witted with a story at the tip of her tongue. But most of all, I wish she were here so I could smell her hair—and stare at her a little too long.

A whistle has us all freezing. Under the cover of the tent, we don't know where the mortar is coming from.

"Take cover!" I shout.

We move as one in all different directions, just as the mortar hits our tent. Shrapnel cuts the exposed skin of my arms. My heart races against my breath. I can't tell if I'm badly injured or if the adrenaline is all I feel.

The tent caves in with poles blown apart, its sharp edges threatening to impale anyone who tries to get out. Smoke billows from a pile of torn canvas as a fire starts.

Fuck!

Hilderbrand's agitated shouts are what bring me out of my trance.

"Medic!" I shout to the top of my lungs.

"Parker!"

It's Graves's voice.

"Parker! You better still be breathing, asshole!"

My coughing prevents me from talking. I push the pile of rubble off my stomach and call for the medic again.

"Who has eyes on Hilderbrand?" I manage to shout.

But it's drowned out by a second mortar exploding close by.

I LEAP OUT OF BED, throwing the covers off. The darkness disorients me. Only a small sliver of light illuminates the hardwood flooring. The light flicks on, and just as I'm racing toward the door, I slip on something on the floor and crash with a sound resembling a herd of wild elephants accompanied by, of course, a shouted curse.

"Jay?"

I lie on the floor and stare at the ceiling in disbelief. *I'm home now.* I slowly sit up and study the room. There's a white blouse at my feet, and Annabelle launches herself out of bed, ripping her blouse out from under my feet and throwing it in the direction of the walk-in closet.

"God, I'm so sorry. Are you all right? What happened?"

My head sings from the contact with the floor. No, I'm not all right. *She's always been messy. You went into this knowing that.*

"Fuck," I bite off, cradling my knee close to my chest. We're silent for a beat as the throbbing in my knee starts to fade.

"I know . . . I'm a total hot mess express. I'm sorry," she coos, running her fingers through my hair and then grimacing when she pulls back to find her fingers coated in my sweat. "What's going on?"

"It was just a bad dream, Blondie. It's nothing to worry about."

But it felt so real!

She studies me with concern, her eyebrows forming a deep *V*. "Do you get these bad dreams often?"

"No," I lie through my teeth.

Hilderbrand died that night. One of the poles fell and impaled him when he ducked for cover. Three days later, Jones died trying to help a little kid.

My chest closes in and breathing becomes increasingly difficult. The rain of sweat doesn't stop, and my need for a hug and for a thousand miles of space—at the same time—go unanswered.

"I need some air." I stand up on shaky legs, and she follows suit. We walk silently through the house and onto the front porch, her porch swing calling my name. She curls up next to me, her head on my shoulder, and she gently sways us with her right foot.

That was six years ago. Six years, and I still can't get that image out of my head.

"Jay?"

"Yeah, Blondie."

"I love you."

Yeah, I know. "I love you too."

When the morning rolls around, I'm the most nervous I've ever been. After my nightmare last night and hurting myself on Annabelle's clothes, I ended up calling it quits trying to get any sleep and started cleaning the house.

I'm coming face-to-face with the Parkers for the first time since I left for the Marine Corps. I'll deal with Uncle Jeremy as best I can. I won't fly off the handle when he tries to goad me into blaming my father's abuse on him. But in order for this town to have a fighting chance at being *safe,* the cleaning up has to start at the town's most valuable resource: the police station.

No kid should lose faith in the good guys when their dad is beating up their mom. No woman should stay in an abusive situation because she knows the police won't help her. I haven't lived here in thirteen years, but I refuse to let the cycle continue.

I drive into town with Annabelle's truck. Her annoying country music blares over the speakers, reminding me she needs to expand her musical horizons. A little Paul McCartney has never hurt anyone. Or Van Halen for God's sake!

As I enter town, flashes from my adolescence flicker in my head like a movie. We were asshole teenagers who didn't give a rat's ass about the future. We egged cars and streaked down Main Street. We sat in the middle of Rhonda's Diner and sang obnoxiously off-key to the top of our lungs to the same song in the jukebox while the older clientele glared at us and alerted management. *That* was what Uncle Jeremy put a stop to. He threatened my career with the Corps and promised Chris he'd be locked up for life. And we stupidly believed him.

I drive around the station looking for a parking spot. Just like this town, the cop shop hasn't changed a bit. It's the same, red brick building with a parking lot that's too small for the amount of police officers with the last name of Parker.

I end up parking on the street, and when I step onto the sidewalk, I tuck my dress shirt into my dress pants and trudge toward the front doors. I cringe to know what's waiting for me on the other side of the doors. Maybe they found my father in the middle of town square and arrested him for indecent exposure. *Don't hold your breath.*

I build all the courage I possess and open the door. The receptionist's desk is stacked with case files and boxes that cover the front of it. I can barely see if anyone is on the other side of the desk.

"Hello?" I ask quietly.

A brunette ponytail pops up from behind the files. She wears thin glasses and is kissed with a small smattering of freckles. Her thin pink lips purse, and when her brown eyes fall on me, recognition sets in.

"Welcome to SCPD. I'm Roberta. How can I help you?"

"Ah . . . yes, I'm Jay Parker. I have an interview with the chief at nine."

She nervously starts tapping away at her computer, desperately searching for *something.* "Are you sure it was for today? I don't have anything in the calendar . . ."

My hands seize at my sides. I clench and unclench to eliminate some of the tension. My heart pounds in my ears, fighting off the adrenaline pumping through my veins at the mere thought of Jeremy Parker. "I spoke with him directly, if that helps. The chief is"–*stop cringing*—"my uncle."

Roberta stammers and clumsily reaches for the phone, knocking over a cup full of mismatched pens and pencils.

"Jay!"

I turn around to see my cousin Clay strolling in through the front doors. He's bald by choice and ripped because he's a gym rat meathead. He beams at me and claps me on the shoulder.

"Hey, Clay," I reply, less than enthusiastic.

He's Uncle Jeremy's only son—one that should be far, *far* away from being allowed in a uniform. Everyone in town knows to stay out of his way. I'm sure if you looked up "police brutality" in the dictionary, his ugly mug would be front and center.

"Roberta, this is my cousin Jay. Don't worry, I've got it from here."

The family resemblance is a little uncanny. Clay has the same jawline and crooked nose. When he was younger, we had the same dark hair that he grew out to the point he could put it in a ponytail.

Worst of all, he reminds me of William, my dad. He's always been a bully. He was always the one who got in trouble at school and would get suspended for days on end. The principal couldn't even expel him because he was the chief's son. Nobody wants the be on the chief's bad side. So naturally, there wasn't a soul around who wanted to touch that with a ten-foot pole.

He leads me through the bullpen. Merv, the cop that's been around since I was a kid, is *still* here, sleeping at his desk with his arms crossed on his big belly. There are case files stacked high on everyone's desks. The walls still have that cream-colored paint but have yellowed slightly from the years of cigarette smoke inside of the building.

My other cousins watch me as I come in. None of them have amounted to anything. Jason, Rhett, Brody, and Bryce all watch on with amusement. The idiotic foursome with Clay as their leader.

Not. On. My. Watch.

My cousin Jared, on the other hand, watches me warily as he pours himself a cup of coffee in the break room. He sets the pot down and offers me a wave, which I return. He's the only Parker who has ever been decent. Probably because his father, Michael, saw how corrupt his brothers became and got the hell out of town while he had the chance.

"How have you been, man? I didn't even know you were in town." Clay finally breaks through the silence.

Did the Chief not even tell them I'm here to interview?

"I've been great, thanks. I actually just got out of the marines. I'm home for good."

His eyes widen, and he nods once.

When Clay opens the door, Chief Parker's office is . . . worse than the actual fucking bullpen. Of course, Jeremy Parker sits at his desk, asleep. His salt-and-pepper hair is now stark white. He's a cynical, disgusting Santa Claus now.

Since he's asleep at his desk, much like Merv, I can't help but think this is on-brand for SCPD. He reeks of bourbon and cigar smoke. His uniform is rumpled and wrinkled. His snores fill the office more than the open case files do.

"Pops!" Clay shouts.

Chief Parker jolts awake, his electric-blue and bloodshot eyes darting from Clay to me.

"What the fuck," Chief growls.

"Jay's here."

"Get out, Clay," Chief barks.

Clay gives him the one-finger salute and strolls out of the office, slamming the door behind him. The glass rattles behind me. It's a maze just to get to the chair across from him, but even so, the chair is full of folders, loose bits of paper, cigarette butts, and a half-empty bottle of Hennessy.

"Just move that shit to the floor," he growls carelessly. He sounds like he smokes three packs a day.

I move the pile to the floor, unsure of where to put it since there's literally no free space. This is why I'm here. The chaos stops right now.

"Thanks for meeting with me on short notice," I offer politely, even though I don't mean a single word of it.

"So you left the Corps, huh?"

The way he shortens the name pisses me off. He never was in the military. When William shipped off, they didn't even care if he'd return or not. They didn't even bother seeing him off at his own going-away party. But then again, that's a story from a drunk narcissist.

"I did. I was ready to come home."

He nods and pretends to type on his computer. Little does he know, I can see his screen, and it's shut off.

"Where are you staying? With your mom?"

"I'm living with Annie McKenzie. We've been together for two and a half years now."

I don't think this surprises him much, but I was hoping to avoid this conversation. The Parkers and the McKenzies have had a multigenerational war since Sage Creek was founded. I was in the right place at the right time and learned how to separate the good people from the bad people at an early age.

"Really? Annie, huh? She's the tall one, right? Blonde hair, big tits?"

My hands tighten around the arms of the chair. The splintered wood bites into my palms, reminding me if I don't get a grip, this could all go sour way too quickly. I don't even dignify that with a response.

"So you leave the Corps, and then you come home and shack up with a McKenzie. Now what?"

"I wanted to join the police force. I don't know what I want to do with the rest of my life yet, but I know the transition isn't easy."

Uncle Jeremy winces because we all saw what the war did to William.

"The police are the next best thing until I can figure out my next move."

"And you're so sure I'll say yes?"

You've said yes to the rest of your spawn. "No, sir. I'm not sure. My military record speaks for itself. I don't play games. I protect my guys and make sure the surrounding people are safe. Serve and protect. That's what we're here for."

He steeples his index fingers and rests his wrinkled mouth on them. "You'll have to go to the academy."

"I figured as much. I've been studying, if that's what you're worried about."

"What about your head, huh? You were a grunt. If a gun goes off in the office, are you going to lose your shit under your desk?"

Deep breath in, deep breath out. "Why would a gun go off *in* the office?"

He shrugs. "Humor me."

"I'm used to having weapons being discharged around me. You're right. I'm a grunt. I know how to respond under pressure while also ensuring the safety of the guys under me."

"I'll need a psych eval."

Of course you will. "I had one done before I left. I can have the records sent to you."

"I don't have the room for another officer, Jay. We're fully staffed."

But he'll keep on Merv while he sleeps at his fucking desk.

"I love you, kid. But we're full enough as it is."

"That's not what you said a few weeks ago when we talked over the phone. You said you had plenty of room to bring me on."

He squints in challenge, waiting for me to be the first one to start throwing shit. I won't stoop to his level. "Have you talked to your father since you've been home?"

There it is. "No, and he doesn't matter in all of this."

"Call him, Jay. He's a different person now."

"No."

"How about this?" He leans over his desk and looks straight into my soul. "Have lunch with your father, and I'll hire you."

My hands ball into fists. His arrogant smirk has me standing up and ready to knock him out. I'm not doing this. My sanity is not worth this job.

Meeting my father after twenty-one years isn't worth the damage it would do to all of the progress I've made.

"You're paying Merv to sleep at his desk. I'd be a good officer. I can help make this town *safe.*"

"Those are my terms, Jay."

It's crystal fucking clear to me that this is Jeremy's way of fucking with me. My mom pissed off the Parkers because she told on my dad when he was beating us. I piss off the Parkers because I'm with a McKenzie. Now he has what I want, and he's dangling it in front of my face.

I'm done. No more games.

Without another word, I storm out of his office. My cousins laugh behind their hands. Roberta calls out to me as I storm out of the building, but it isn't until my cousin Jared races to meet me that I stop to look back.

"Jay, wait!"

He's Michael Parker's son. Fair-skinned, even-tempered, and *kind.* I don't think any of us hold *that* gene. His black hair matches the black in his uniform. He's the only other Parker who is a black sheep. He hates this town, but he came here to wrong a right. And he's the only one who has kept in touch with me since I left for the Marine Corps.

"Not in the mood, Jared."

"Shut up and listen to me for a second."

I shove my hands in my pockets and stare at him expectantly.

"Eight months ago, when Aria McKenzie and Zoey Hawthorn were kidnapped, the FBI swooped in."

"Yeah, I know all of this."

"This cop shop is a joke. Internal Affairs is refusing to look into us because of the connections the chief has with them. Aria has connections within the FBI, right?"

My gears start turning. "I think so . . ."

"Roberta and I have been collecting evidence for the last year. The investigation of their kidnapping is still ongoing. That gives the FBI all the leeway they need to start investigating this police station."

He nervously glances at the front doors. Clay waves to us as he hops into his police cruiser and zooms away, peeling out of the parking lot with a loud shriek.

"We're righting wrongs, yeah? Help me with this. This town deserves a reliable police station."

"*We're* Parkers. They'll fire you."

He shrugs. "Maybe. But like you, my record speaks for itself. Just . . . think about it." He claps my shoulder and squeezes. "It's really good to see you back, Jay. I'm happy for you."

I hop into the truck and start driving. Derek and his band of assholes have an entire arsenal to bury the chief. What are the odds of it actually happening? What are the odds of them helping me when I haven't done anything in return? Two whistleblowers in one police station. How many other officers who don't carry my last name would come forward and tell the truth? What kind of jail time would Jeremy get?

My phone vibrates in my pocket. I reach for it and nearly blow chunks when I see my father's name appear on the caller ID.

This is war.

My drive has me pulling into the parking lot of the shelter my mother opened. Once upon a time, it was a paper mill. An unsuccessful one at that. It closed nearly a decade after it opened and was abandoned after that.

But when things were bad with my parents, this was my safe haven. In the house my parents shared, there was a crawl space that had a weak wall. It was missing about twenty bricks. It became my hiding place when my father was looking to teach me a lesson.

I'd crawl out of the house and run until I puked. More often than not, the old paper mill had always been my shelter. It housed rats and roaches, but it was the only place besides the McKenzies' house that provided safety.

I study it as a thirty-three-year-old man. The red bricks are pristine and power washed. The windows aren't broken and dingy but are rather clean and large. The front steps hold pots of bright and colorful flowers.

It's a slap in the face.

This is what should've been here in Sage Creek when my life was raining around me. It's not that I'm not amazed at what my mother has created, because I am. But why is it that *she's* the one who comes to everyone's rescue when she couldn't come to ours?

"Are you just going to stare, or are you going to come in?"

From the side door, I find my little sister hanging out of the doorway, waving me in with Troy on her hip. I reluctantly turn off the truck, pissed that I got caught, and follow her in through the side. I'm sure some hulking man with an angry scowl on his ugly mug would be off-putting to the women and children who are trying to start a new life.

Her office is decorated with a love seat, a pack and play, and a large desk in the middle of the room. At least a dozen pictures of her favorite people in her life hang around the office. There's the one of us at a summer camp in town and another where she's being held by Chris when she was a premature baby, barely four pounds. Then I see it—the picture of all of us at the lake house Steve used to rent every summer.

"So, Adam Broody, to what do I owe the pleasure?"

"I was just driving."

Troy pops up from the pack and play and bounces for attention. She scoops him out and allows him to crawl on the floor. He regards me carefully, like he doesn't fully trust me just yet. *Hey, I don't blame him.*

"How was the interview?"

"It went as well as you'd expect it to."

None of this is a surprise to anyone. For years, people have taken matters into their own hands because they don't trust SCPD. And for a shelter like this that could typically depend on the police to back them up should unwanted company arrives, it's not exactly surprising.

"That bad, huh?"

"He said he'd hire me on if I went out to lunch with my dad."

Aria freezes, her kind amber eyes suddenly lighting on fire and promising retribution. "Are you serious?"

I nod. "It's not happening. I won't do it. But . . . Jared approached me when I left. He said that he and the receptionist have been collecting evidence against the chief and the other officers. Internal Affairs doesn't want to get involved because of the connections they have with the chief."

A small smirk appears on Aria's face. "What are you asking me?"

"Are you still in contact with that Nate guy?"

"He's Derek's best friend. Of course I am."

"Do you think maybe . . . he'd put the cop shop under investigation?"

She shrugs incredulously. "I don't know. He's not allowed to talk to me about what's going on with the investigation. But . . . maybe I can see if Derek could nudge him in that direction."

I look around the room while she studies me. This place makes me uncomfortable. When this was my home away from home, there were huge holes in the ceiling. When it rained, it rained in random spots in the building. There weren't any refrigerators or microwaves. For a little boy who feared for his life from the people he was supposed to trust, this was the perfect situation.

"It's okay to hate this place," she says softly. "Sometimes I hate it. It should've been here for people like us when we were going through it."

"Yeah, but Momma put her blood, sweat, and tears in it."

She shrugs. "You know, I still haven't stepped into the cafeteria. Eight months have passed. It was single-handedly the most terrifying experience of my life, but at the same time, it was where my son was born. It was where I finally admitted to Derek that I was in love with him. It's also where I looked that monster in the eye and shot him until his heart no longer beat in his chest."

"There's good in that room."

"There's also a lot of bad," she replies with a reassuring smile. The dark reality hangs in the air. She's a people pleaser. She can dress me down with one look and can tell when I'm lying. But still, she changes the subject. "How are you? I'm being serious. I know it's only been about a week since you've been home. Are you coping?"

"I'm fine." The lie drips of denial, and I think she knows it. "I know you're still coming around to the idea of your sister and I being together, but I get to live life out in the sun with her."

She smiles and shakes her head, a light laugh escaping her lips. "I'm on board with you and Annie. I always have been. I just didn't like it being a secret. Take it from somebody who used to hoard secrets about her own well-being. They're not worth it. They fester and then it turns into resentment. If you're going to be with her, be loud and proud about it."

"When did you become so wise?"

She giggles. "I don't know if you know this, but I lived with a man who tortured me for the fun of it. I've learned a lot of things about human behavior along the way."

The pang in my stomach is tough to digest. She talks about her abuse like it's a distant memory. Isn't there something they say about grief? That it's different for everybody. She had the closure of killing him. *Where is mine?*

The last night I saw my father, I watched through swollen eyes as Uncle Jeremy pulled him into his cruiser. Momma was awarded a restraining order just so Jeremy could get her off his back, and we moved in with the McKenzies. There wasn't a trial. Whether Momma dropped charges or not, I don't know.

"So . . . William."

I chuckle. "It's a dumb idea. It's been over two decades, Peanut. I've moved on."

She narrows her eyes and leans back in her chair. "You do what's best for you. You don't have anything to prove to him. You're a good man, JJ. You forged your own way. You had a successful career in the Marine Corps. You're with a woman who has loved you since you were kids. You have a support system that would steal the stars from the sky for you. We wouldn't hate you if you decided to meet up with him, you know. Just for some closure. Hell, I'm sure Daddy would go with you to get his own licks in."

I can imagine how it would go. He'd blame me for pissing him off all the time. He'd blame Momma for never doing anything right. He'd somehow compare our time with the Corps and brag about how he never had to deal with the transition. Then it would end with Steve getting carted away by my uncle for knocking him out. The thought makes my blood boil.

"Be real with me. I know today was a disaster for you. But are you okay?"

I nod. "Yeah. I'm okay."

Her amber eyes hold me captive. She doesn't believe a single word that tumbles out of my mouth.

"You and Derek should go shooting or something. It would help get some of that frustration out."

I chuckle. "Yeah, maybe."

I glance over my shoulder, somehow expecting my mother to be waiting around and listening in to this conversation.

"We had a new family come in today. Your mom is getting them settled, but she should be done soon."

"Eh. I'll call her later. And thanks . . . for the talk."

"Any time, big brother. Don't be a stranger, okay? Trauma has a funny way of worming its way into your brain when it's been dormant for so long."

I nod once and make a funny face at Troy who breaks into a wide, two-toothed grin. "See you at home."

I walk out the same way I came in. The heat from beneath the pavement heats through the soles of my dress shoes. I'm not looking forward to barn chores, but I do what I have to do to get it done.

While cars drive past the shelter, I see that same silver car. ELO's *Strange Magic* blares out of its speakers. It stops in the middle of the road, dozens of cars behind it slamming on their horns to get him to move. The window rolls down, and Dominic Reese's face focuses into view. He smirks and gives me a two-finger salute and pushes forward.

I wonder if that's something I have to be worried about.

9

DOMINIC REESE

The shelter holds two of my targets: Aria McKenzie and Josephine Parker. My job is to eliminate *one* of them. However, if I eliminate more than one, then I'm one step closer to exacting my revenge and completing the overall goal.

Make. Him. Pay.

The people that meant most to me were brutally taken away from me. And being that *he* did the same to Banks, so *they* say, our goals are aligned.

Imagine living in a world totally alone. Only those who want to witness your drowning are around. Mark my words, he'll face the most excruciating torture, and I won't even have to lay a finger on him.

But there always seems to be *one* person standing in my way every time I'm doing recon, and that's Jay Parker. He always seems to be exactly where I need to be, and it's infuriating. He protects Aria simply by being around. The sister, Annie, who he's staking a claim to, follows him around like a lovesick puppy, which takes her out of the running.

It's too risky. Not while he's around. He's observant. Probably from his training with Marine Corps. I just need to exercise a little more stealth.

He stands near his truck as I drive by, staring me down as if I'll tell him everything, as if his beady eyes are intimidating.

I smirk.

I'll make Jay Parker fit into the plan. He'll just be one more person out of the way, one more person to hurt *him.*

10

ANNIE

"I've been to Boston three times this year, Autumn. What more can I possibly write about the place?" I bark into the phone. Autumn Sanders, my insufferable editor, can't get it through her thick skull that she is slowly killing my creativity.

I itch to get out of Sage Creek, even if it was just for the weekend. But Boston . . . I wouldn't even know what else to write. I think I'd rather be locked up in my house for an eternity than go back to Boston.

That's not true. Way too extreme.

"You have the whole state to explore. You don't have to stay in the city. There are coastal towns, there's Salem, there's the Mayflower . . ."

"No, I get all of that, but the last time I went to Boston, I visited practically every city I could. I've been to Salem. I've been to the Mayflower. Autumn, there are at least six states I haven't visited yet—"

"I'm going to stop you right there because I want to review your job description. The travel correspondent will get their locations from the editor at the editor's discretion. The travel correspondent will provide an exciting piece for the reader's enjoyment—"

"Okay, let me stop *you* right there. I know what my job is. I've been doing it for the last seven years without a problem. I'm telling you that if I write another article about Boston, I'm going to lose readers."

"My hands are tied, Annie. Boston for two weeks. I'm sure you can find something to do, and I'm sure you haven't done *everything*. You'll figure it out."

"Can I at least have Mara come with me?"

Autumn scoffs. "Mara is in sales."

"Mara is wanting to become a travel writer, and it would be a fresh take since I've written about it twice."

"I'll talk to Nick and Geoffrey, but don't get your hopes up. Mara still has a job to do, and writing an article isn't part of it."

"Fine," I seethe. I slam my laptop closed.

"Check the attitude, Annie. We still have to work together."

Unfortunately. "Right. Well, if that's all, I'll need to get going."

"I'll email you when I have travel dates. Talk to you later."

I itch to throw my cell across the room. My job never used to be stressful. But when Elliot, my mentor, retired, Autumn was promoted and embarked on a major power trip. I wish I could take her down a few pegs. That would make me feel a lot better.

Jay walks through the front door a minute later looking haggard and annoyed. He kisses me on the cheek and drags his feet into the bedroom. I follow him in, eager to hear about how his day went with Jeremy.

I climb onto the bed and straddle his lap, lowering myself to wrap my arms around him. "You look tired, baby."

"That's putting it mildly," he replies darkly.

"How did it go?"

His jaw ticks against my shoulder as his mind races a mile a minute. "Jeremy did what he does best. He's a bastard. Don't get your hopes up, Blondie. I doubt anything will come out of my meeting with him today."

I frown and squeeze him tighter. "But he said he wanted to hire you on . . ."

A silence envelopes the room, waiting for one of us to say something.

"Yeah, well. Judging by what I saw when I stepped into his office this morning, he forgot. Or didn't intend on following through with it."

My heart aches. He was so hellbent on turning this place around. For his own sake, maybe for his own closure with his childhood, he *needed* to turn this place around. And now that Jo will be here any moment to drop the bomb on him . . . There's so much I need to tell him. His mom is about to go through the fight of her life, and he knows nothing about it.

"Rightsville is always an option."

He scoffs. "I'm not about to drive an hour out of the way for a town I don't care about. The plan was Sage Creek."

"I hate to be the bearer of bad news, but sometimes, plans change."

Jay grimaces, and a fire burns in his eyes.

"Can you give me some time to process this?" he snaps.

My heart catches in my throat at the sudden hostility. "Jay—"

"I'm not like you, Annie. I can't just let it slide." He sits up urgently and scoots off the bed.

"Hey, I didn't mean for it to come off like that."

"God, I could have avoided this part altogether had I just stayed in the fucking Corps," he growls, taking off the dress pants and pulling on some basketball shorts.

He's regretting coming home. *Oh, god. This is what I was worried about.* "I'm not asking you to let it roll off your back, babe. I'm asking you to see the silver lining."

He scoffs, pulling his dress shirt off in one swift movement, the buttons flying in every direction. One smacks me in the forehead. I curse under my breath, soothing the dull pain with my hand. He glares at me with contempt and a touch of sadness.

"What fucking silver lining is there anyway?"

"There are other ways to serve your community for one. The shelter doesn't rely on SCPD. They rely on Derek and whatever goon he has with him at the time."

"I'm not relying on him," he glowers.

"Then who are you going to let help you get your feet on the ground?

Because it's obviously not me!" Tears fill my eyes. More from the pain than anything.

"Come on, Annie . . . Don't be like that!"

I storm out of the room, slamming the door behind me. I rip the front door open and step out on the front porch. My bare feet against the sanded wood remind me I don't have anywhere to go.

Chris would tell me "I told you so." Aria would try to fix it. And if I brought this to my Momma . . . Well, I feel like her reaction would be much like Chris's.

I collapse on the porch swing while stray tears escape down my cheeks. Imagine loving someone so *fucking* much that when the weight of the world is on their shoulders, when the walls are closing in and there's no escape, the only thing you can do is watch helplessly.

After fifteen minutes of wallowing, Jay invites himself on the porch, studying me with a grimace and moving my feet so he can sit down. He massages my calves as we sit in the uncomfortable silence.

"I don't have the right tools to immediately find the positive in every situation." He turns to look at me, but I'm looking everywhere but him. "Annabelle, are you listening to me?"

I roll my head so that I'm facing him. But I'm not happy about it.

"I don't need you to fix everything for me." He gently squeezes my hand and offers me a weak smile. "It's not your job to fix me."

I sigh impatiently. "This is who I *am.* I see a problem, I fix it, I move on."

"Baby, that works for you. But it doesn't work for me." He pulls me up by my arms and folds me into his chest, his nose burying in my hair. "Sometimes, things can't be fixed. You don't control Jeremy or what he does. You *can't* fix that. And sometimes, I need to mourn something that doesn't pan out the way I wanted it to."

"How do you live like that?" I ask in a broken whisper.

I can't imagine living my life in constant sadness. Who would *want* to?

He chuckles in my hair, his hard chest bouncing with laughter. "You ever wondered why people called you an ice queen in high school?"

I push off him and create as much space as possible between us, staring at him scandalized. "I know you're not calling me an ice queen, Jacob."

He grins and pulls me back into him. "I love you, Annabelle."

"I love you too."

He heaves a content sigh and pecks me on the spot of my forehead where his button hit me. "I'm sorry for hurting you with my incredible strength."

I roll my eyes and laugh. I pull myself away so I can properly look into his pretty jade eyes. He's fucking perfection, and I'm the lucky one who gets to admire that bitable jaw.

"It's you and me against the world, remember? We don't *have* to stay here. We could go somewhere else."

"Germany isn't an option," he teases, pecking me on the lips.

"I'm just saying, Jay, we have time to figure it out. Nobody's forcing you to get a job right away."

"I know that," he presses, keeping his tone level. "But my whole point in coming home is to give you the life you deserve. Part of that was taking out whoever is in SCPD."

I kiss his forehead when his grip gets tight on my ass. "I love you for that. Have I ever told you that?" I gaze up at him. The wistful look in his eyes has me wondering what he's thinking about.

He smiles. "I know you were mad at me."

I arch an eyebrow, not entirely sure where he's going with this. "Which time? You're going to have to be more specific."

"Ha-ha, smart ass. I'm talking about senior year when I brought Marie Dawson to prom. When we were in the living room taking pictures, I saw you on the staircase. You were glaring at me like you were ready to rip my head off."

I giggle. "Yeah. I wanted to. I don't know why, but you make *that* so incredibly easy."

He removes a hand from my ass and gently pushes my hair out of my face. "I had a terrible time at prom. I lied to you when we got back."

"I could tell. That's why I spent the night in the treehouse. I knew you'd come and find me and, for one brief moment, be brutally honest with me."

He found me. We argued until we fell asleep. It was the first time I ever slept in somebody's arms. At fifteen, I knew I was going to end up with Jay Parker. I knew he was leaving in a matter of weeks. I knew he'd be a different person when he got out of boot camp. But part of me always knew that our love could stand the test of time—no matter what.

Because even though he was denying his feelings for me, he felt the same. I could tell by the way our gazes would meet while we did barn chores. I could feel it in his hugs when we ran into each other in the halls. Love is a feeling, yes. But it's also something so profound and tangible in its own sense. It can hurt as much as it can heal.

"I knew right then I was going to marry you," he says softly. He kisses my smile and caresses my cheek. "I'm a grumpy fuck. I know you deserve a lot more than what I can give you. But I promise I'll make a good life for us. We might just be a little late getting there."

"A good life doesn't always mean job security and money out the wazoo. How many people can say they live in a house on four hundred acres of land in a house that's already paid off?"

He chuckles. "I suppose there's a whole town that doesn't have the luxury of McKenzie security."

My face falls. He chuckles and pecks me on the lips.

"We have our whole life to figure out what we're going to do."

"He had a condition, you know."

I arch an eyebrow. "Who did?"

"Jeremy. He said he'd hire me on if I had lunch with my dad."

Of all the ugly, idiotic things that man could do . . . "What did you say to him?"

"I don't want to see him. I haven't seen him in twenty-one years, Annabelle. No run-ins at the grocery store, no bump-ins while I was in town. Hell, I even know he knew about boot camp graduation, and he didn't show up. What happens if I see him again?"

"Baby, is it really worth it?"

"My *home* is worth it. I knew the risks of coming back here. I knew I'd inevitably bump into him."

"People like that don't change. You said that."

"But *I've* changed. The Corps made me into a man. I don't believe in the bullshit Jeremy was peddling about how he's a changed man. I'm strong now. He can't get inside my head like he used to."

My stomach drops. This is one of the worst things that could happen right now. The pit in my stomach pulls tighter. What if this all goes wrong? What if they bury the hatchet? What happens to Jo?

Jo.

I swallow nervously, and Jay studies me closely.

"If you have something to say, baby, just say it," he encourages quietly.

"It's not that I have something to say . . . I just worry. Have you talked to your mom about this?"

He shakes his head. "I don't think that would go over well."

No, it certainly would not. Not when she fought through hell to get them both out of his clutches.

"My old mentor, Elliot, before he left the magazine, used to tell me all the time that we, as humans, are equipped with three reliable things: our hearts, which tell us what we want; our brains, which tell us what we need; and our guts, which tell us what is *right*. What's your gut telling you right now?"

He presses his lips in a hard line, contemplating his next words. He wages a silent war in his head. Meanwhile, I'm doing the same: In *my* heart, I don't want him to go through the heartbreak of his father again. My head tells me I *need* to let him make this decision on his own without my input. And finally, my gut tells me that the *right* thing to do has nothing to do with his father at all and *everything* to do with what his mother is keeping secret.

"My gut tells me I can save this town," he murmurs quietly. "We said we wouldn't have kids, right? But we have Troy. We have Zoey. And knowing what's out there, what happened to Aria, I *know* the right thing to do is to take out any old Parker influence. What's *right* is to play Jeremy's game and meet with William. I need to swallow my pride and meet with him face-to-face so I can make this town what we always dreamed it to be."

I stroke his cheek with my thumb and paste the best smile I can on my face. He's a hero. *My* hero. This town's hero. "You're a good man, Jay. The best I've ever known."

"Why does it feel like you don't agree with me?" His jade eyes darken as they study my hesitance.

"You have a gut made of steel, babe. I trust you. But . . . if things go south . . . if you feel like you can't cope . . . will you please share that with me? It would kill me if you hid that from me."

He nods, placing his hand on the back of my head and pulling me down to his level. His lips press to mine and urgently demand entrance. "I love you, Annabelle. More than my next breath. More than life itself. I won't hide anything from you."

I wish that comforted me. I wish his words didn't cut me up like a dagger to a sheet of paper. Because all I can think about right now is a different Parker—one who asked me to carry a bomb without any training.

11

ANNIE

It's been a week since Jo was supposed to come over and tell Jay the news. She's been avoiding us. Well, me, mostly. Jay's been going over every day for the last week so they can catch up. And every single time, she hasn't said anything to him. My stomach has been in knots the second I accidentally found out about her secret. I swear I'm going to form an ulcer by the time she finally tells him, and at this rate, it will probably be when it's too late.

On Tuesday morning, when I take a shower after morning feed, her truck is in the driveway, and she's waiting on my front porch. I don't bother drying my hair because I've been *dying* to talk to her. She grins at me through the window and shakily stands up from the porch swing. Has she always been this pale? Has she lost weight?

"Mornin', sweet pea," she greets with a kiss on the cheek.

"Good morning, Jo," I reply hesitantly.

"Is Jay around?"

"No, he went on a run with Derek."

I've never known tension in the air when Jo was around. It's always rainbows and butterflies. Apple pies and chocolate milkshakes. Now it's top-secret information and pretending what I saw wasn't real.

"Well, I hope you don't mind. I thought you and I could have breakfast together . . . and talk."

"Um . . . sure. I just need to be back by ten. I have a Zoom meeting with my editor."

Jo grins. "No, baby. I brought some staples with me. I thought we could cook together."

Every cell in my body immediately revolts. I *don't* cook. Cooking isn't something *I* do. I poison people and make everything inedible. "You've seen me cook. Do you think that's such a good idea?"

"Baby, I brought a box of pancake mix and fresh fruit. It's extremely difficult to mess that up. Come on over and grab an apron."

I ignore the urge to vomit. She's here, and she wants to talk. Maybe I can do some talking of my own and convince her to tell him.

"I was thinkin' some eggs too. Doesn't that sound good?"

How can she be so calm about this? I know if I were diagnosed with breast cancer, I'd be sailing around the world and seeing whatever this planet has left to offer me. "Sure. I have no preference."

She winks. "Good. Scrambled it is. Go ahead and measure the ingredients for the pancakes. The directions are on the back of the box."

As I measure, I hold onto my breath. I have to say something. "Jo . . ."

"It was a few months ago . . . shortly after Aria's engagement. I don't know if you noticed, but I haven't been around a lot. I'm tired all the time, so getting up to drive this far is a bit of a challenge."

I stop what I'm doing and slowly turn around. I need to see her when she drops this bomb on me.

"Stage two. That's what they said. They caught it early enough, and they're optimistic."

"Does Momma know?"

She takes an impatient breath. "When I was a little, the C-word was something you didn't talk about. It was bad juju, an invitation for the devil to take you away. I suppose now that I'm older, I know that's all bull-honky, but

—" She turns to face me with tears blinding her eyes. "—I *refuse* to let people see me as anyone other than Jo Parker."

She sniffles.

"I had parents who worked themselves to the bone. I had sisters and a brother who were much older than I was and didn't give a hoot about me. Then I married William *Fucking* Parker because I didn't want to be a spinster, and now look," she sobs.

I close the distance between us and embrace her gently. "I'm sorry," I whisper. "I need you to know I wasn't snooping when I found that."

"I know, honey." She pulls away from me and gently pats my face. "We've lived a hard life. Jay is finally coming into his own, and he can *finally* be with you. If I tell him this, his mind will go to the worst-case scenario, and he'll derail all of his plans. I can't let that happen."

Bile rises in my throat as the truth of this visit dawns on me. I'm being asked to continue keeping a secret that will certainly destroy Jay's newfound freedom. As if the interview with the police station couldn't have gone any worse, he's now actually considering meeting with the man who nearly killed him after twenty-something years of not seeing him as well as putting his marine life to bed.

Why did I go into that office? More importantly, why didn't I tell him?

"Jo, you have to tell him. He'll be so angry when he finds out . . ."

"No. Honey, I know this isn't fair of me to ask you to keep this to yourself. I'm okay, honestly."

I don't believe that. She's far from okay. "Is there something I can do for you? Who is bringing you to treatments?"

She shrugs nonchalantly.

A chilling thought comes to me. Who would she call if she wanted complete secrecy? Who wouldn't fawn over her like she's living her last days on Earth? Certainly, it wouldn't be us.

"Jo . . ."

"I asked William."

Oh my God! My mind screeches to an abrupt halt, struggling only for a moment to take in this newly discovered, *awful* information. "What?"

"Who else was I going to ask?" she shrieks. "Your mother would fall apart. The Parkers are off the table—"

"William is a Parker!" I've never raised my voice to her, and yet, I feel like my whole life is spiraling.

"He's sober."

I bet he is. I wonder how he got that way? Perhaps Jeremy threw him in the old slave quarters and let him detox it out.

"It's not like we're back together. I needed someone to bring me to and from the appointments. I needed someone to take care of me after—"

"I'm not trying to be an asshole, Jo. I swear I'm not, but you have *us.*" I meet her watery jade eyes. "We would've been that support system for you. Hell, we still can. You don't need William, especially after what he put you through."

"Listen. I'll tell Jay. I'll tell the family. But after my next follow-up, okay? I want to make sure I can give them good news before I go breaking hearts."

Hearts are already broken, whether she tells them or not.

"Please, baby. I know I'm not being fair. I kept your secret for two years. *Please* keep mine. Just for two more weeks."

I swallow the lump of tears and nod.

A secret for a secret. Fair's fair, isn't it?

WHEN JO LEAVES for the day, I do something I haven't done since I was a teenager. I pack a backpack with Lunchables, a few sandwiches that will make the grazing steer pay me a little attention, and enough water bottles to last me the afternoon.

I'm relieved to find the barn completely empty. I take Archie out of his stall, slinging my backpack to the ground, and clip him into the crossties. He's a thoroughbred—one of those who spent his formative years running around a track for other people's enjoyment. When Daddy found him, he and I formed an instant connection.

I suppose at the end of the day, he was fast. But he didn't *look* like the other thoroughbreds on the track. Whereas most of them have dark coats, his is more chestnut colored. He has kind eyes. Almost like he's witnessed a world of hurt and is grateful for the reprieve he gets here.

I'm tacked up in no time. I slide the bridle into his mouth and secure the straps. Five minutes later, we're heading to the other end of the property.

There's something about riding in the middle of the day. The sun is out, and it's pretty hot. But the entire property is *silent.* The guys are five miles away, harvesting whatever's ready to harvest. The stalls were done early this morning, so I suppose Derek is out doing his real job of healing other people's animals as this town's only equine veterinarian.

And me?

I took this time off to be with Jay. I thought he'd need me. I thought we'd have enough time to reacclimate to each other. His ambition is admirable. He's a hero in everyone's eyes—except for his blood relatives.

The heat of the sun beats down on the back of my neck. My ponytail isn't thick enough to cover it, but I love it. Archie walks on with a pep in his step. I'm sure the monotony of being either in a stall or out in the pasture gets boring. It feels like old times.

Our property is big enough that we don't ever have to venture outside of it to find some other park to trail ride to. With a property this big, nothing is ever too similar, especially when the creek runs through the middle of the pasture and patches of thick woods spread themselves out. It makes for fun cattle drives.

My phone vibrates in my pocket. When I see it's Autumn calling me *again,* I ignore it.

A smile plays on my lips when we ride across the other steer who graze obliviously. When I was a kid, this was the next best thing when I needed to get away. I wasn't old enough to take the world by storm, and other than the lake house getaways or the *one* time Momma brought me to Florida, it was like I was Louis and Clark discovering a new frontier.

When I reach the creek, I drop my pack to the ground and take the bridle off of Archie. He walks away, chomping at the grass while staying close in case he needs a quick getaway.

My boots are the first thing to come off. Typically, when you ride, the attire is jeans, ugly tube socks that reach your knees, and boots that will stand the weight of a horse stepping on your toes. But today, I dress in shorts that would make my father blush and a green tank top that barely hides the bikini underneath.

I lathered up with suntan lotion before I left home, so when I strip down to my bikini, the hot sun feels like magic against my skin. I reach for my phone, play country music, and sing along with only Archie and the steer as my audience.

Songs of broken hearts, revenge, and sweet love echo into the pasture. I've heard somebody say before they couldn't stand being within four walls all the time. The world called to them, begging for space to roam free and fresh air to fill their lungs.

I get it. I don't think there's anything more that could ever speak to my heart the way that did. Except for that one time . . .

Annie – Fifteen Years Old

When I finally hear my parents' door close, I give it a fifteen-minute buffer before I sneak out of the window. With summer not quite here yet, the air outside is still cool when the sun goes down, so I dress accordingly. I slide a hoodie over my blue, spaghetti strap tank top that Aria swears makes me look like I just stepped out of a tanning booth, and my blue and white checkered sleep short that I've rolled up at the top. Slipping on my flip-flops, I head out the door.

Besides, I know Jay will eventually come looking for me. Maybe then, after he's danced with Marie and she's shoved her tongue down his throat, he'll finally realize that the girl he'd rather make out with has been in front of him the whole time: me.

I hoist the backpack full of stolen snacks from the kitchen over my shoulders and tiptoe out of the room, silently closing the door behind me. My heart pounds so hard I can feel my pulse in my neck. I wait for Momma and Daddy's bedroom door to stop swinging open. After a prolonged period of silence, I go for the window and shimmy down the drainpipe.

One day, my parents will find out about this little hack Chris came up with, and when they do, I see my time at the barn vanish into thin air. Daddy will make me harvest with Hank, the operations manager. No, thank you.

I traipse through the property confidently. Passing the house that will be mine as soon as I turn eighteen, a swirl of excitement consumes me at the thought of not having to sneak around. But also because I can't wait to be in college.

It takes me about thirty-five minutes to hike down to the creek. When I get there, I carelessly toss my backpack down to the damp grass, kick my flip-flops off, and stick my feet in the icy water.

This part of the property always smells so fresh. A lone oak tree on the other side of the creek stands proudly rustling its leaves. The patch of woods fifty yards behind me, where Jay and Chris have their dumb treehouse, holds the secrets of every member of this family.

Except for me.

"What the hell are you doing out here?"

I jump at least three feet in the air, clutching my fluttering heart. There aren't any lights around, but with the brooding tension in the air and his voice getting deeper by the day, I know I'm not in danger.

"What are you doing back so early?" I counter, resituating myself so that my feet are submerged in the water.

He sighs and sits down next to me. From my peripherals, his dress shirt is untucked from his pants. His bow tie is undone and hanging loosely around his neck. He smells of the crisp cologne he put on earlier with a slight scent of beer wafting in the wind.

"It's late, Annabelle. If your dad finds out you snuck out, you're going to be in deep shit."

I'm past the point of caring. I needed to be outside where the sky is the limit. I turn to face him, and my stomach drops with anxiety.

"Did you have fun?" I ask, pulling my knees to my chest and hugging myself in case he tells me they did the dirty. I don't want to know.

"It was all right." He drops the parental tone and lies back on the grass. I open my mouth to warn him that the grass was wet, but a content smile spreads across his lips. "They played a lot of country music which really sucked, but the food was good."

"Did you dance?" I already know the answer to this, but what can I say? I'm a masochist.

"Yeah. We danced a few dances, and we went to Henry Fox's after-party." It's a punch to my gut because Henry Fox is one of the most popular guys at school. If the party was at his house . . . well . . . he would have had sex with her. That's what the popular kids do.

I blink the tears away and clear my throat. A fiery, hot rage bubbles in the pit of my belly. That was supposed to be me! How can he just pretend not to love me too?

"I don't really want to hear about the after-party." I purse my lips as my eyes begin to water.

"Why not?"

I squeeze my eyes shut and tamp the jealousy down as far as it will go. "Because."

"Because you're in love with me?"

Simply put, yes. But he doesn't get to beat this out of me so easily. When I don't answer, he sits up and tries to look me in the eye, but my hair blocks him.

"You can't expect me to admit to that," I bark. "It's more than my pride at stake, Parker. Do you think I'd actually admit to it when I know for a fact you'll find any excuse to rebuff me?" Especially when he has someone as beautiful as Marie on his arm. How could he say no to a face like that?

"You can't, Annie."

I hate the way he throws "Annie" around so carelessly. I've never been Annie to him. Ever.

"You don't get to just push me away, Jacob," I spit poisonously, scrambling from my seat and grabbing my backpack. Screw my pride. Women don't get what they want by staying silent. It's so dark out here that I can slip into the treehouse unnoticed, but he grabs my arm.

"Where are you gonna go?" he demands.

"Wouldn't you like to know?" I hate the way my voice cracks with emotion. I hate that I'm even crying at all. I rip my arm out of his tight grasp and gather all of the bravado I can muster. "I've figured it out, I think. You play dumb when it comes to me when we're around other people. You treat me like the little sister who follows you around and worships the ground you walk on. You call me 'Annie' in hopes nobody figures out that you prefer my whole name. But when we're alone, you look at me

like you give a damn." I sniffle, wiping the snot away with the sleeve of my hoodie. "You look at me like you love me too."

"Of course I love you. You are *my sister."*

I scoff and march in the direction of the woods with him hot on my tail.

"You're blowing this out of proportion—"

"If that's how you feel, then go home. I'm spending the night in the treehouse away from everyone. Say what you want about me, but at least I'm honest about my feelings for you."

I race off with him calling after me. He at least has his phone to light his way. I left mine on my nightstand in case my dad had some secret way of getting alerted that I left the house.

I'm getting there by muscle memory. This treehouse has held all of my tears and laughter over the years. And tonight, it gets to seal my broken heart into the floorboards. I climb up the ladder and push the battery-operated push light, only illuminating a square inch of the floorboard. It's been here so long that most of the lightbulbs inside of it have burned out. Nobody has been here in forever to change it out.

I pull a sleeping bag and a small throw pillow out of my backpack to make myself comfortable. Until the sound of shoes on the ladder grabs my attention.

Jay crawls in and sits on his haunches in the door opening. I don't bother looking at him. I said what I needed to say, and I need to catch enough sleep before morning feed.

"I'm sorry if you thought I was leading you on."

Yeah, I bet.

"But Annabelle, you need to understand that our age gap matters."

Scoffing, I hold onto the pillow tighter while my heart threatens to bust a hole through my chest.

"I'm eighteen. You're fifteen. If anything could happen between us . . ." He sighs in exasperation. "Look. This town is still caught up in this multigenerational war between our families. Uncle Jeremy wouldn't have a problem locking me up with a statutory rape charge. Ever since he gave my mom what she wanted—the restraining order—he's been finding any excuse to stick it to her. What better way to get to her than locking me away? The whole town would make our lives a living hell. Then I wouldn't be able to join the Corps."

"We haven't even so much as kissed," I counter.

"It doesn't matter."

He crawls deeper into the treehouse until he's sitting right next to me. I don't dare move in case I'm dreaming this and my movements wake me. I feel his warmth on the back of my neck.

"You're important to me, Annabelle."

"No, I'm not." I sob into my pillow. "Because when someone is important to you, you don't make them feel like shit every single day."

He sighs and lies next to me, staring up at the ceiling. We're silent for so long that my eyes droop.

"Sit up for a minute," he instructs softly. "Come on, Blondie. I know you're not sleeping. Just for a minute, and then I'll leave you alone if that's what you want."

I sit up with a huff. I turn to face him. Under the dim light, I can see him for who he really is, who he hides from everyone but me—the kind, raw Jay Parker, the one whose heart is more tender than he likes to admit.

"You're right. People don't treat people they care about like shit."

"Then why are you doing it to me?" I demand.

He licks his lips nervously. His Adam's apple bobs. "Because I think I'm afraid of how you make me feel."

What the hell does that mean? "Are you just saying that because you want to be in my good graces again? I swear Chris doesn't care what you call me—"

Before I can finish that sentence, he presses his lips to mine. As fast as they were there, they're gone. There was no tongue. No fingers in my hair or wandering hands. But still, the butterflies in my stomach frenzy with anxious energy.

"Jay—"

"Now we know what it feels like," he breathes. The corners of his mouth twitch.

I know what it feels like, and I want so much more.

"Go to sleep. I'll wake you up before everyone gets up for morning feed."

How the hell can I sleep after that?

"YOU HAVE the whole place in a tizzy," a deep voice comes from above me.

I grin at the familiarity of Jay's baritone voice, and my stomach somersaults because it's *him.* Now that I'm not daydreaming of the last time the two of us were out here together, my breakfast with Jo floods into my consciousness.

He crouches down next to me and lowers himself all the way to the ground, sitting crisscross applesauce. He traces his index finger over my stomach and chuckles when I shudder.

"You left without a word. I saw you all packed up when I was turning Tippy out and then you were gone."

He's killing me. "I didn't know you were around. I'm sorry. I would've invited you along if I knew you in the barn."

He whips his navy-blue shirt over his head and scooches in on my towel. The sun glistens off his sweaty, tanned abs. He kisses my cheek and sighs heavily.

"What are you doing out here, Blondie? Tell me the truth."

The truth is a dagger. And if I can save him from being struck in the gut, I'll take his place every single time. "Do you ever feel caged here?"

He ponders that a minute, propping himself up on his elbow and staring at me with concern. "Caged, how?"

"Caged like . . ." I collect my thoughts silently. "Caged like everyone has these high expectations of you. They look past your hopes and dreams and replace them with their wants."

Doubt rolls over him like an impending thunderstorm. I'm not telling him all this to put him off-kilter. But at the same time, I want to get away. I *need* to get away.

"Talk to me, baby. Don't talk in riddles. Am I making you feel that way?"

"No, of course not! I think you're the only one who understands the way I'm wired. I'm just . . ." I sigh. "Somebody asked me to keep a secret."

He smirks. "Aria's pregnant again, isn't she?"

I snort. Very unladylike. "No. She's not pregnant."

His lips press against my shoulder, the contrast of my boiling skin against his cool lips a nice refreshing treat.

"I don't like keeping secrets, Jay. I'm not good at it. It eats me from the inside out—"

"Do you want to tell me?"

I'm grateful for the bug-eye sunglasses that cover the majority of my face. Because if they weren't there, he'd see the tears pouring out of them.

"So badly," I murmur. "But I can't."

He licks his lips nervously. "Is it about *us?*"

"No. I love you, and I love what we have. I'm so happy you're home, Jay. You have no idea."

"What kind of secret is it?"

Do I tell him and betray Jo? Or do I keep my trap shut and allow him two more weeks of ignorance? "Life changing." I sigh deeply and turn on my side to face him.

"When Hilderbrand and Jones died, a lot of the guys were keeping their shit locked up. It wrecked them. It wrecked me." He gazes at me and smoothly reaches out for the sunglasses, pulling them off my face. "You have to ask yourself if this anxiety you're putting yourself through is worth it. And baby, it's okay to unload. Our whole relationship is built on word vomit and clumsy pickup lines."

I giggle.

"Is that the only reason you came out here on your own?" he asks with a raised eyebrow.

God, he knows me so well. I may as well be lying spread eagle, allowing him a gander to know the inside of me as well.

"I was feeling nostalgic. I can't fly anywhere, so Archie filled that role for me." I don't have to look far for my goofy guy. He's grazing a yard away with his ears pointed toward us.

"Yeah?" He flips me on my back and hovers over me. His pink, pillowy lips twitch, and his jade eyes are hidden beneath his eyelids. "What were you thinking about?"

"You."

He chuckles. "Tell me."

"Our first kiss . . . and how I wanted it to be more."

He licks his lips with anticipation, his rock-hard erection pressing up against my core that's covered in flimsy bathing suit material.

"You wanted more?"

"I wanted it all," I whisper. "I wanted what you wanted to give me but forbade yourself to."

His lips crash against mine hungrily, begging for every inch of me. My legs hitch around his waist, crossing at my ankles. My arms snake around his neck, pulling him closer against me.

He leaves my lips, licking the suntan-lotion-infused sweat off the crook of my neck. A moan escapes my lips as my soul leaves my body. His strong hand holds my hip, and the other strokes my hair, letting me know he can be the one to be what I *want* and what I *need.* He's my heart and my brain. And somehow, he's my gut too. Because he's perfectly *right.*

"I wanted all of you," he growls in my ear. "It was wrong. But *fuck,* Annabelle, you will forever be *right.*" I fumble with the button on his jeans, tearing them down and grasping his length in my hand. He groans as I lightly squeeze, stroking him while his want for me seeps out of him.

I lick my lips, wanting to taste him. To taste the desire for *me.* He sits up on his haunches, once again proving he can read my mind without having me open my mouth. I lick the tip, all of the precum of fun he's promised. I take him farther into my mouth until he reaches the back of my throat.

He hisses in pleasure, his hand tangling in my hair and pushing my head down further. My free hand cups his balls, kneading them and pulling out the guttural growls that show me how much he can let go with me.

I pick up the pace, deep throating him whenever I can.

"Fuck!" he bellows. He doesn't finish, but he pushes me down, yanking my bikini bottoms off of me, his fingers tracing my slit and finding that bundle of nerves. My legs clench. His mischievous smile makes my heart race. He reaches for my pack, taking out an ice-cold water bottle.

"You're so fucking hot," he hisses. He unscrews the cap and pours a little on himself before pouring the rest on me. My breath catches in my throat, and before I can come back to Earth, his mouth is on me. It's like he's committing me to memory in case he gets recalled to the Marine Corps or he gets caught by my dad.

My legs lock around his head, his fingers pumping into my soaked entrance. I possibly can't get enough of him. I cry out when he removes his fingers. We lock eyes and he winks, gently inserting his soaked index finger into my puckered hole.

"Fuck, Jay!" I cry out.

"I wasn't like this back then, Blondie. I would've lit candles and played cheesy music. I would've made my bed and sprinkled it with rose petals . . ."

I tune him out as I focus on the pressure.

"Which do you like better?"

"It wouldn't have mattered," I pant. His fingers go deeper. My throaty screams echo into the nothingness around us. "This one!" I cry out.

He removes his fingers and lines his cock up with my entrance. He stares into my soul when he enters me. My body is already spent, my voice hoarse.

"I've loved you forever," he grunts. "Your pussy is so perfect."

My orgasm builds. I squeeze my eyes shut. I want to see all the Technicolor fireworks he brings me.

"Open your eyes, Annabelle," he demands.

I obey because his eyes are even better. I explode around him. He pistons his hips faster until he gives in to his own release. He crashes to the ground next to me, a sated smile on his face.

"You're going to be the death of me," he huffs.

"You're not allowed to die, Jacob. Not when you promised a life full of happiness."

He kisses my cheek. "Do you feel better?"

No. I betray myself by nodding, though my stomach screams at me to grow a pair of ovaries and come clean. I'm better than this.

For the next hour, we dress before anyone comes looking for us and snack on the adult Lunchables I packed. For the most part, we're quiet. I ache from his touch. I'm almost certain he could take me right now without any foreplay with how wet I still am.

"I decided not to meet with William," he says quietly.

I swallow the cracker and glance at him in surprise. "Really?"

"Maybe I can't help on the inside. But maybe . . . I don't know. Aria's in talks with Nate. I can facilitate the meeting between him and Jared." He glances at me and pinches his eyebrows together. "You know what I can't stop thinking about?"

I wait for him to continue.

"For twenty-one years, my momma never went running back to him. She knew the can of worms she would open if she did, and look at her."

Stop talking! Please, stop fucking talking!

"I don't need to meet up with him to know that I'm a good man. I saw war, but I came out the other side wanting to help people, not hurt them. So I'm going to take a leaf out of her book. I can be patient. I can help around here until the investigation ramps up . . ."

I'm going to puke.

"What do you think about slipping away to the beach for a weekend?" he asks, taking me completely off guard.

"That sounds heavenly," I reply, closing my eyes in frustration at the innuendo.

"I'll set it up. Don't worry. You and I are going to reset. We'll put the stupid SCPD behind us and start building our future together."

12

JAY

"Jacob!"

My name sounds so foreign. I'm Jay. I've always been Jay.

"Jacob!" It gets louder, and the voice behind it holds so much anger and hate. I've locked the door. I've pushed the chair under the door handle. He can't get in. Not again. "If you don't open this fucking door right the fuck now, I'm going to make sure you never see the light of day again!"

I jump into action.

Except, when I jump out of bed, my feet hit the ground heavily. The Thomas the Tank Engine pajamas I wear are too small. I catch a glimpse of myself in the mirror. I'm not a little boy. I'm Jay Parker. I'm an adult.

But why is there still so much fear?

I duck into the closet and lock the door behind me. I do what Momma told me to do all those other times before when Dad would get angry. I hop up into the storage space in my closet. I stash myself behind boxes of Christmas and Easter decorations. I crawl all the way back until I hit the end of the space. A blanket and pillow await me. The banging gets louder. But then, everything goes quiet.

"You have two options, you little shit. Option one, you face me like a man and

take your punishment, or option two, you cower and become a useless piece of shit for the rest of your life."

I'll take option two. I know I'm not a piece of shit. I hold my breath, desperate for him not to hear my breathing.

"Option number two will be worse than option one. Option two will have twice the punishments."

I press my lips together, my lungs screaming for relief.

"Remember the song, Jay," Momma's voice rings in my head.

Something about storms and holding your head up high.

The bedroom door is kicked open with a muted growl. I let go of the breath I'm holding. To my horror, the boxes of decorations fly out of the storage cutout. William stands in the opening with a sinister grin on his face. His hair is graying, reminding me of Jack Dawson from The Shining. *The bitter hatred mixed with anger in his blue eyes is petrifying. I can't move a muscle. The sweat rolls down my back as I pull my legs up to my chest.*

"It's just a dream, Jay," I say to myself. Only, it's not my voice. It's my voice as the scared eight-year-old kid.

I peer out from my crossed arms. Dad doesn't move a muscle. It's like he's a wax figure of himself. That smirk on his face, the thinning hair . . . He doesn't move.

His eyes snap wide and he jumps onto the ledge.

"Time to play, Jacob!"

THE THRASHING around isn't what wakes me up. It's Annabelle on the floor, the moonlight bathing her in the slightest amount of light. Her bluebell eyes are wide with fear as she presses up against the wall.

The thrashing continues even though I know I'm awake. I sense the fear in her eyes and the uncertainty in the air.

"Jay?" she says cautiously.

She summons all the courage she can and rises from the corner she's hidden herself in. She crawls back on the bed and puts her hand on my chest. My body goes still. Her palm is cold on my sweaty chest.

"Was it about Jones?"

I close my eyes in frustration as I try to catch my breath. "Did I hurt you?"

She shakes her head and helps me sit up, fluffing my pillows behind me. She's had a front seat to my nightmares off and on for the last two years, but this is the first time William has ever shown up. Like always, she straddles my lap and pushes herself close to me, enveloping me in a tight embrace while I catch my breath.

"You scared me, that's all. I thought you were being killed."

It sure fucking felt like it. "I'm sorry. I didn't mean to scare you."

"Do you want to talk about it?"

"No," I murmur.

"Come on. Let's go cuddle on the couch. I have some rosé in the fridge that will help take the edge off."

I don't want wine. Every time I blink, I see his cold eyes staring at me. So waxy, so evil.

She climbs off of me and takes me by the hand. We enter the dark living room, and she turns on the dimmer and seats me on the couch.

"Can you make it a beer, Annie?"

I don't make it a habit by calling her by the name everybody else calls her. "Annabelle" is solely for me . . . or if she gets in trouble with her family. But I don't miss the surprise when it rolls off my tongue so naturally.

She nods and pours herself a glass of wine and pops the top off a beer. She pads into the living room, my T-shirt brushing against her creamy thighs. She sits down and wraps her arms around my left bicep. She hugs me close and kisses my arm.

"Are you sure I didn't hurt you? You were across the room . . ."

"You didn't hurt me," she murmurs. "The thrashing started and I got out of bed to get out of the line of fire. Honestly, I'm okay. What about you?"

"I don't know." My admission comes out with a hysterical laugh.

Her doorbell rings, shocking me into sitting straight up, gripping my beer. Annabelle peers through the peephole in the door, her shoulders slumping with relief.

"Oh, it's just Derek. Let me get rid of him and I'll be right back." She leaps out of the cushion, almost like she can't get away from me fast enough.

I can't make out their muttered words. Like a bucket of ice water, the sight of Derek looking at me like he knows *exactly* what I'm going through makes me want to punch him through a wall.

"Hey, buddy," he says softly.

"I'm fine, Hawthorn," I bark.

"You sure? Because the whole neighborhood is too afraid to make their way over here. You're lucky Steve lives four acres away."

Fuck.

"What's going on?"

"I don't want to talk about it," I hiss. My legs contract, my toes curl, and my fingers itch to extend as far as I can let them.

"You don't have to talk about it then. Go get dressed. Let's go for a run."

"What do you say, handsome? It might give you a chance to catch your breath," Annabelle soothes.

"Hey," he says, trying to get my attention. "Just a run. A mile at the most, and we'll come back home. I promise."

I want to be out of here. I don't want to close my eyes and see his face again.

"Okay," I croak.

"We'll be back. I have my phone on me. I promise you I won't let anything happen to him."

Reluctantly, I shuffle into our room, leaving the beer on the dresser. It's one o'clock in the morning. By the time I get back, we'll have maybe an hour of sleep before we have to get back up.

"Jay . . . ? Are you sure you want to go for a run? It's the middle of the night."

I snort. "I doubt the good citizens of Sage Creek are going to jump me in the middle of the night, Blondie. Plus, I have the good doctor to keep me company."

I don't miss her scowl or the way she disapproves.

"Okay," she murmurs sheepishly.

"I'm sorry," I say softly. I close the distance between us and kiss her forehead. "The run will do me good. I'm sorry for scaring you, Annabelle." Annabelle McKenzie is not one to back away from a fight, especially not when she can be her authentic, argumentative self around me.

"Come back safe, okay? I'll be waiting up for you."

I don't want her waiting for me. She should be in bed, sleeping it off.

Derek waits for me outside, his arms crossing his chest. I wonder if I woke the kids up too . . .

"Start stretching, big boy. Shake the bullshit out," he coaches.

I wave him off dismissively.

The worst part about this is that my best friend, my brother from another mother, trots down the front porch steps of his house, geared up and ready to run.

"What are you doing?" I demand.

"Running."

"Let's go, pretty boys. Let's see if the old man can beat you."

We run in stride with Derek slightly ahead of us. My breath comes out in short puffs, like I can't race to meet it. My heart races erratically in my chest, and with it is the pain of everything slipping out of my control.

"Come on, Parker. Step it up, Gunny," Derek coaches.

Twenty-one years. That's all it took. A quick trip to the cop shop to bring all of those memories back.

"You all right?" Chris breathes.

"Peachy."

In the dead of night, with three grown men running for their lives on an old country road, it almost looks like something out of a horror movie. Where are they running? *Why* are they running? Why are the two young guns trailing so far behind the old guy?

It was a dream. I was myself, but . . . not. And William . . . I've never seen him like that.

While my body screams at me to go back to bed, my mind encourages me forward. I've had mile markers hidden out here when I was first getting ready for the Corps, and Steve kept them around. So when we sail past our one-mile mark, I keep going.

I'm escaping William. I'm escaping that house I spent too much time fearing for my life in. They say you shouldn't be afraid of the dark. But all I've ever known is terror when it's dark out.

The abuse.

The kiss I had with Annie when she was too young.

Hilderbrand's death.

Jones's death.

The aches in my legs go ignored. I don't pay attention to the way my lungs seize under my speed. Chris falls behind, but Derek hits his stride right next to me.

"Slow down," he coaches.

"No."

He jumps out in front of me and slams my chest with open palms. I come to a screeching stop to avoid knocking the both of us over.

"Hands on your head. Breathe."

I swear my pulse is not only in my ears or my throat, but I feel it *everywhere.* My blood is coursing with adrenaline. The creepy smile of my father's wax figure is still there, taunting me.

"Fuck off."

Derek shuts up, finally. Chris catches up and looks like he's about ready to puke.

Annabelle was in the corner of the room staring at me in a way she's never stared at me before. It sends me on my ass, literally. I hit the ground and bury my face in my hands, unleashing a guttural scream.

"Talk to me, Parker. What happened?" Derek says firmly but gently. He meets me at eye level, sitting comfortably on his haunches waiting for me to spill my guts. "Close your eyes."

We're not there yet. He may be marrying my baby sister, but we're not blood. We didn't serve together.

"Are your eyes closed, fucker?" he barks.

I nod, though it's not remotely true.

"You're in the middle of the pasture where you had your dirty sex with Annie the other day."

Chris interrupts him by growling.

"You're under a tree. You hear the creek. Acknowledge. Do you hear the creek?"

I squeeze my eyes shut. I banish William the best I can, but I still feel his presence.

Annie's voice flits into my mind. *"I have a secret . . ."*

Suddenly, I'm there with her. She lies on my arm, her head turned toward me and staring at me like I'm the best thing that's ever happened to her. The trees rustle on the warm summer breeze. The steer graze nearby, ignoring our presence completely. And sure enough, the rushing water of the creek can be heard just a few feet away.

"I want you to look up at the tree, Parker. Find a leaf, and watch it float down toward you."

A green leaf, nothing spectacular, detaches itself from the tree and swirls on its way down. It gets picked up by the breeze and lands on Annie's chest. Our eyes meet and a soft smile touches her lips. She closes her eyes and basks in the sun, the heat tanning her perfect skin.

"Open your eyes, buddy," Derek reminds me softly.

When I open my eyes, I'm back in the dark, sitting in the middle of the road.

Chris watches on with hesitant amazement. My lungs no longer seize in my chest. The sweat isn't pouring out of me anymore.

"You good?"

It seems I've lost my words, or at least the actions to string sentences together, so I answer with a nod as he helps me up. We walk back toward the property in utter silence. My nightmare woke up the entire neighborhood. I don't know whether to be impressed or terrified. Maybe a little bit of both.

When we start down the driveway to Steve's house, Derek claps my shoulder and stops us. Chris stops too, but reading the expression on Derek's face, he bids us goodnight and heads back to his house.

"Talk to me."

He isn't going to leave me alone unless I spill my guts.

"The nightmares don't stop."

His blue eyes lock onto mine. "Yeah? What kinds of nightmares?"

"It's a mix. Ninety-nine percent of the time, they're my memories of Afghanistan. It's my guy trying to take off a bomb strapped to a kid's chest. It's a mortar coming out of nowhere and blowing up our tent." I swallow. "I haven't thought about William in twenty-one years," I breathe.

"Your dad?"

I nod. "My uncle wants us to meet. That was his condition in hiring me on the force."

Derek lets out a heavy sigh. "Nate's working on it. He said there's an investigation open and he's testifying personally about how dysfunctional that night with Aria was." He drops his hand. "Do you want my two cents?"

I nod, but only because he's dealt with the pain from what happened with Aria. I don't pretend I don't hear the screams from her nightmares too.

"Your father isn't worth your sanity. I promise you that the police station is going to get stripped of everyone who works there and get rebuilt from scratch. But don't rely on the likes of Jeremy Parker who has his own ulterior motives up his sleeve. You got out, Jay. You and your mom. You both got out and live a good life. Fuck William Parker. Leave him in the past."

It's easier said than done. Not when you close your eyes and wonder if your father is going to hack you up with an ax.

"I'm sorry for waking everyone up."

He waves me off dismissively as he starts down the cobblestone path back to the neighborhood. "We've all been there, buddy. Find a therapist. I promise you it's the only way it gets better. You're not the first marine to need help after getting out."

I mentally roll my eyes. Finding a therapist is a ridiculous suggestion. I don't need to hold anyone else down with my baggage. Sure, a therapist is paid to shrink my brain, but why does everyone think I want to sit down and relive everything? I have the nightmares to show me how useless I was. Regardless of what anyone says, I could have saved Jones, and I should have been able to protect my mother from a monster.

When I don't say anything else, Derek pats my shoulder and sighs.

We bid our goodbyes. I walk back into our house and find Annie waiting on the ugly green sofa, bundled up in the burnt-orange throw blanket. She gives me a watery smile as I fill the space next to her.

I don't like scaring her. I don't like her being afraid of me.

"Did it help?" she asks softly.

"A little," I reply honestly. I take a deep breath, my lungs aching. "Are you afraid of me, Annabelle?"

"No," she says almost too quickly. "I was afraid of not being able to help you."

She shouldn't be the one shouldering my bullshit. Maybe Derek's right. Maybe I should be seeing a shrink.

"Are you tired?"

I nod. The beer on the coffee table is warm now. I take one last swig before launching off the couch. When she moves to lead us back into the bedroom, I grab her waist and pull her close to me. She'll never know how much she saves me every day. How much just the memory of her got me through all the bullshit overseas.

She's the love of my life. My soulmate. The savior of my whole fucking universe. But even the strongest of heroes have their weaknesses. And they can't be around to save you every time you need it.

13

JAY

I've been home a total of a month. Annie is finishing up her trip in Boston and will be home tomorrow night. While she has the time of her life, I'm picking up her slack around the house and feeding her animals. I love the woman with every fiber of my being, but she's a disaster. I've cleaned every inch of this house, and I've done her laundry, cleaned all the bathrooms, and even deodorized the place.

Most nights, I've eaten with Steve and Betty Lou. Though Peanut has invited me over a few times for dinner.

However, there's another thorn in my side. There's been a change in the eldest McKenzie sibling. He's warmed up to me, but I can't understand why. So when he invites me over for a beer and *Call of Duty*, I'm fearing for my life. Will he initiate fight club? Will he lose his mind and make me drive to Jackie's house so his apologies will fall on deaf ears?

When I arrive at Chris's house, I take a seat on one of his leather sofas that he got from Randall Gross, one of the metrosexual "cowboys" who lives in an apartment in town. Chris's idea of an appetizer spread are premade dips from the grocery store, a sub platter, and a case of lukewarm buffalo wings. Whatever. I'm not complaining.

There's never been an awkward silence between us. I rocked his world in the worst way, but I don't like being in the line of fire, especially when it can be easily fixed.

"So . . . how's work?" I ask, desperate for conversation.

"Remember Tommy Keller?"

"The asshole PE coach? Yeah. I hated him."

Chris snorts. "He retired. Anyway, the administration thought he was bluffing and didn't bother hiring anyone to take his place. So not only is the asshole assistant coach, Franklin, taking on both classes, but they just opened up spots for volunteer coaches." Chris wriggles his eyebrows excitedly.

"Yeah? You signed up?"

"I did, and they offered it to me. It's an extra stipend, which is great, but now I can finally fix what that asshole Keller ran into the ground."

I can't imagine Chris coaching. Don't get me wrong. He's a great teacher. His students love him. But football? Let's just say that when he was the star quarterback, he got under a lot of other people's skin which landed him a mutiny. "Good for you, bud. That sounds awesome."

We reach a beat of silence. Chris stares at the TV blankly. I can hear his gears turning from here.

"You ever wonder what would've happened if we married our high school girlfriends?"

I choke on my beer. Being married to Marie Dawson sounds like a deserted cruise to hell. Absolutely not. "I take it you have?"

"Megan Livingston. She was a fox," he says with a drunken smile.

"She also picked on Aria."

He scrunches his nose. "Aria could always take care of herself."

It's *those* statements that make us freeze every time. She was a tough kid. But were we not watching close enough? Were we ignoring what she was going through because we were thinking with our dicks?

"I mean . . . when it came to girls like Megan. She didn't take their shit."

Probably because she's stronger than we all give her credit for.

"Anyway, she got married last winter to Eric . . . You know, the farrier?"

"Senior or junior?"

Chris chuckles maniacally. "Senior! Anyway, it got me thinking. Maybe I should stop living like an eternal bachelor."

The thought alone is comical. The guy has been around town at least twice, and if his tryst with Jackie has anything to do with this new revelation, I have a feeling she'd kick him to the curb before he could even cross the street.

The last time I saw her was briefly when we FaceTimed during Aria's engagement and again at my welcome home lunch. Since then, she's avoided us, not that I blame her.

"Do you have your eye on someone?"

I know the answer. He knows the answer. Regardless, a small smile forms on his lips, but it's soured by regret and bad choices. "No, I don't think I do. But kids would be kind of fun."

Not my scene. "Well, if that's what you want to do, what's stopping you?"

"Well, she refuses to even talk to me, for one."

It seems like Jackie is on somebody else's mind tonight too. Her boyfriend, Sam, for one. I don't blame her. Chris was a grade *A* asshole to her. "She's dating that vet, you know. The one who Derek hired. I think his name is Sam."

Chris shrugs. "It wouldn't have worked out anyway. We're too different. She's so young. She isn't even out of her twenties yet."

But that girl has lived her whole life being more mature than all of us combined. "Did you apologize?"

"I tried to. I took two steps into the office before she went off on a tangent about how I should go fuck myself in front of the whole town so they can witness."

I snort to myself. I love Jackie. She's never afraid to speak her mind. "Did you go over there because you were sorry for your actions, or did you go over there to mend fences before it got back to Aria?"

He licks his lips nervously. "Can't it be both?"

I sigh impatiently. "I don't get it. You're one of the smartest people I know, Christopher. I don't know why you thought that would be appropriate."

He scowls at me, pissed that I'm not on his side.

Christopher McKenzie—the Golden Boy, the Casanova—has always been scarily intelligent. The guy could drink us under the table on a Thursday night and fly into school on Friday bright-eyed and bushy-tailed to ace the chemistry midterm without studying for it. If he'd just apply his book smarts to his common sense . . . he could make someone so happy.

"Jackie was a mistake."

I smirk. "I don't think that's the case with you, buddy."

The front door flies open. Derek strolls in with a six-pack and a shit-eating grin.

"What are you doing here?" Chris asks.

"I wouldn't let you fools have a boys' night without me." He sets the beer on the coffee table and crashes next to me on the couch. He winks at me and cracks open his own.

"When is your friend moving here again? Because this nightly drop-in is getting intrusive," Chris asks, referring to one of Derek's best friends from his time in the navy.

"I'm not sure," he answers with a grin. "But why do I need him when I have you?"

"I think you're just trying to force an in with me because you're marrying my sister."

Derek cackles maniacally and grabs the controller out of my hands. "You're not wrong. Anyway, what's going on with you and Jackie?"

Jackie is going to go on a murder spree.

"Nothing!"

"She and Sam are good together," Derek states simply.

I'm sure they are. I bet he's some nice farm boy who treats her like a queen. He treats her the way a woman should be treated.

"Good for her," Chris grumbles.

"But she's avoiding my fiancé, so you see where that puts me?"

"She's not avoiding Aria. Are you kidding me? They went two years without seeing each other, and they're still attached at the hip. Don't think I don't know they eat lunch together every day."

Oy.

"How do you know that?" Derek challenges. "Because I know for a fact you haven't been at school since it let out, and you haven't been seen near my office since she told you to fuck off."

I wish I could stop grinning. Chris glares at me, softly calling me a traitor under his breath. Seeing him being put in his place is quite enjoyable. *I can't wait to talk to Annabelle about this!*

"Look. I'll admit it was a mistake. It was supposed to be a one-time thing, and she got confused."

A year ago, Derek was that guy. He was the one mothers threw their daughters at. He knows how to play the game, and he knows Chris is full of shit.

"Or you realized you had feelings for her and chickened out."

"This is the most fun I've had in days," I offer unhelpfully.

"Fuck off," Chris snaps.

"Anyway, I'm going to have to insist you mend that bridge fast. Aria wants her in the bridal party, and she won't have her be uncomfortable throughout the entire wedding because you couldn't keep it in your pants."

As Chris turns this over silently in his mind, I glance at my phone and find a picture message from Annabelle. She's bundled up in her hotel bed and blows me a kiss.

Annabelle McKenzie: Call me for bed tonight. I thought we could have some fun

Insatiable. But I love her for it.

"In all seriousness, Aria told me about the guy who came to the barn a few weeks ago."

The thought of Dominic Reese makes my hackles rise. There's something off about him. The fact I saw him scoping the place out when he thought we were all asleep is making my stomach churn.

"She didn't tell you that day?" Chris asks.

"She told me bits and pieces. But now that I'm thinking about it, I find it interesting that they sent a Dodge Enterprises representative to talk to her."

I raise my eyebrows. "Why would they send out a representative when they're under investigation?"

Derek shakes his head. "According to the business card, he's some higher up that swooped into Charlie's place. He said the board wants to help put Senior away for life. Anyway, Nate's looking into it and recording it under the right protocols. I was wondering if you could tell me any more about him?"

I love when I can use the tools the Marine Corps gave me. "He made sure the girls were alone."

Derek nods once. "She said he wore an earring."

"A diamond stud on his right ear."

"That doesn't seem to be very CEO, don't you think?" he asks.

That's exactly what I said!

"What else?"

"He wore a suit. Maybe not as high end as someone in the Dodge Enterprises caliber would. He had dark hair that was slicked back, real Italian-Mobster-like. Brown eyes, about five ten . . ."

"Did you see what he drove?"

"A silver Audi, but he was fast. I didn't catch the license plate number."

He leans back into the sofa and stares at the ceiling.

"This trial can't end fast enough."

I know how he feels. I know what it's like constantly looking over your shoulder, waiting for the other shoe to drop.

When the night concludes, Derek and I walk out of Chris's house together. We walk in silence in the same direction until Derek stops me. I turn to face him, the lone streetlight illuminating our spot, making it look like a cheap drug deal.

"Did you do any surveillance while you were in?"

I shrug. "Some. Nothing like what you did."

"Are you looking for work?"

My spirits soar. This vigilante group he has going on is what I've wanted to be a part of since somebody in my unit mentioned it to me. "Are you offering?"

He chuckles. "It's an off-the-books thing, but Aria deserves a fairy-tale wedding. This . . . *guy* roaming around looking for her is putting me on edge. She doesn't want me getting involved, and if I'm being honest, I don't think the FBI wants me getting involved either. Think you can trail him the next time you see him?"

"Yeah. I can do that."

"Good. Report to me when you find something. Get some rest. I'm sure you'll need it for when Annie gets home tomorrow."

I want to laugh out of hysteria.

This is a turning point. Something I can get behind. It protects my family, and it allows me to use my skills. Now to trap the fucker and see what he's really in town for . . .

14

ANNIE

Boston Commons at nine o'clock in the morning is a magical sight. It may not be as big as Central Park, but my heart soars when I see happy couples walking with their baby-filled strollers.

Boston Commons at nine a.m. the morning after your young protégé drags you to a nightclub you're *definitely* too old for—well, that's a whole other beast. I cling to my coffee with two extra shots of espresso for dear life. Checkout's at eleven. Our flight doesn't take off until four o'clock this afternoon. I don't want to be here.

But the warm air against my skin is a blessing. I people watch the happy families who walk their dogs or the kids playing Duck, Duck, Goose in the grass. My mind inevitably goes to Troy and Zoey. They have the perfect parents: people who know what it's like when life throws onions and tomatoes at you for no good reason.

Jay and I said no kids. I stand by that. I like being able to leave at the drop of a hat. I'm lucky to have a job where I can do just that. Having kids would put a stop to that. And I think I'd turn into my mother—not that it's a bad thing. It's just not *my* thing. I wouldn't be a good mother anyway. I'm selfish and flighty.

But . . . I'm a kick-ass aunt. And if I'm being honest, that little butterball has me reconsidering my decision.

My phone rings, and speak of the devil, Aria's name flashes on my screen, asking to FaceTime. I oblige willingly and answer the phone, only to see Troy's chubby cheeks smiling back at me.

"Well hello, handsome," I greet with a giggle.

He babbles, telling me all his troubles. I listen on while Aria giggles in the background. Soon the phone is taken away from him, and Jay's handsome face fills the screen.

"Good morning, baby," he greets with a sleepy grin.

"Good morning. You seem happy today."

"Well, I got a visit from Zoey early this morning. Seems like Dr. I-Think-I'm-So-Pretty is hungover, and Peanut wanted more sleep, so I came and ran interference."

He'd be such a great dad. The love in Troy's eyes as he rests on Jay's hip is apparent.

"Hungover, huh? Maybe they were practicing making another baby."

Jay's face twists in disgust while Zoey shouts, "Ew!"

"I'm never getting pregnant again, Annabelle. Keep it in your pants," Aria's voice carries from the kitchen.

Jay sits on their sofa while Troy reaches for the phone. The angle on his face continues to get higher the more Troy climbs over him to get it.

"So you played babysitter?"

"I think Zoey wanted a few extra minutes of shut-eye, so I came over and made breakfast. Peanut's awake, but pretty boy is still sleeping."

"You must have had a wild night playing *Call of Duty*."

He smirks and shrugs his shoulders nonchalantly. "Maybe. I can tell you one thing. Your brother doesn't have the same southern hospitality your momma does. I ate cold sandwiches and cold wings all night."

"Yeah, well, I was dragged to a nightclub by Mara. She's twenty-four, and the girl can party." I sigh and set my coffee down. "I spent most of the night at the bar nursing one tumbler of vodka while I babysat her."

I yawn and stretch my arms over my head. When I realize I have to fill this day with something, I frown. Too bad it isn't winter yet. We could go ice skating. I'd pay a good amount of money to see hungover Mara try to handle herself in ice skates on Turtle Pond.

"Are you excited about coming home?" The longing in his voice is painful. It never used to be like this. This was our way of life. But we went from spending maybe a weekend a month together to now where we're spending every single day together . . . It makes me wonder if he's regretting this at all.

"I am. Do you miss me?"

His dimples pop from his face. He winks at me and nods. "Of course I do, Blondie. What would I do without you?"

"Well, being that I can't cook to save my life, I'd say you're doing pretty damn fine without me." *Living in your ignorance-is-bliss world. For that, I envy you, sir.*

"Oh, stop. You're my best friend, Blondie. I'd die without you."

My eyes water as I look away from the camera, scanning the park before me. "Have you visited your mom since I've been away?"

"Yeah, we've had dinner a couple of times. Hey, have you noticed she seems more tired lately?"

Yes. "A little. The shelter must be taking a lot out of her." *I'm an asshole. I'm the worst person alive.*

He shrugs. "Yeah, maybe. Anyway, I was thinking when you come home tonight, we can go grab some dinner in Richmond, canoodle under a table . . .?"

That sounds amazing. But at the same time, I'd rather hide under a rock. "Sure."

He heaves a sigh. "Blondie . . ."

"Hey, don't expect too much out of me. I'm nursing a hangover with gas station coffee."

He chuckles. Just then, Troy grabs hold of the phone with all of his might and sticks the camera in his mouth. I giggle while Aria shrieks in the background.

"I'm not buying you a new phone when he ruins yours, JJ! Take it away from him!"

I giggle as they wrestle the phone out of his grubby hands. The tiny terrorist is whisked away by his mother, and Jay wipes off the camera with his shirt.

"Is everything okay?" he asks seriously.

"Remember that secret I told you I'm holding?"

He nods seriously. I wish the word vomit would take me now. I have so much to tell him. But my father always told us that there's monetary currency, and there is the currency of your word. Money is always nice, but it holds greed. Anyone can be paid off. What is more valuable is your word, no matter who it's to. Your word is the most valuable resource you own.

"Are you ready to talk about it?"

I chew on my bottom lip as I turn over the situation in my head. I should tell him. He'd want to know. He'd want to take care of her.

"I don't think I can," I reply hoarsely. "I want to, Jay, but I don't think I can."

His understanding nature kills me. I don't deserve him. I wish I could fly out to London and let the shit hit the fan while I'm there and hide out in a flat somewhere. I don't want to be the middleman. This isn't fair.

"Do you remember when we were kids and your dad always sat us down and lectured us about the weight of a promise?"

So speaks the devil. But regardless, I nod.

"Somebody asked you to make a promise, Annabelle. You're not the judge. You can't make that decision for someone else. *Even though* I'm dying to figure out what it is."

He won't after Jo's told him. He'll wish for this ignorance.

"But what if it affects other people? Don't you think the affected parties would have the right to know?"

He shrugs. "This is why you have to choose your people carefully," he teases. "I don't like secrets. They have a way of chewing you up and spitting you out. It isn't fair they burdened you with this. But if I were you, I'd keep the secret. Wait until they're ready to share it."

He's going to eat his words. When he finds out I was holding the skeleton key to his mother's health, I'm going to be public enemy number one.

"So again, I'd love to take the love of my life out for dinner tonight when she gets back home. I want to stare into her pretty eyes and fondle her under the table. What do you say, Blondie?"

Despite my despair, I giggle. "Fine. But I like dark corners and seclusion, Parker."

He chuckles.

"That's disgusting!" Aria shouts from behind him.

"Mind your business, Peanut!" I call back.

Her house is a zoo. But my heart yearns for that chaos, though I tamp it down. I've always wondered what a baby between Jay and I would be like.

But we can't. Our lives are too chaotic. Not to mention Jay doesn't want to pass along more Parker genes.

"I'll see you soon, baby. Keep in touch, okay?"

I nod and blow him a kiss.

Glancing at my watch, I decide to start walking the commons. I come across some pop-up shops that garner my attention. I end up buying homemade soaps in the shape of seashells and lobsters and loading up on chocolate to nibble on while I walk the fashion district.

"Annie? Is that you?"

I turn to face the familiar voice and find Elliot, my old editor, at one of the outdoor cafés sipping his coffee.

"Hey, you! What are you doing here?"

I don't need an invitation to sit down. While Elliot is in his mid-sixties, we're still the best of friends.

"We moved here for Barbara's new job. She got tenure at Harvard."

I wriggle my eyebrows and touch his arm. "Congratulations! It's beautiful here. This suits you."

"Thank you. But I suppose I could ask you the same question. What on God's Earth are you doing here?"

I snort. "Again? I'm sure you wanted to add that in there. This was Autumn's idea. I've got Mara from sales with me for a fresh take, but this is where she wanted me."

He rolls his chocolate eyes, hidden behind his thick, black-rimmed glasses. He looks great. Happy. Healthy. The stress of the magazine is no longer on his shoulders, and he can live his life.

"I told Nick and Geoffrey that putting her in my position was going to be a mistake."

The waiter appears at the table and asks if I want anything. I ask for an omelet and a coffee because this is the first time throughout this trip that I sort of feel in my element.

"I'm sorry, kid. I really tried looking out for you."

I shrug. "It's not your fault. The gal's got ambition. I'll give her that."

"And a head full of hot air," he adds with a chuckle.

He isn't wrong about that.

"Can I ask you something?" My gears start turning, and if my old mentor can point me in the right direction, maybe I can take this to Nick and Geoffrey, bypassing Autumn altogether.

"Sure thing."

"Have you been keeping up with the other magazines like us?"

He nods contemplatively.

"I've been wanting to revamp *A Fish Out of Water.* In this day and age, everyone is watching videos. They don't want to read whole articles. They want to see things beyond a picture and some carefully crafted words. I really wanted to give making it a web series a shot . . ."

His face lights up. "Not a bad idea. People are always on YouTube these days rather than watching cable. Have you thought of an angle?"

"Well, look at me," I shrug with a bashful smile. "I'm a country bumpkin with a weird accent. I've worked on a farm my entire life. If I could learn how to make Greek wine or work in the back of an Italian kitchen in Bologna . . . I don't know. I think I can add flair."

"You need something more. These trips you do now, they only last a few days to a week, at least. Sure, putting yourself in an unknown situation will garner attention, but what if you asked yourself how you can make it harder on yourself?"

Like a light switch, my brain turns with new ideas. They rush past me at the speed of light, exciting me to new heights.

"Sort of like Survivor Man. Okay. What do you think? I get dropped in the middle of Iceland. Or China. I'm given an amount of money. I have to find accommodations on the spot, learn just a little bit of a language I don't know, and eat food I've never tried."

His grin lights up my world.

"That sounds like something an old guy like me would watch."

Is this happening? Am I out of the rut?

"What does Autumn think of all this?" he asks.

Just like that, my good mood swirls down the drain. She'll never go for something like this. It'll be too much money. It'll scare away readers. She doesn't like the idea.

"She's been adamant that she doesn't want anything like this on the magazine."

He sighs impatiently and leans back in his seat. "You're a charming woman, Annie. You are one of my brightest protégés, and I think if *anyone* had the potential to make this a reality, it would be you. Have you thought about pitching to cable networks?"

I scrunch my nose. "I have a literary agent, and that's about it. Pitching to networks like the *Travel Channel* or whatever is intimidating for someone who doesn't know the industry."

"Tell you what. I have some contacts. Would you be open to talking with them? Are you ready to leave the security of Nick and Geoffrey?"

My mind races to Jay. Would he be okay with this? Is it wise to spend all this time apart for something that might flop?

"Yeah. I think I would. Besides. My contract is up next month."

"Perfect. Let me get in touch with some friends, and I'll forward them your email address and phone number. And Annie?"

I pause right as I'm about to dig into my omelet.

"I've said this before, and I'll say it again. You are an incredible human being. I'm very proud of you."

15

JAY

I arrive at the airport a full hour early. The airport police have been watching me like a hawk because all I can do is pace and check my watch every three minutes. The older couple sitting in an otherwise empty row of seats whisper about me, saying I'm making them nervous. Finally, I'm asked to take a seat or wait in the cell phone waiting lot. And there's no fucking way I'm going to wait in a parking lot when I can have her run into my arms without a cop telling us to get out of the way and get off the curb. No thank you.

The arrivals screen updates, saying that her plane is at the gate. The last two weeks have been painful without her. Sure, I had dinner with Steve and Betty Lou most nights and the occasional meal with either Aria or Momma, but the more time they left me to my own devices, the more I would get hung up on the fact that I'm not doing *anything.*

At least in the Corps, I was always fighting for that promotion. Or I was helping another guy at the gym or PT or something. I was doing something for our country. And yeah, the bullets through the extremities were a real bitch, but that was a price I was willing to pay.

I'm realizing I'm not going to be a part of the SCPD. That dream of William was enough to remind me I never want to see or talk to him again. If I'm being honest, even if I *did* meet Jeremy's requirements, I still think he'd tell me to kick rocks.

But now what?

I left the best job I ever had. I created a family with a bunch of badass men who have been to hell and back and have been my rock through every significant moment of my adult life: The deaths. Annabelle. War.

Why the fuck did I leave?

My chest aches in the worst way. My heart races at the speed of life, and suddenly, I can't catch my breath.

What the hell did I do wrong?

"Jay?"

Before I know it, she's straddling my lap and pulls me close. Annabelle runs her fingers through my hair. The rhythmic thumping of her heart helps time my breathing.

"You're freaking everyone out. What's wrong?" she asks softly.

"It's nothing, Blondie."

It's *everything.*

She pulls away and searches my face with concern. "It's not nothing," she chastises. "Come on. Let's go get my bag and go home."

She laces her fingers with mine and pulls me up. We take the escalator down to the baggage claim in a silence that weighs so heavy that I'm sure the other people around me can feel it. Her bag is one of the first on the carousel. She pushes through the throng of her fellow passengers and yanks her bag off the belt. She squeezes my hand in reassurance, and then we step onto the elevator to get to the garage.

"What were you thinking about?" she asks.

"The Corps."

She nods, dropping her gaze to the gray flooring, rolling the wheel of her suitcase with the toe of her boot.

"Listen, Annabelle, I'm okay, really. I made us some reservations downtown close to our hotel. I'd really love to spend the evening with you, fondle you under a table or something."

She smirks, and the doors to the elevator open. I take her bags from her and step out. Her truck is just a few spaces away. I carefully place her bags in the bed of the truck as she slides into the passenger seat.

"Where did you make reservations?" she asks when I hop into the driver's seat.

"Graves told me about a speakeasy downtown. It's dark, there's a jazz singer, sexy dancing . . ." My voice trails off when she blushes and giggles.

"Well, if Graves told you about it, it must be good."

The fucker knows a good party.

"What do you say, Blondie? Let's get freaky in the dark."

She tries so hard to hide her smile against her pursed lips. "Okay. You've convinced me. Let's go."

I press my lips to hers, threading my fingers through her wavy, golden locks. Her palm slides up my right thigh, her fingers brushing my dick. She smiles against my lips when I growl. I'm not going to be the idiot who takes her in a public garage, especially when I know the people who are checking the surveillance tapes—aka her father.

I pull apart from her, pecking her one more time on her pillowy lips before pulling out of the parking spot.

"How was your flight?" I ask, desperate to change the subject before I have half a mind to pull over and live out my fantasy of dominating her in public.

"It was fine. There were two young girls behind me arguing about a boy they both liked. I was here for the drama for the first fifteen minutes, but then they wouldn't shut up about it."

"Could be worse. You could've been sitting next to Graves when he passed out and snored so loud the flight attendant had to wake him up, insisting he didn't go back to sleep."

She groans. She and Graves have a sibling relationship even though they don't see too much of each other. But when they are together, they argue like cats and dogs. It's a little weird to see my life before and after the Marine Corps mesh together.

"So . . . there's something I wanted to talk to you about," she starts hesitantly, her eyes boring into the side of my head as I pull onto the highway.

Is this the secret she's been keeping? Is she finally going to tell me?

"You know I don't like the pretenses. Come out and say it."

She licks her lips and turns her whole body to face me. "Elliot was in Boston while I was there. We had breakfast together this morning."

I grin. Elliot Handler is Annabelle's former boss and one of the most respected editors in the country. He's one of her favorite people. It broke her heart when he left the magazine.

"Yeah? Did he ask you to work for him?"

"No, he's retired now. But I mentioned the web series to him, and he loved the idea."

Of course he did, because she's always been able to tell a story that could captivate a rowdy group of three-year-olds.

"Okay . . . I'm at a loss here, Blondie. What does this mean for you?"

"Well, he thought it might be a good idea to think beyond a web series. He said he had a few talent agents he'd reach out to and get in touch with me. He thinks I should pitch it to the big networks."

I can't stop the giant smile. When we stop at the red light, I pull her face to mine, planting a loud, obnoxious kiss to her cheek. "Holy crap! That's amazing, baby! I'm so proud of you!"

Her eyes soften. "Do you mean it? Because a TV show is totally different. I'd be gone a lot, but my time in between would be longer so we could still spend a lot of time together."

"Hell yeah! Come on, Annabelle, this is a *huge* deal. This is what you've been working toward. And if that means me holding your sandals while you revolutionize the travel industry, then I'll do it in a heartbeat."

The thought seems to punch both of us in the gut. She rears back as if she was just slapped. My stomach drops with guilt and self-pity.

"Jay . . . you know I don't think of you like that . . ."

But that's what it would look like, wouldn't it? Without a fancy degree from a fancy college, my skills don't necessarily transfer over to anything. Am I going to let her go to Europe on her own with a sleazy camera crew ready to devour her? *Absolutely not.* I'd be right there, being her biggest cheerleader. I just wish it didn't make me look like the trophy husband.

"I know. It was a stupid thing to say. I'm just so stoked for you." I offer her a reassuring smile and reach for her hand, bringing it to my lips and planting a kiss on her cold knuckles.

We both sit in the awkward silence, waiting for the light to turn green, not knowing what to say. I've never had to hide my true feelings around her. Part of me envies her for knowing exactly what she wants out of life. The other part of me wonders if I could be the arm candy.

"What did you do while I was away?" she asks, desperate to break up the ugly tension.

"Barn chores, mostly. I helped Hank out with fertilizing the corn for the first couple of days. I spent some time with Momma, and your parents and sister invited me over a lot, so I wasn't completely alone. I think they're afraid of me falling down a pit of despair since the SCPD thing fell through."

Her face falls, and she reaches over and squeezes my knee. I wish she'd stop looking at me like that. Like she doesn't believe a single word coming out of my mouth. Though, I suppose that's warranted.

"You're coping, though, right? Have you looked into finding a therapist?"

"It's not for me," I quickly cut in. I smile at her. "Seriously. I'm fine. And I want to take you out because I've missed the hell out of you. Now scoot over and cuddle into me so I can smell your hair."

She gives up on fighting it and scoots across the truck's bench seat. She snuggles into my chest, and I take a deep inhale, devouring the jasmine shampoo she uses. *This is home.*

"I've missed you too. I should've brought you along instead of Mara. I could've taken a different angle for couples."

"Hindsight is twenty-twenty."

She sighs. "Yeah. Anything new at home? Has Aria found a dress yet?"

"I don't think she's gone shopping yet, and if she did, she didn't tell me about it. Nothing new, except for the new rescue your dad brought in from West Virginia."

"Tell me about him."

"His name is Spirit. He has a deep swayback, and Derek says he'll never be rideable. His feet haven't been done in at least a year. Eric took a brief glance at him because Spirit wouldn't allow him to get close, but we could smell the infection in his hoof without even having to pick it up."

Eric Jr., the farrier we all went to school with, concurred with Dr. I-think-I'm-so-pretty. He said if the smell was that bad, he probably will spend the rest of his life healing.

"Wow, poor thing. I bet Derek will have his hands full with him. What about Archie? How's my boy doing?"

I chuckle. Earlier today, I had to pull Archie into a stall because he escaped and broke into the feed room.

"Archie's fine," I reply.

I pull into the dark parking lot of an office building. Annabelle peers up at the building through the windshield, staring at it in disbelief.

"Are you sure this is the right place?"

"Yes. It's a speakeasy, baby. Get into it."

I help her out of the car, and we enter the office building hand in hand. As soon as we walk into the dim foyer, Annabelle's whole demeanor changes. Bouncers stand next to the interior door with sunglasses. She gives them the password with a giggle, and when they open the door, I'm amazed at what unfolds in front of me.

It's dark. Extremely dark. The only bright lighting are the spotlights on the stage. The rest of the room is dimly lit on the lowest setting. The tables are separated by tall, velvet curtains that give quite a bit of privacy. The jazz singer on stage looks like she's stepped out of the twenties with curly chocolate hair pinned back and a black flapper dress. Her fire-engine-red lips wrap around every crooned note. It's beautiful.

The host ushers us to our table on a raised platform in the middle of the room. He places a bowl of truffle popcorn on the table, draws the curtains slightly, and walks away. I pull Annabelle closer to me, her skirt sliding effortlessly across the leather of the booth. A bright smile replaces the uncertainty that was just there a few moments ago.

"This is nice," she whispers to me.

"I didn't get to tell you earlier. You look beautiful."

She rolls her eyes and bashfully grins. "No, I don't. I've been sitting at the airport for hours. I look like a tired hag."

"I wasn't going to say *that* . . ." I tease.

She slaps me on the chest and giggles into my arm.

"Let's play a game, Blondie. Tell me who's on a first date."

She scans the room with an amused smile, her eyes settling on a couple close to the stage. Those tables don't have the fancy curtains like we do. They're a middle-aged couple. The guy, in his late thirties, wears a crisp gray suit and hasn't looked away from the singer since they sat down. The woman scrolls aimlessly on her phone, occasionally smiling and flirting with the waiter.

"They're not on a first date," she whispers, "but they've been married seven years. They both have the seven-year itch, and she's serving him with divorce papers tomorrow."

"Jesus Christ," I choke on my laughter.

She grins victoriously and nudges me in the ribs. "Your turn. Tell me a story."

I already found the couple I wanted to roast, spotting them when we walked in. "The couple by the bar. They're on a first date. She's with her best friend's brother, but he's *super* gay, and she doesn't realize it yet."

Annabelle arches an eyebrow in challenge. "What are you talking about? He's been staring at her chest this entire time."

"He has familial obligations, Blondie. His father is a politician—he can't have a gay kid. It'll ruin everything. He's staring because he's trying to make himself feel something."

"Oh my god. You've put too much thought into this," she laughs.

Finally, the fun, happy, bubbly Annabelle comes out to play. She takes a deep breath and shrugs her sweater off. She's wearing a black button-down blouse, her cleavage begging me to take a taste. Her scent is inviting, and it's taking every morsel of willpower to keep my lips off her neck.

"That guy over there," she says, smirking when she realizes I haven't looked up from her boobs yet. "He's been stood up. He's over there wondering if he should leave to take the pity off of him or make a scene because he's been waiting around for the last hour for a table so he can get something free out of it."

"How do you know it's been an hour? We've only been here fifteen minutes."

She shrugs carelessly. "You told me to tell you a story, so I'm telling you a story."

I watch the man she's talking about. He's been standing at the hostess stand since we arrived. If I were a woman, I'd be intimidated. He has the whole mob-boss thing going. The suit he's wearing is a couple of g's, and his hair is slicked back with enough product to make him an artificial helmet. His scowl is off-putting. Whoever he's meeting, I pray they have a sense of humor, at least.

Annabelle places her cool hand on my cheek, turning my attention to her. She smiles seductively and leans in. I press my lips to hers and revel in her intoxicating jasmine scent. She pops open one of the buttons on her blouse, her black lacy bra peeking out. My fingers thread through her hair, and I pull her head back, exposing her long, graceful neck. My tongue glides up the arch, savoring her sweet taste.

Her erratic pulse thrums against my lips. My left hand slides up her thigh under her skirt, and I'm welcomed by her heat. *She's not wearing panties.* I trace her slit with my fingers. My eyes open to find her smirking at me. She's going to be the death of me.

"Slow down, Blondie. We have all night."

"You said you'd fondle me under a table, Parker. Live a little."

From the corner of my eye, the interior door opens again, and the man who walks through sends a bucket of ice water over my head.

Dominic *fucking* Reese. The "CEO" who visited Aria in the barn.

Annabelle is none the wiser.

He scans the room, and before his beady eyes can land on me, I yank Annabelle onto my lap and smash my lips against hers. She grinds her core against my dick, and I swear to whatever god is out there, I see stars.

Focus!

The host ushers the men to the table directly behind us. Annabelle whimpers against my lips and reaches between her legs, stroking my erection.

I'm going to fucking lose it.

"You're late, Reese."

If I can keep Annabelle busy, I might just be able to figure out more about this idiot.

"There was traffic on the highway. Calm down."

The other guy growls. "You are skating a very dangerous line. Banks isn't happy and wants you back at headquarters."

I quickly lay Annabelle down in the booth, kissing every inch of exposed skin I can get my lips on. I reach up her skirt, teasing her clit. She bites down hard on her bottom lip. It's so dark in here that nobody can see what we're doing unless they walk up to our table.

"I don't give a fuck about Banks," Reese snaps. "Besides. All of my research has paid off. I have everyone's routines down to a *T*. I've mapped out the perfect times to—"

"Jay," Annabelle hisses. Her body vibrates beneath me. "Let's get out of here, please?" she begs.

"I thought you wanted me to live a little," I reply with a smirk. I dive under her skirt, and the scent that's so perfectly Annabelle permeates my senses. She's close. My cock presses painfully against my zipper. The need to be inside of her tight pussy and the need to hang on Dominic Reese's every word are polar opposites, and I can't do anything rash without alerting them.

Her hand moves out of my hair, and with her muffled moans, I can only assume it's over her mouth. I lap her up, savoring every drop she has left to give.

"You better be right about this," the other guy snaps. "There's a meeting tomorrow. Banks will be there. You better make sure that what you have is ironclad. Otherwise, I'll be forced to take your life."

Annabelle finishes and shudders in the booth. I unearth myself from under her skirt and hover over her. I press a kiss to her pillowy lips as she tries to catch her breath.

"Jay, please. I need you."

Movement behind us has me smashing my lips to hers again. If Reese doesn't see us, we're one step ahead of them.

"Let's get out of here, Blondie," I say, helping her sit up. The men are gone, which gives us the perfect opportunity to leave.

Whoever this Banks is . . . Well, they're not finished with Aria.

16

ANNIE

"Miss, you're holding up the line," the cashier pleads with me while the line behind me grumbles under their breath and shoots me death stares. I was the first one up this morning after the wild night we had, so I decided to grab us some breakfast from the bakery across the street. Sue me for walking in here blind and finding everything appetizing.

"Ugh, fine. Just a dozen donuts, then. Surprise me. And I'll take a four count of the cinnamon rolls and two black coffees." We have sugar and cream back in the room. I wouldn't want the patrons of this fine establishment to murder me because the poor barista had to take an extra step.

"Your total is $25.67." I hand the teenager my card and slide over so the next person can start with their order. She hands my card back to me, and I wait at a table for my name to be called to pick up my order.

"Ah, Ms. McKenzie. What a surprise."

I turn to face the smooth and slimy voice, and when I lock eyes with Dominic Reese, my blood runs cold. Rolling my eyes and turning around in my seat, I silently hope he gets the hint and leaves me alone.

Unfortunately, I'm not that lucky.

He pulls out the chair across from me and sinks down. His beady black eyes scan me up and down, savoring every inch of me.

"Mr. Reese, I don't have a lot of time to sit and chat with you. Besides, I'm sure you could go around and annoy *anyone* else."

His arrogant smirk sends warning bells and sirens all around me. I need to get out of here.

"I'm sure that's true. However, destiny has given us the opportunity to clear the air."

I *highly* doubt that's what he has in mind. Judging by the way his gaze keeps falling to my cleavage, there's another asinine suggestion he's going to make that is going to land him on the floor covered in coffee.

"That or you're following me."

"Are you that vain? Perhaps I live here. Did that thought ever cross your mind?"

Nope. And I don't care if he does, either. He's a Dodge goon, according to his business card, and last time I checked, Dodge headquarters is located in Chicago. I'll eat my shirt if he truly lives here.

"And what, pray tell, do you have to say that would change my mind about you?"

He leans forward on his forearms, his face dangerously close to mine. "You and your sister were so quick to make me out to be the bad guy."

"Well, you look like you just left a meeting with the mafia, so pardon us for jumping to conclusions."

"I'm not part of the mafia," he declares, clutching at his imaginary pearls. "I wasn't asking her to marry me. I just wanted to sit down and have a talk with her."

I arch an eyebrow and lean back in my seat. *Talk.* The danger in that one syllable alone makes me want to run the other way.

"It's not going to happen, Mr. Reese. So I suggest you stay out of Sage Creek because you have her fiancé ready to burn down the town to make sure you don't go near her again."

"Annie!" the barista calls from behind the counter. I stand up and push my chair in, casually nodding to him.

"Anyway, thanks for the chat, but nothing is going to change."

I grab the bag full of our treats and the two coffees and stroll out the door without a second glance. The cool air puts pep in my step. Boston was my last trip until the holidays, and until then, I'll be visiting lesser-traveled cities around the US. More time to spend with Jay.

The hotel is two blocks away. When I turn the corner, I'm met by a rough-looking man with a gun pointed at my forehead. My stomach is hollow, and I can't seem to find the scream that is clawing at my throat to get out. It's hard to look anywhere else, especially when his hands shake and his grimy index finger trembles in the trigger guard.

Stay calm.

"I want everything in your purse," he demands shakily. It's like he doesn't want to do this. Tears well up in the corners of his eyes. I swallow nervously and nod. It's then that I suddenly realize how heavy everything is: the bag of cinnamon rolls and donuts weigh down my left arm, the plastic handle of the bag digging into my flesh while the coffee warms my hands.

The coffee.

Everything my father taught us as kids is slowly coming back to me. Incapacitate him and run like hell.

"Okay," I reply courteously, willing my voice to stay level.

I'm not afraid. I'm not afraid. I'm not afraid.

The mantra is useless. I'm terrified. I'm dead if there's so much as a loud boom in the distance.

My thumbnail finds the lip of the plastic lid, and much to my annoyance, the lid topples off the coffee and onto the ground.

Our eyes meet, and it's then I notice the petrifying fear that lives inside his dark pupils. He's just as terrified as I am.

"Don't do it, bitch!" He brandishes the gun around violently, and much to my horror, a shot rings out. It ricochets off the newspaper locker behind me, and I'm not sure where it goes after that. People around us scream, and still, mine is lodged in my throat.

"Okay! I'm sorry!" I shout. I place the coffee down and slowly sink to my knees on the sidewalk. "Please don't hurt me," I plead. "My sister is getting married, and I'm her maid of honor. She's already had such a crappy time in life. Please don't take me away from her."

"Shut *up*!" he roars.

Footsteps emerge behind me. *Whoever is listening, please let it be the police. I'm not ready to die yet.* My body shakes uncontrollably. I've picked a spot on the sidewalk, and I wait for the inevitable pain he's going to inflict.

Another shot rings out, and my attacker crumples to the floor. A river of crimson streams from his head. His eyes remain open, but the life has been drained from them. A bloodcurdling scream has me scrambling up. I turn to find the culprit, to see who is hurt. The building just behind me has a wall of windows, and when I turn to face it, I realize *I'm* the one screaming.

Someone grabs onto my shoulders, and I swing around, my fist colliding with my attacker's jaw.

"Ow! Stop it! I just helped you!" Dominic Reese bellows.

The glint of the gun he used to kill this man sends another scream up my throat. He slaps his hand over my mouth, shushing me violently.

"There are witnesses. Do you see them?"

I glance around me, people on both sides of the street watching in horror. The man who was going to kill me lies in the middle of the sidewalk like a bad sideshow. *I've never seen a dead body before . . .*

"They've already called the police."

"But I-I didn't do anything wrong!" I exclaim. "They'll see it on the street footage. I was just walking—"

"You're still going to get questioned, and I don't want to be around when they come looking for me."

I can finally focus. He's going to pin this on me! "I'm not going down for you! I don't even know you!"

"I'm sure we'll see each other again, Ms. McKenzie."

With that, he stalks away, turning down a random alleyway, disappearing into the abyss. *What the actual fuck?*

THE POLICE BARRICADE this section of road. One of them called Jay for me, and before I know it, my father is blowing up my cell phone. I can't bear to answer it. I don't want to hear all the ways I disregarded his self-defense lessons when we were younger. Just when I think he gets the hint that I won't be picking up for him, the rest of the family follows suit.

Jay is let in through the barricade and wraps me up in his beefy arms. He kisses the crown of my head, though I can feel the anger radiating from his hot skin. I've been checked out by the paramedic and deemed "good to go." So when Detective Mathis circles back to check on me, he gives me the all clear to leave Richmond.

We walk in a painful silence all the way back to the hotel. He stares at me with concern, waiting for me to say *something.* All I can see is the life draining from that man's eyes and Dominic Reese telling me to take the fall.

"Talk to me, Blondie. Tell me what happened."

A hysterical laugh escapes my lips. Tell him what happened? Did he *just* hear me give my statement to at least eight other cops?

"I told you everything." He purses his lips in disapproval. "Hey, you know what sounds like fun? Why don't we go to Busch Gardens today?"

Anything to get me out of going home and facing the vultures.

"You can't be serious," he says in shocked amazement.

"Why wouldn't I be? It's an hour away, and we had nothing planned today, anyway. I'm sure Aria and Chris can handle feed for one more day."

"Annabelle, do you understand your situation? He almost killed you today—"

"I know! I was there," I snap.

God, doesn't he realize I can't live like this? That I don't *want* that image in my head anymore? That's what the roller coasters are for!

"Meaning we should go home and try to relax—"

"You know, all of you have your own ways of coping and, for some reason, it's what *you* deem correct. You like to wallow. Aria keeps to herself and you never know what she's thinking. Chris blows up at anything and everything. I can't *live* like this! I can't live in the sadness and fear like you can, Jacob. *I. Don't. Want. To. Go. Home.*"

He furrows his eyebrows, hanging onto every clipped syllable.

"I have to take you home, Annabelle. Your parents are worried sick, and they need to know you're okay, but you're not answering your phone."

And what do I do when I get there? Pick up where I left off? Mucking stalls, giving lessons, and feeding? This isn't what I signed up for.

"I'm sorry, baby, but we're going home."

17

DOMINIC REESE

From what I'm told, Dominic Reese was a mobster. He died in the Capone days in some massacre that I don't give two shits about. Borrowing his identity comes with some issues, though. Which is why when the witnesses call the police, I don't want to be around for them to throw me in the slammer, not to mention I'll be sent to ICE in two seconds flat.

Banks won't help me. Neither will Wren Ramirez, my direct "supervisor". I'd be a liability. Being the fall man ensures my death whether Banks's revenge has been satisfied or not, which is why I don't make mistakes.

Killing this man was not a mistake. This was just a message.

I want Stephen McKenzie to know I'm coming for his happiness. I want him to know that his daughter can easily die, just like this homeless fool did.

Twenty-five years ago, he killed my mother and father right in front of me. Their blood sprayed onto my clothes, and I spent the next three days crying for somebody to help them.

That was in London.

Nobody cared. Nobody came looking for me. The police treated me like a suspect.

I was five years old.

I made a promise to my parents all those years ago that I would avenge their death. Fortunately for me, Wren Ramirez found me two years ago and shared a plan with me that would ensure Stephen McKenzie paid for the carnage.

Come hell or high water, come death or torture, he will die at *my* hands.

"What was that?" Wren's voice filters through my rental car's sound system.

"It was necessary. Let me remind you, Ramirez, *you* sought *me* out. It's a little late to question my motives."

"Your job was to keep a low profile."

"When they look up Dominic Reese, they will find a dead, old, Italian mobster. They'll look through the CCTV footage your team will have gotten ahold of and doctored. I'm not worried, Ramirez. Neither should you be."

I hang up the phone and steer the car in the direction of New York. I'll take a week or two to disappear, to get the heat off of me. Then I'll return and take what's mine.

18

JAY

The entire two-hour trip from the hotel to home has been the most uncomfortable the two of us have ever been around each other. She's stewing and hasn't taken her eyes off of the scenery outside her window. She didn't even want to stop for lunch.

I can't fathom the idea of going to an amusement park after she was nearly killed. Who would want to go on a roller coaster when the man who was obviously a part of—whatever *this* is—is still on the loose?

When we get home, she storms into the house and locks herself in the master bedroom. I text Steve to let him know we're home and that she doesn't want to see anyone. He'll be pissed about it, but he'll get over it.

Since she's been in Boston, the house hasn't been cleaner. I cleaned out the fridge while she was gone, chucking a ton of spoiled food into the garbage. From where I stand in the living room, staring at the bedroom door longingly, I can already hear the mess she's making, slamming dresser drawers shut. Immediately, my peace flies out the window. She'll wreck the room out of spite. Any semblance of sane people in this house will be gone.

How does this woman function? How can she not have any self-preservation whatsoever?

I flick the TV on and collapse onto the couch while I wait for her to make an appearance when she's ready to start yelling at me again. ESPN plays in the background while my mind works overtime.

The club last night was dark, especially with the red velvet curtains around us. There's no possible way he could've seen us.

My phone vibrates with a text, and when I see it's Derek, I'm hopeful he already has one of his guys looking into what happened.

Dr. Pretty Boy: Look at your email.

I reach out for Annabelle's laptop and crack it open, firing up my email. There's one from an unknown sender, and despite my military training and watching videos on YouTube of people scamming scammers, I open it up.

It's a video.

I click play and hold my breath. The homeless guy who threatened Annabelle is in the alleyway, sleeping. Another man, one in a suit and a 1920's fedora hat, enters the alley and crouches next to him.

What am I watching here?

The man reaches into his pocket, pulling out a fat stack of cash and handing it off to the homeless man. He accepts and holds his hand out for something else.

What are you doing, guy?

A glint of a gun shines as it's pulled out of the man's suit coat and placed into the hands of the homeless man. The homeless man takes the gun, but the other man grabs his wrist quickly. He says something to the homeless man before standing up. The homeless man looks terrified. Just as the man is walking out of the alleyway, seemingly aware of the camera, he tips his hat and holds out a peace sign.

Me: He was set up.

Dr. Pretty Boy: Looks like it. And I have an idea who it was.

Dominic Reese.

I glance down at the time stamp on the video and notice it was just after the time Annabelle said she walked into the bakery.

This doesn't make sense.

Tossing my phone to the couch cushions, I brave whatever wrath I'm going to get from the love of my life and tap on the door. I enter with an answer and find her lying down with the covers up and over her head.

"Go away," she groans.

"I don't want to."

She turns over to face me, narrowing her eyes. I'm not welcome here, and if I know what's best for me, I'd leave before she gets into *Snapped* territory. But what can I say? I'm a dumbass.

"Baby, I just want to talk."

"I don't. I'm being forced to lie here and wallow. So I'd appreciate it if you left."

Good God! She lays on a guilt trip better than a Christian momma.

"Do you really think it would've been a good idea to go to a theme park right after you'd been held at gunpoint? Think about it, baby. The cops are going to be looking into you to make sure you're not a suspect. What would've happened if they looked into your credit card statements and saw what we did right after a man died at your feet?"

She blinks her tears away and shrugs.

"Baby, I'm just looking out for you. You're safe here."

I'm dying to ask her about her conversation with Reese. She told them what they talked about in the bakery while she waited for her food, and they promised they'd look into him. But there's a sinking sensation in my gut. I already know they're not going to find anything on him. That would be too easy.

"I know you are," she admits. "But damn it, Jay, you have to understand I don't operate like you. I don't want to sit here and cry about what happened. I want to get it out of my head as fast as possible."

But that doesn't solve the problem!

"You can't erase it, Annabelle. It happened, and it's traumatizing. You pretending it didn't happen isn't healthy."

She chuckles darkly and turns away from me. "Let me know where you got your license, Dr. Google. I could make a killing with everyone's problems around here."

And we're done. "I'm going to make lunch. When you're done with your pity party, come find me."

I storm out of the room, slamming the door behind me. Her feet thunder against the hardwood floors. She wrenches the door open, her face red with rage.

"So you admit it's a pity party!" she bellows.

"I'm not doing this, Annabelle," I warn, entering the kitchen and ripping the fridge door open. I'm not looking to start a fight.

"Of course not! Why would you? You'd actually have to tap into your true feelings for once!"

"Are you done? You got your jabs in, right?"

"No, I'm not done." She hoists herself onto the counter, crosses her ankles, and glares at me. "You don't allow me to cope the way I *need* to. So when I try your method, it's a pity party. For fuck's sake, Jacob, you can't have your cake and eat it too!"

Her method was going to get her arrested!

"Someone had a gun to my head this morning, and the one thing I wanted to do would get me away from here where I'd be forced to think about it. Okay, so we couldn't go to Busch Gardens. So what! There are a thousand other things we could've done. But you had to be a dumb caveman and bring me back to my dad to get punished."

"Is that what you think this is?" I close the distance between us and wrap her in my arms. "This isn't a punishment, Annabelle. This is us protecting you. That guy in the alley was paid to ambush you."

She pushes me back to the counter directly behind me. "What are you talking about?"

"That guy was paid and given a gun to ambush you. *You* were the target."

She gapes and closes her mouth, and it goes like this for several moments before she's collected her thoughts. "I haven't been on social media. I haven't even posted where I was."

He had to have seen us last night. That's the only explanation. "I don't know why or how. But if someone could track you down in Richmond, they could do the same at Busch Gardens. Or Boston. We have a home-field advantage here."

She nods and takes a hesitant step back.

"Let's put on a movie. Or we'll play a board game or something. I'll even entertain a trail ride if you're up for it."

The fact she can't even look me in the eye is evidence enough that she's shaken to her core.

"Let's watch a movie," she murmurs.

AFTER DINNER, she sinks into the bath, and I sneak to the house next door to talk to Derek. He meets me outside with a grimace and Troy on his hip. Troy snuggles into his chest with his eyes drooping. Derek sits in the rocker and gently rocks back and forth, playing two separate parts in two different worlds.

"His beef is with Aria," I reiterate as I sit in the accompanying chair.

"That's who he sought out first. Maybe he thought he could make some headway with Annie?"

That's not enough. There's something more at play. Why shoot a man for a woman you're not even after?

"The common denominator is us. You guys have your share of enemies. Couldn't it be from another job you guys pulled?"

He shrugs at a loss. "I don't know. Without the fucker tied up in the basement, I can't exactly ask him, now can I?" He sighs, scrubbing his hand over his face. "I don't know of anyone who would come searching for us through Charlie. We don't have loose ends, Jay. We don't have *ends,* period."

The night has fallen, and the only soundtrack to the night are the crickets and Troy's suckling on his pacifier. And yet, it's deafening. I can't hear myself *think.*

"I could try to get into his hotel room."

He shakes his head, immediately shooting down the idea. "Jay, he's not going to leave his whole master plan out in the open in the hotel. We need to get ahold of his phone. Better yet, we need to level up. He's the bottom of the totem pole. He's only doing the grunt work."

"How do you expect us to level up if we don't have any information from him?"

Troy's eyes finally droop closed and Derek stops rocking. "Those cameras caught him. He's as good as gone. We don't have leads on who this guy is."

"So you expect us to sit here and do nothing, then." *Unbelievable.*

"No, I don't expect you to do that at all. However, Nate and Tanner are running facial recognition, and that takes time. Give them forty-eight hours. Besides, he isn't going to just kill a guy and disappear without taking what he's really come here for." He shoots his gaze over to my house. "He targeted Aria because she's vulnerable in preparation for the trial. He targeted Annie because she was under his nose."

Because he saw us at the speakeasy. "He met somebody last night. He was standing near the hostess stand, and then, when Reese arrived, they were escorted to the table behind us."

He nods. "He saw you."

I blow out an uneasy breath. The rest of my world is about to shatter. The last time I felt like this was the night my mother and I were leaving my father. I feel that dread in my bones.

"This affects all of us, Jay. We're not just sitting here and twiddling our thumbs. We're working every resource that's available to us. I'm not going to let anything happen to our girls, okay?"

"I want more responsibility."

A small smile spreads across his lips. It's almost proud, like he's been waiting for me to ask all this time.

"Okay. We can do that. First things first, okay? Tanner needs time to track him down. As soon as we have a location, you can come with us to get information."

I nod once. This family is done being stolen from.

I bid goodnight to Derek and head home. Annabelle is out of the bath and cuddled up on the couch with a glass of rosé in hand. I snuggle in next to her and inhale her jasmine scent. I'm so glad she's home.

The thought of almost losing her today has me crippled with fear. To think that I wouldn't be doing this with her right now had that first shot hit her makes bile rise in my throat, but her soft touch has me coming back to reality. She smiles sweetly at me and kisses me on the cheek.

Dominic Reese will not have the last laugh.

19

JAY

When a super-secret meeting of the McKenzie family, plus the honorary McKenzies, commune at Rico's for dinner, I can already tell something is going to go down. Especially since Chris is the one to call the meeting. Now that he's coaching football, it only means they're demanding backup and they're not taking "no" for an answer.

Steve is a tough nut to crack, and I've been around him my entire existence, which is how I know he can tell something is up. His eyes narrow as if he's trying to find the hidden meaning behind every sentence or any hint as to what's going on.

He'll fight against the farmhands. He'll inevitably ask me to take over, though I don't want to. He'll come up with any excuse to keep the place running. But when it comes to hiring on people he doesn't know, that's when things become dicey.

Momma is sandwiched between Betty Lou and me. She doesn't drink tonight and is more quiet than usual. She looks exhausted. I'd say "haggard," but I don't want to be on the receiving end when she smacks me with her giant purse.

Derek watches a dynamic he's only been a part of for maybe a year. And sure, maybe he knows a little more about what's going on, but he doesn't understand the foundations of our friendship. When I'm around my family, I feel like I've finally come home. I can finally relax and let all thoughts of Dominic Reese fade away. My dream with the SCPD is dead in the water, especially since Jared hasn't gotten in touch with me since that day at the police station.

"Hey, handsome," Annabelle whispers in my ear.

"Hi, beautiful. Do you want to dance?" She nods eagerly and slides out of the booth. The dining room is dark and reeks of beer and cigarettes. The country music playing over the speakers adds to the ambiance. When Annabelle twirls in my arms and my hands land on her full hips, my cock revs to life. My girl wears a halter top, and there isn't a bra underneath. Her nipples harden at our contact, and it's *so* obvious with what she wears.

I've never needed to communicate with words with her. Somehow, a look in the eye or the tension in our posture could always warn us how we were truly doing on the inside. While Annabelle dances like a beautiful ballerina, she's still tense. Not even the upbeat music relaxes her. Still, she dances with me. Her cool hands rub my chest, and her smiles are made just for me.

"How do you think he's going to take it?" I ask her honestly.

"Prepare for World War III, Parker. Stephen is going to go on a rampage."

She's probably right. But it's one that would probably be enjoyable to watch.

When the song ends, we head over to the bar. Annabelle gets another margarita, and I get another beer. If I'm going to witness a shit show, I at least want to be somewhat sober for it.

The bartender slides Annabelle's margarita down the bar and winks. She smirks at me and kisses me on the cheek.

"I'll go back to the table and order your food. Come back when he finally starts paying you attention." She winks and walks away. Her hips sway as her long legs carry her to the table. She glances over her shoulder and winks at me. I could take a bite out of her round ass. I'd love it even more if it was on my face . . .

"Jacob!"

The familiar voice has me snapping to attention. I turn around to stare the most dangerous man in the room in the eye.

William Fucking Parker.

The sound of his voice sends my heart screeching to a halt. Despite my mind's vision of him now, he looks . . . different. His dark gray hair is thinning at the top, but it's longer than where his ears sit. His skin is tanned and . . . clear. When I meet his gaze for the first time in twenty-one years, my stomach sours. Gone are the eyes that held so much hate and contempt. They're replaced by a set of eyes who have seen too much.

I refuse to feel sorry for him. I won't.

Anger is the emotion I'm most comfortable with when it comes to him. My balled fists shake with rage at my sides. My jaw is clenched so hard that my teeth are buckling under the pressure.

"Get the fuck away from me," I seethe. "I don't know you. You don't know me. If you know what's best for you, you'll get the fuck out and leave us alone."

I hate the way he doesn't flinch. He stares at me like I'm the most interesting thing in the world. "I just want to talk—"

"I'm not interested, William," I snap. "I'm here with my family, and you're not a part of it. Get the fuck away from me."

William stares at me with a blank expression. I'm not sure if he's gathering his courage to deck me or if he's surprised that I'm much bigger than him and wouldn't mind shoving him through a window.

"When Jeremy said he saw you, I wanted to come down to the station to see you. It's been a long time, son."

My stomach hollows. *Don't call me son!* "Right. Because the last time you saw me, Jeremy was shoving you in the back of his cruiser while a paramedic was trying to revive me."

Hurt flashes in his eyes.

"I'm not interested, William, for the last time. Get away from me before you regret it. And tell Jeremy he can take his offer and shove it up his ass."

I pass on the beer and stalk off toward the table. The McKenzies are in deep discussion, and Momma looks like she'd rather be anywhere else. If she's seen him yet, she hasn't said anything. Regardless of my need to get out of here and sit in the tranquility of my truck, I think better of it and slide back into the booth. Momma doesn't want to be here either, but she needs my support.

"Daddy, I have a full-time job other than the farm work I do," Annie explains.

"I love the shelter, and we've already done so much good. You can vet the farmhands yourself. Besides, Derek will be around to keep an eye on things," Aria reasons.

William stares me down in a way that makes my skin crawl. This is a new form of torture. He's gotten under my skin, and he knows it. Yet he does nothing about it.

"It would be a rotating seasonal thing. Football season is up in December, and then I can help out again."

I tune Chris's voice out as I watch William. He doesn't drink anything. No beer, no cigarette in his hand . . .

What game is he playing? And why is he waiting until now to make a move?

"This is a family-run business," Steve smarts.

"Of course it is, Daddy," Aria groans. "We're not abandoning you, but we need extra help."

Betty Lou shrugs. "You could spend extra time at home," she says with a flirty smile.

Nope. That's my cue. I do *not* want to hear the meaning behind that innuendo.

I apologize to Annabelle and slip out of the booth. I need air. I need a minute to myself where William isn't around to fuck up my life. Outside, a pack of people smoke their cigarettes and laugh obnoxiously about a joke that probably isn't that funny.

When Jones died, we had some therapist come around to teach us grounding techniques. I sink to the ground and place my palms flat on the sidewalk. The ridges and unevenness scratch my fingertips.

I itch to call Graves, but I don't want to be *that* guy. I'm a progressive man. I don't enjoy living in the past. But when the past comes knocking . . . I'm losing my grip on reality, and I don't appreciate William coming back to fuck with my head.

"Hey," Annabelle's voice breaks through the silence. She sinks to the ground next to me and rests her head on my shoulder. "Is this too much? I can get our food to go if you want. We can go eat in front of the town hall."

I shake my head and turn to her. I'm sick to my stomach. "I'll come back inside in a few minutes. I just need a minute to breathe."

"I'll sit with you then."

I love her, but I want to be alone. I just don't have the heart to tell her.

"Are you okay with all of this? I mean, I know you're still transitioning and things haven't been . . ." Her voice trails off.

Things haven't been great. Especially with Dominic Reese on the loose. She thinks I'm not giving her enough space. I think she's being entirely too cavalier with her safety. We're still getting used to each other. I long to still be in the Marine Corps, where I fit in seamlessly.

"But maybe it would be a good idea to see someone. What do you think?"

"You need to stop pushing the shrink thing, Annabelle," I reply darkly.

She sighs. "Aria didn't think it would work either. But who knows? Maybe it would help with the nightmares or something."

It won't help with the carnal need to tear William Parker apart.

Footsteps sound from beside us. Annabelle's gasp gears me up for a fight. I turn to find William approaching us. In a fraction of a moment, I'm up with my fists clenched and the adrenaline rushing through my veins. It's like I'm the Hulk, ready to rip him to shreds just so he'll get away from me.

"Jacob, just hear me out—" William starts.

My fist flies out before I can even stop it. Annabelle screams, and the group of smokers run this way. Somehow, my cousin Clay comes into my line of vision and pulls William away. Jared grabs my cocked arm, shouting at me to knock it off.

"I told you one and one time only, William. Fuck. Off. I don't want to see you. I have no interest in your half-baked apologies or excuses. Live with the shit *you* put yourself in and leave us alone."

"Jay, stop!" Annabelle shrieks.

William straightens and shrugs out of Clay's grip, rolling his shoulders.

"For once in your life, kid, think about what you're doing," William snaps. "Is this what you want? You want your girlfriend to watch this?"

"Leave her fucking out of it! I got away from you. *You* sought *me* out and continued over to me when I told you to go away."

"Is there a problem here?" Steve's voice sends a chill down everyone's spine. It's sort of like when a little kid gets caught by their parent doing something wrong—only Steve is a hell of a lot more terrifying . . . and dangerous.

Jared's grip loosens on me as Steve approaches. His hard, amber eyes bore into William's skull, begging him to do something stupid. Like the boy wonder he is, Derek is on his six, ready to fight if he needs to.

"Steve—"

"Save it, Parker. I'm not in the mood." He turns to me. The trust in his eyes is a welcome relief. "What's going on?"

"He approached me at the bar. He wanted to talk. I told him to kick rocks."

Steve dangerously turns toward William and squares his shoulders.

"The last time we spoke, William, you and I had a conversation about consent. Do you remember that?"

Even with the loud music behind us and the throng of people watching on with bated breath, it's eerily silent. My mind wanders to that night. I remember seeing Jeremy's cruiser. I remember William being pushed into it. But . . . was it Jeremy who shoved him in there?

"Jay told you to leave him alone, did he not?"

William swallows and nods.

"Your restraining order is still in effect. Believe me, I've been keeping an eye on it. You have two options, William. You can either leave here and not come back or you can say what you need to say, and then you and I can have that *same* conversation about consent."

I'm not even the one in trouble, and I'm the one terrified. Steve's threat hangs in the air. This has turned into a three-ring circus, and I'm the main attraction.

William turns Steve's words over in his mind before he spits on the ground. He turns to the crowd and zeros in on someone. To my horror, I follow his gaze and it falls on my mom.

"Tell him."

That's all he says. What is that supposed to mean, anyway? Clay pulls him away and throws him in his truck. They're gone. The people scatter when the show is over, leaving me dumbfounded against the building while I try to piece together the last twenty-one years in my head.

"Sweetheart?" Momma asks gently, approaching me and placing her hand on my cheek without any hesitation.

"Get in the car, Jay. Let's go for a ride," Steve announces.

"Daddy, wait—"

"Come on, son. We're just going around downtown. We'll be back."

I glance at Annabelle who, for once in her life, has nothing to say. Momma bursts into tears and falls into Annabelle's arms when Steve yanks me forward.

"Keep an eye on him," he says to Derek. "If he leaves wherever he is, I want to know about it."

Derek nods and leaves us without another word. I climb into the cab of the old seventies Ford and shut the door behind me. The seatbelt is old and smells like mothballs, much like the weathered upholstery on the bench.

I'm transported back to my teenage years, driving around town with him doing odd jobs. Only this time, I'm a grown man wondering what the hell he did to my father.

Steve drives with the windows down. The town speeds past us in a blur.

He took William somewhere that night. How did he do it? Why didn't he say anything?

"Talk to me about what happened," he pushes gently.

I stare at him in bewilderment. *I want to know the same thing!*

"He was thrown in the back of Jeremy's cruiser that night."

Steve presses his lips in a hard line and doesn't remove his gaze from the horizon.

"You said the two of you had a conversation about consent . . ."

"Your mom finally fessed up that night. I had my suspicions, and I couldn't do anything about your dad until she told us. Not to mention I was gone a lot in those days. I told her to come live with us until she could get on her feet."

I swallow the lump in my throat.

"The two of you were going to leave that night. For good. I'm not sure how he figured it out, but when the two of you stepped out of the house, he was there. He was ready to take your life."

This isn't happening.

"He figured if he couldn't have the two of you, nobody could. Though, I found that out later. By the time word reached us, the police were already at your house. I had to get creative, but your lives meant something to me. They still do."

My heart sprints in an unbeatable race against itself.

"Jeremy was going to throw him in holding for the night and call it a day. He would've gone back to his old ways the second he got out."

I believe it. "So what did you do?"

He's silent for a beat, but the silence speaks volumes. He won't ever admit to it. But I can only imagine the torture he subjected William to. I almost wish I would've been there to witness it.

"You know about the group."

It's not a question, but a statement. A loaded one at that. Derek and his band of brothers are legends in the Corps. We all know they're part of some vigilante group, but they constantly deny it. Rightfully so in case anybody higher up found out about it. That's how I knew about it. Color me surprised when I found out my surrogate father is the ring leader.

"Yeah," I stammer.

He nods. "I also know Hawthorn put you on an assignment."

I nod again. He turns onto Western, and we pass the shelter. I want to shout at him to turn around when parks in the parking lot.

"What have you gathered so far?"

"Not much. He isn't staying in town. I happened to run into him last night when I picked Annabelle up from the airport. He was in the same restaurant and sat behind us."

I'm not about to tell him I took his daughter to a speakeasy. And good thing too because Annabelle's mention in this makes him stiffen.

"The kids aren't supposed to be involved, Jay," he warns in a dangerously low tone.

"I swear to God it was purely coincidence. I wouldn't do something stupid to put her in danger."

He doesn't speak, nor does he relax.

To save my own skin, I continue. "He met with an older man, around early forties. They were talking about the family and schedules. I hid Annabelle as best I could. I didn't think he saw us."

He glares at me. "Jay, he's behind that idiot who put a gun to my daughter's head."

"It wasn't until Derek sent me the footage that I put two and two together. Hell, I didn't even realize she left the room. I swear to God I'm sorry. I'd never put her in danger."

Steve nods. He's done talking about it. Now I just have to keep my shit straight and my head down.

"Steve . . . what did you do to William?"

He smirks. "We had a conversation." The weight behind those words isn't as concerning I thought it would be. As a kid, I daydreamed about William dying at my own hand. But I *know* Steve would do anything for Momma and me. He's proven it so many times.

"For how long?"

He shrugs. "About seventy-two hours. It had Jeremy chasing his tail for a few days," he replies with a chuckle.

I can't believe William thought I'd want to talk to him. After twenty-one years, he couldn't have just spotted me and moved on?

"I know you're angry, and I know you're wanting him to pay for what he did to you and your mom. But you're a different man now."

When we reach one of the only traffic lights in town, he turns to face me.

"You joined the Corps. They stripped you of the boy you were and turned you into a man. Since then, William has left you alone and you haven't had the burden of worrying about him all this time. He's a product of his upbringing. But I promise you, he isn't worth your concern anymore. He's a miserable old man living in a run-down house with the demons of his past. Let him suffer."

He backs out of the parking spot and turns the truck in the direction of Rico's.

If Steve got to him all those years ago, then he *must* have suffered for it. I don't see Steve letting him get away with it.

That part of my life is over. I'm a new man. *A man who doesn't know who he is anymore.*

We reach Rico's and park. Annabelle waits nervously outside and relaxes when she sees I'm not a raging lunatic anymore.

"He left. I made sure of it," she says softly.

Steve gets a kick out of her boisterous personality, but it only makes me worry about her more. The last thing I need is her pissing off William and him retaliating.

"What did you do, Blondie?"

"I gave him a piece of my mind," she replies with a wink.

"You're going to get yourself killed one of these days," I groan.

She shrugs and nudges Steve with her elbow.

"I doubt that," Steve replies.

We return to the table. Everyone seems to have lost their voices. Momma's mouth barely moves, and when it does, you can barely hear what she has to say.

"Are you all right, Momma?"

"I think I want to go home. Can you drive me?"

We say our goodbyes and walk at a snail's pace to her truck. She grips me tightly. As I close her door, a figure appears next to me. I want to explode when I glance over and see William, but Steve's words echo in my head. *He isn't worth it.*

"You really don't get the hint, do you?" I ask pointedly.

"Your mom is sick, Jacob. I want to help."

I arch an eyebrow, my stomach somersaulting at the implication. But I'm not having it. She would've told me.

"You know *nothing.* This is the final time I'm going to say this to you, and if you don't listen, I'll let Steve have a *conversation* with you. Leave us alone. You've done nothing but shit on our lives. We're doing great without you. Go be miserable anywhere else."

"I've been taking her to her appointments. She won't tell you, but I will. I think if she can forgive me for the pain I've caused, so can you."

What the actual fuck?

"Talk to her about it. I'm a different man now."

"Let's go, Parker," Derek snarls, making William jump. Derek grabs him by the scruff of his neck and shoves him in the opposite direction.

I jump into the driver's seat, eager to put this day behind me. Derek stalks behind him, and I don't care if I run William over, but now I'm wondering if he's telling the truth.

Momma rests her head against the window and closes her eyes. She's exhausted, and whether or not he's telling the truth, there's a seed of doubt that starts in my gut.

"You have three tools. Your heart to tell you what you want. Your brain to tell you what you need, and your gut to tell you what's right."

I allow her the peace on the drive back. When we get back to her house, I start a kettle for her while she gets comfortable on the couch.

"Are you all right, baby?" she asks when I bring over her mug of tea.

"I'm fine." It's not a lie. I'm fine for now, but I fear what comes out of her mouth next.

"Listen, honey . . . we need to talk."

Please don't let William be right. I don't think I can handle a truth bomb from him. Not when it has to do with the only woman on the planet who has put me ahead of herself this entire time.

"He said you were sick."

I meet her jade eyes. They fill with tears, and she lets out a shaky breath.

"Yeah, baby. I have breast cancer."

She tells me in detail what she's been through. She tells me of reaching out to William because she was too embarrassed to ask the McKenzies for help . . . again.

My stomach feels hollow to the point that if I were to bend over and throw up my guts, nothing would come out.

"Momma, there are at least a hundred other people who would've been happy to help—"

"He wasn't always a monster," she whispers.

No. I'm not listening to this. He's a monster. He isn't a human being. He gets off on bringing pain to other people.

"Before he went to war, he was sweet."

"I know you're sick, but you can't go back to him. Do you remember what he did to us?"

"Of course I do," she whispers. "I lived through it, Jay."

"Momma, I'm begging you to go no contact with him. He isn't worth our time—"

"Don't worry. I already asked Annie to take over."

My insides freeze. My world comes to a screeching halt. Annabelle knew about this, and she didn't fucking think to mention it to me?

"What are you talking about?"

It's like she realizes her mistake and clamps her mouth shut. Her face blanches, and the waterworks begin.

"Annabelle knew about this?"

"Honey—"

I can't take this. I race out the door. Our relationship was built on trust and communication, and she didn't think to fucking tell me my mother is dying?

I drive with the pedal touching the floorboard. I'm dodging potholes and speed bumps. If Jeremy is watching, well, he can take me away. It'll be better than what excuse Annabelle has for not *fucking* telling me.

When I reach the McKenzie property, it looks like everyone is still in town. I charge into the house I share with the person I'm supposed to spend the rest of my life, still befuddled as to why she kept a secret this big from me. I itch to hang onto any morsel of sanity I have. I won't be William. But how could she not fucking tell me?

She paces in the living room, and when I wrench the front door open, she spins, guilt written all over her face.

"Jay—"

"I've used the entire drive here to think about *why* you would keep something this big from me, and I'm coming up fucking empty."

Her eyes water. "She asked me not to say anything. She made me promise

I wouldn't say anything." Her tears spill over, and she buries her face in her hands.

She told me she had a secret, and she couldn't say anything. She told me that! And I fucking told her to keep the secret.

I rake my hand through my hair and sit on the hardwood floor. Just like I did hours ago, I place my palms flat on the floor, attempting to ground myself. Annabelle approaches me cautiously, but I stop her.

"I need you to get out of my space, Annie."

Her bottom lip trembles. "Jay, I'm sorry I couldn't tell you . . ."

"I can't talk about this right now," I growl.

My world is being torn apart from the seams. Everyone around me is lying to me, and I don't even have a place to call my own. I share a space with the McKenzies. I can't go to my momma's because looking at her makes me so incredibly dejected and angry all at the same time. I don't even have something to *do* to get my mind off it.

I race outside with Annabelle on my tail.

"Where are you going?"

"I need to get out of here."

Don't be William. Yeah, I'm trying really fucking hard not to be!

I stop and turn to her. "I'm so fucking livid with you, Annie. I need to be alone. I'm getting a room in town. I need the night to myself."

She sobs into her hands. "I'm sorry," she wails.

"Give me the night. We'll talk about this in the morning."

20

ANNIE

I sit in utter disbelief after Jay leaves for the night. My loyalties were off, and I'm the most horrible person on the planet. Jo kept my secret for the last two and a half years, and if I were Jay, I would be beyond pissed too.

I can't sleep a wink. He texted me to tell me he got to the hotel okay, though he didn't tell me where he was staying. For most of the night, I stayed on the porch swing and marinated in the early morning chill. Derek comes home around two in the morning. He barely regards me, and Chris comes home shortly after. He sees me sitting alone, and against his better judgment, he joins me.

"Jay found out. He knows that I know about Jo."

Chris leans against the back of the swing, gently rocking us with his feet. "Where is he?"

I shrug. "He got a hotel for the night in town."

"He what? Isn't he the one who always wants to talk about everything until everything is ironed out and smoothed over?"

A sob racks through me. He's so angry. He'll never know the anguish I went through to hide all of this.

"She called me when he left. She let it slip that I knew, and then she told him about William bringing her to appointments."

Chris breathes out heavily, hanging his head. "I didn't know about William," he says softly.

"As soon as she told me, I wanted to tell him. But when I started to, he told me to keep her secret. God! I'm such an idiot!" I rake my hand through my hair, wishing I could yank it all out.

"This is the first time I've seen him in years," he admits.

Yeah, me too. Apparently, he and Daddy had a conversation, one I'm sure didn't involve many words.

"I hate him," I seethe. "He couldn't leave well enough alone. Jay was already struggling, and he had to swoop in to finish the job."

"You should go in and get some sleep."

"What if this is the straw that breaks the camel's back? What if he can't get past this?"

"The what-if game is dangerous, Annie. He's been in our lives since day one. He's not just going to dump you because of one bad night."

He doesn't get it. When it comes to Jo and Jay Parker, there is no keeping secrets about each other. They're all the blood relatives they have. For too long, it was the two of them against the world, and I made a stupid decision to keep a secret that would break him.

"Did you know he came and found me after prom?"

Chris stares at me blankly, though the tension in the air thickens.

"I was so angry at him. But he still came to find me at the end of the night to tell me . . ." He couldn't even say he loved me. He hid that part of himself away from me for so long. He comforted me. He hugged me while I cried. Then he made sure I got home safely.

"Jay and I have always had this connection. We were so attuned to each other's feelings without having to say a word. When he went to boot camp, I wrote him every single day. At boot camp graduation, he ignored Cindy What's-Her-Name, who insisted they were together, and spent most of his time with me." I take a deep breath and look my brother in the eye. We're so much alike. Same blond hair, same bluebell eyes. But we can't be any more different on the inside. He'll never understand. "Through deployments, I kept myself busy in between phone calls because I was secretly terrified he wouldn't come home."

"Annie—"

"This isn't just one bad night, Chris. This is betrayal. This is a crime against him, and I don't know if what we have can fix it."

"Then fight for him."

I shut my mouth in surprise. I expected him to explode about all the secret meetings we had as kids. The softer side of my brother is something I don't expect.

"He's a man of honor. He's upset because he's taken responsibility for his mother since he was a kid. I love Jo, but he became her parent, Annie. He was a broken kid who turned into a broken adult trying to be the parent of *his* broken adult. Yeah, this secret we kept from him is betrayal. But you're his girlfriend and one of the only constants he's had in his life. Give him the space he's asked for, and when he comes back, talk to him."

He's right. And I hate that.

A few minutes later, Chris turns in for the night, but I stay outside. I have no plans of moving until Jay's back under the same roof as me. Until then, I'm a slave to the night.

WHEN MY EYES CRACK OPEN, the sun is already high in the sky. A thin blanket and a sheen of sweat covers my body. I sit up, my tongue swollen in my mouth from having dry mouth. Chris's truck is gone, and Jay's boots are in front of the front door.

I bound out of the swing and into the house. He stands in the kitchen over the stove, cooking. He doesn't bother lifting his gaze to meet mine. Normally, I require coffee to make me into a human person, but I make an exception by racing into the kitchen to await my punishment.

"Hi," I greet timidly.

"Hi," he replies curtly.

The silence is awkward. Saying "I'm sorry" won't cut it. I don't think there's a good explanation out there. Now I await the fate of our future while he flips a strip of bacon.

"You wanted to tell me."

My breath explodes from my mouth, my tears a close second. "I wanted to, Jay. God, I was going to tell you that day in Boston—"

"But I told you to keep it."

His voice is razor sharp. If he's trying to hurt me, he's succeeding. I've only seen him angry to the point of uncomfortable silence once. I *hate* being on the receiving end of it.

"I begged her to tell you. She came over one morning to have breakfast with me, and she promised me she'd tell you."

But she didn't. She waited until her ex-husband came around to fuck everything up.

"I'm angry," he grits.

"I know. I'm so sorry, Jay."

He turns slowly to face me, his eyes narrowed. "My mom is dying, Annabelle."

His voice cracks, and the second I see him crumbling, I'm rushing to his side, collecting him in my arms and letting my gentle giant feel his feelings for a minute.

"She's getting treatment."

"I went back over there last night. She's dying. The tumor isn't shrinking."

My heart splinters into a million pieces. His muscles flex under my hands. The tension in his shoulders keeps him upright.

"What?"

"They want to take her right breast. They're already scheduling surgery for it."

I can't believe this is happening.

"I went off on her, Annabelle. I yelled at her for reaching out to William, for involving you—"

"You have every right to be angry." I'm not sure what the proper protocol is for being angry with the woman who has been your second mother for the last almost three decades. I love her so much, but he's right for doing it. "She should've told you."

We sink to the ground. Big, fat, salty tears dribble from his eyes as he cries on my shoulder.

"What the fuck do I do if I lose her?"

"We can't think like that," I say, trying to comfort him. "People beat breast cancer all the time. Your mom is a fighter. She survived your dad. She's not going to let her own body take her out."

We're quiet for a beat.

"I'm sorry for the role I played. I need you to know that. I would've told you that day if she would've let me."

"I know," he croaks. "New rule. You can keep secrets for my mom. But if it's something regarding her health, then you need to tell me regardless of if she asks you to keep it a secret."

I can live with that. As long as we're together, we can get through anything.

21

ANNIE

There's something funny about forgiveness. Sure, you forgive whoever wronged you and move on. Sort of. "Forgive but never forget" seems to be the driving force pushing Jay through life these last two weeks. As for Jo . . . Well, I haven't exactly made the effort to see her.

It makes me a terrible person, I know. But I'm so *angry.* Keeping her secret is one thing, but making me keep the other half of the secret, of William being in the picture . . . Let's just say that if I were in Jay's shoes, I wouldn't forgive myself either.

To everyone around him, he's adjusting well enough. He's working hard around the farm, he's paying visits to his sick Momma every day, and the smile on his face is contagious.

Behind closed doors is a different story.

The guy stays up until the wee hours of the morning avoiding whatever awaits him when he closes his eyes. Last night, he made the mistake of falling asleep on the couch. I awoke to his urgent shouting and thrashing. Jones was making his presence known yet again, and for whatever reason, he's focusing in on Jay.

"So . . . I was thinking about taking a trail ride down to the creek today. What do you think?" I ask, turning off the blender for my smoothie—aka my sad attempt of "cooking" my own breakfast.

He sits at the bar, scrolling mindlessly through his phone and not paying any attention to me at all.

I sigh impatiently, which oddly grabs his attention. Finally, I get to see those jade eyes he's been hiding from me for so long.

"What was that?" he asks.

"I wanted to go on a trail ride today. What do you think?"

He shrugs, not a care to be given.

Must be nice.

"It's a beautiful day. Might be nice to get some alone time," he replies.

My smile can't be hidden. He desperately needs to get out and forget his troubles for a few hours.

"Great! I'll go get Archie ready and meet you in the arena in half an hour?"

He arches an eyebrow in confusion. "No, Annie. I meant for *you*."

Again with the *Annie* business!

My face falls, and I turn around so he can't see the waterworks. I'm not a crier. I don't do *crying*. I'm Annabelle *fucking* McKenzie for God's sake!

"Fine."

His impatient sigh is enough to make my blood boil. I turn on my heel and get at eye level with him.

"I'm sorry, Jay. I'm sorry I didn't tell you about your mom. Nobody hates me more than I do at the moment, and this walking on eggshells silent treatment you have going is *killing* me—"

"You think I hate you?" he asks in surprise. He studies me in genuine concern.

"Yes!" I wail, throwing my hands up in exasperation. "My stomach has been in knots for the last two weeks, and I've been trying to make up for it—"

"Okay, wait a minute," he stops me by leaping out of his seat, crossing the bar, and placing his hands on my shoulders. "I don't hate you, Annie."

The way my eyes widen makes him crack a smile, but it only makes things a thousand times worse for me.

"How could you not? And you keep calling me 'Annie.' I've never been 'Annie' to you."

"I'm sorry, babe. I've just been . . . preoccupied."

With fucking what? "How am I supposed to know that? I'm not a mind reader! You won't talk to me, you haven't slept in the same bed as me—"

Before I can list anything else, he presses his lips to mine, and quickly pulls away.

"I love you, Annabelle. I'm sorry. I've just been busy."

"Are you going to elaborate?"

He smirks. *Smirks!* "I wish I could, but I can't. Anyway, I'm going into town for a bit, but have fun on your ride."

With a peck on my forehead, he strides out of the house and pulls out of the driveway. Meanwhile, I stand stuck in the middle of the kitchen, dumbfounded and not feeling *any* better.

I NEEDED to do something with my hands, which is why I'm in barn number three rearranging the tack room. The center aisle of the barn is filled with saddle racks and bridles galore. Saddle pads rest neatly on top of stall doors as to not get dirty, and the grooming caddies sit in a neat line in the feed room.

The plywood floors have been around for decades, and though they still hold up pretty well, years of dust and dirt blanket the floor. I sweep it all out, making a new pile of dust and dirt just outside the door. The saddle racks that hang on the wall are wiped down with Clorox wipes and dried.

"Annabelle?"

I ignore my father's voice, eager to get the rest of this done before Aria gets home and insists on reorganizing herself. I love the girl, but sometimes I need to have things my own way. What could Daddy want from me, anyway? I swear . . . Sometimes I think he forgets I'm alive.

"What are you doing?" he asks, his broad figure darkening the doorway.

"Chores," I reply darkly.

He nods once and scowls at the clutter in the aisle. "You're cleaning out the tack room?"

I meet his amber eyes and narrow my own. "You can't have your cake and eat it too, Daddy. You can either bitch at me for putting my job before chores or you can be grateful I'm pulling my weight."

He chuckles. "I *am* grateful. Just surprised."

I make an unintelligible noise to let him know I heard him, but I continue with my task, wanting to be left alone. But damn it, he doesn't leave. I stop and turn to him, arching an eyebrow.

"Can I help you with something?"

"I was hoping you'd come for a ride with me."

Something's wrong. Stephen McKenzie doesn't willingly spend time with his children.

"Oh yeah? Am I in trouble?"

"When you get older, you're going to learn life isn't worth gambling away. I wanted to spend time with you. Is that such a crime?"

Yes.

"Let me put the tack room back together. Then I'll get Archie ready," I groan.

This is usually the part he bestows some of his famous Stephen McKenzie knowledge upon us. My father is a quiet man. Always observing his surroundings. Always ready with an escape plan. It's something I've tried to hone myself since I started globe-trotting like my mother did at my age.

What is there to say? What did I do wrong?

It takes me an hour to get everything back together. The place is spotless, and the cobwebs that once adorned the corners of the room are now a distant memory.

I grab Archie out of his stall and groom and tack him up. My father meets me in the covered arena on Ricky, one of the "newer" horses he bought a few years ago. He's jet black with a white blaze down his nose. He's sweet when there isn't a saddle on him. Otherwise, he's in the mind to work and doesn't tolerate many horses around him when he's being ridden.

We start down the pasture. I study him with a sidelong glance. I've always been closer to one parent. And that's not saying I wasn't close with my dad. I've heard that it's difficult to bond with a kid when you have multiple. It didn't help that I demanded attention. I'm a typical middle child, though I'm sure that isn't a good flex.

"What did you want to talk about?"

I'm the first one to speak. The silence is painful. It's uncomfortable and pointless. I don't like it.

"When was the last time we went on a ride together?"

I shrug. "I don't know. Probably when I was a teenager." *Enough with the riddles already!*

Daddy grins and relaxes his reins. Ricky lowers his head and walks lazily ahead with his ears relaxed and flopping with each step.

The sun beats down on us. I'm lucky to be wearing a ball cap, but the sun won't be too forgiving on the exposed skin on my arms.

"How's work?"

Did I mention I hate small talk? So pointless!

"Fine . . ."

What is his angle?

"You knew about Jo."

Mm-hmm. Always an ulterior motive.

"I'm surprised you didn't. You always seem to be on the up and up."

He shrugs incredulously, a frown pulling at his lips. "Believe it or not, I don't actively go looking for everyone's deepest, darkest secrets."

Maybe. But it always seems to work out that way. "But yes. She told me and swore me to secrecy."

"Parents have a funny way of forgetting their kids aren't their friends." He glances over at me. "She shouldn't have made you keep her secret. It isn't right."

My stomach swirls as I think about that last meeting. William looked straight at her and demanded she tell Jay. I wasn't privy to that conversation. It wasn't something Jay rehashed later with me.

"I don't like secrets. Especially when they involve people I love. She made me an accomplice, Daddy."

"People do drastic things out of fear. Jo has only known fear her entire life."

Put a drunken Parker in the middle of it and you have yourself a fatal concoction.

"People do drastic things out of protection too," I counter. Like Derek inserting himself into a hostage situation to deliver Troy while Charlie held Aria at gunpoint eight months ago.

"Sure."

And we're back to silence. I'm envious of my sister. She can live through the darkest period of her life and welcome silence like an old friend.

For me, the silence is deafening. I don't like having to guess what everyone is thinking. Just say what's in your head and we'll talk about it.

"Can I ask you something, and will you give me a no-bullshit answer?"

His eyes spark amusement, something I don't see often.

"Ask, I may not answer," he replies cautiously.

"What did you do after high school? There's a whole chunk of your life that we know nothing about. I know you had the farm and everything, but surely that's not all you did . . ."

He chuckles. "The answer would surprise you. It's not as glamorous you kids suspect."

I press him silently with my eyes.

"I traveled."

I roll my eyes. That's Momma's wheelhouse, not his.

"To where?"

"Europe. Asia. Russia. I mostly stayed domestic."

He's killing me. "What did you do in all of those places?"

"You know, when you were a kid, you used to look through the photo albums your mother put together. I always thought it was strange because we had a library of books for kids that told much more fascinating stories than those old pictures did."

"Says you. Momma has a rich history. She defied her parents and sought out what the world offered her. Nanna and Poppa wanted her to marry a Parker."

Daddy scowls. "She got me instead," he growls victoriously.

I giggle. "I can honestly say she got the better end of the deal. You're not doing anything shady."

He rolls his eyes. "We McKenzies have a code. Honor. Truth. Justice."

I take this time to challenge him. "How truthful are you being right now?"

Nobody challenges Stephen McKenzie. But what can I say? I'm a unicorn. I know where the limits are, and most of the time, I can touch my toe to the other side. This is one of those times.

"It's not proper for your kids to know *everything* about you. What secrets are you leaving yourself to discover when I'm dead?"

He's got me there. I laugh through my nose and roll my eyes. I take my feet out of the stirrups and let them hang as Archie walks along.

"There's a whole side of you I don't know about."

"I can say the same about you," he counters with a sinister grin. "You kept a secret from your family for two and a half years. And then another one about a member of our family. When do the secrets stop?"

Yep. Not going to live that one down. "If I told you right off the bat, what would've been your reaction?"

He shrugs indifferently. "I don't know. You took that away from me."

Ugh.

"But since we're on the subject, are you happy?"

We're not on the subject, and he knows it. Honestly, I was waiting to see how long it would've taken him to call me out on all the secrecy, especially the parts that included Jay.

"Yes." It comes out of my mouth so fast. But my stomach rebels. Something isn't right between us, and all the uncertainty has me doubting things. "He's a good man, Daddy."

"I know who he is," he replies.

He doesn't know him like I do. I know all of his skeletons in the closet—his deepest, darkest fears, the things that keep him up at night. I've had a front-row seat ever since I can remember.

For most of my life, I was the one they didn't need to worry about. I had good grades. I was home running the barn and giving lessons. After all that time, when I look at my father, I don't even know if we've had a true moment alone together. Not like this.

"Do you know who *I* am?"

Our eyes meet. The fact he can't answer right away makes me sick. He doesn't know me either. I've spent so much time running away from this place when Jay wasn't here.

"I think you keep the important parts of you hidden away. Maybe that's my fault. I haven't given you much of an opportunity for you to show me who you are."

I drop my gaze. "I'm not sure if that's supposed to make me feel better or worse . . ."

"I've watched you pine after him since you were a teenager. There's a lot you don't think I know, but I know a chunk of your life has been spent wishing for a life with him."

Sweat beads in my hairline at the implication. *Pining?* I don't *pine.* But . . . I always wished for him. Is that the same thing?

"What are you insinuating?"

"The whole point of bringing you out here wasn't for you to question your life with him, Annie. But I want you to stop—" he reaches over and grabs hold of my reins and stops Archie.

We face the open pasture. The afternoon sun is starting its descent. The light it provides illuminates the grassy field. Large oak trees are scattered in random places that provide little shade. What am I looking at? What is *so* important about this spot?

"—and look around you."

The breeze ripples through the long-bladed grass. A small pond acts as a natural watering hole for the steer that live in this pasture.

"This land was purchased before the turn of the century. Your great grandfather envisioned you. And your brother and sister. Maybe it wasn't *you* specifically, but he always imagined that this land would be crawling with McKenzies."

"Doing the farming thing," I retort, giving him the I'm-not-having-this-conversation-with-you-again look.

"He came from Scotland and wanted to give his family the freedom to choose the life they desired."

I turn to meet his gaze. Is this the life I chose? Is this the life I wanted for myself?

"When you think of your life together, what exactly do you see?"

I see me . . . and Jay . . . and *nothing else.*

My heart stops beating in my chest. What exactly is the plan for us? Now that I have him, what does the rest of our life look like? What are we working toward?

"I see us."

He nods. "And? Do you plan on having a family? Do you see yourself moving off the property? What is it you *see?*"

I hesitate before answering with, "I don't know. It isn't something we've talked about at length yet. We more or less follow the 'we'll cross that bridge when we get there' territory."

"I worry about the three of you. Chris is wandering around, still sneaking girls in like we don't notice. Aria almost died. And you . . ."

"What about me?" I ask with urgency. *What am I doing that's so horrible?*

"You're floating, Annabelle. I worry that you've made yourself into the woman you thought Jay wanted and forgot yourself along the way."

His words cut deep. I promised myself I wouldn't turn into *that* girl. I'm too strong to be that girl!

A poisonous laugh escapes me. Leave it to my father to just magically know when I'm doubting everything.

"And you wonder why I didn't tell you when we first started dating." I push Archie forward and turn him around to go back to the barn.

"Annie—"

"I've always been one hundred percent authentically myself, Dad. Unlike you, I don't hide who I am. I open my mouth at the wrong times, and I ruffle a lot of people's feathers, but I have never had to change myself for a man. Including Jay."

I think.

I push Archie into a canter. Ricky's hooves thunder behind me as Daddy tries to catch up.

This just proves that nobody knows who *I* am.

"Annabelle, stop!" He cuts in front of me, and Archie screeches to a halt. "I wasn't trying to hurt your feelings—"

A poisonous laugh escapes me. "Weren't you, though? That's what goads you on, isn't it? When things are going a little *too* well, you have to stop by and stir the pot." I growl in frustration. "Why are you choosing *right now* to question my judgment? I've been around the world at least twice now, and you didn't question if I was going through an existential crisis. But the second I come clean about my feelings for Jay Parker, *I'm* the one that's crazy!"

"When was the last time you did something for *you?*" He narrows his eyes and challenges me. "Tell me. When was the last time you did something for you that had nothing to do with Jay?"

My eyes spring with tears, because honestly, I can't answer that question. Everything I've ever done was done with Jay in mind.

"Does it matter?"

"Do you want to be a travel writer, Annie? Can you see yourself traveling now that Jay's home? Can you see yourself answering to other editors?"

I hate him. I hate him for planting the seeds of doubt.

"I'm done talking about this with you."

I'm grateful he gives me a head start. I gallop back to the barn and cool Archie off in the arena. After untacking and rinsing him down, I turn him out to the paddock and race home. Jay's truck is in the driveway, and for the first time ever, I wish we weren't home. I wish he would be anywhere else.

I storm through the front door, slamming it behind me. Jay lounges on the couch and stares at me wildly when I storm past him and lock the bedroom door behind me. I need a minute to myself.

I strip out of my clothes and start the bath. The hot water tap is on as far as it will go. Pulling my hair into a messy bun, I sink into the scalding hot water. My skin stings, but I don't care. My joints and muscles ache. I play with the taps, finding the perfect temperature to lose myself in. Jay pounds on the bedroom door, but I tune that into a rhythmic beat.

What is my father's end game, here? Why is he making me question my relationship after all this time? Did I piss him off that much that he had to wait to get his revenge?

I end up staring at the textured ceiling. I point out shapes with each textured stroke. The pounding on the door stops. I think he's got the hint.

Ever since I could remember, I knew I didn't want to become my mother.

I envied her for her stories. She had the opportunity to lose herself in the world and discover who she was before she settled down.

I know who I am. I'm Annabelle McKenzie. I love traveling the world. I love my family with the fiercest intensity. I found the love of my life at an early age . . . and started planning our future before I even had my first kiss.

Oh my god. I'm that girl, aren't I?

Terrified, I jump out of the tub and empty the water. Jay sits on our bed, watching me with wide eyes as if I just lost my mind.

"Annabelle, what's wrong?"

I wrap the towel tighter around me and root through my dresser without acknowledging him right away. *Just let me freak out, won't you?* "Nothing."

"Come on, Blondie. We're not those people. We talk about what's bothering us, remember?"

Ha! What a joke. We're not those people, yet he's the one refusing to talk to me about anything! My heart hammers in my chest as I rake my hand through my hair and look anywhere but at him. I laugh, but only because I'm borderline hysterical now. He hasn't talked to me about what's bothering him. Why should I be the bigger person?

"Jay, I need a minute alone."

Once upon a time, if we needed space, all we had to do was end the call. Now his fight or flight is activated, and he wants to stay here and fight. He wants to be the protector, the provider. All I want to do is lie in my bed without anyone touching me and banish my father's seeds of doubt in peace while watching *Community* to banish all crappy thoughts away.

"Alone, huh?"

He hops off the bed and crowds me. I gently place my hand on his chest and push him away.

"Talk to me," he begs softly.

"Not right now," I seethe. "I'm begging you to give me some space."

"Fine. If that's what you want."

He turns on his heel and slams the door behind him. The alarm chimes, alerting me that he's left the house.

This went so unnecessarily horrible. I just wanted space. I wanted to sort through my feelings before having him doubt us. How am I the bad guy?

22

JAY

I'm tempting fate by coming back to Rico's. With William on the loose and begging me to talk to him, I should stay far away from downtown altogether. But here I am at the bar where he approached me last time. I'm here because the elusive Dominic Reese has been sighted. I lock eyes with Derek's reflection through the mirror behind the bar. Troy sits in a high chair at the head of the table, and Zoey sits by herself in a booth talking across the table to Aria.

Aria laughs at something Zoey says, but I can't break my gaze from Derek. I follow his eyes to the end of the bar where, lo and behold, my target sits without a care in the world, nursing a whiskey.

I nod my acknowledgment to Derek and focus on the salt-and-pepper shakers in front of me. In the mirror, I'm able to keep an eye on him without him noticing too much.

"What can I get you?" the bartender asks.

"Beer. Surprise me." She winks and pops the top off a Corona.

"Hard day?" she asks.

"Something like that."

Just that Annie is going through something and she's shutting me out. My stomach growls, reminding me I haven't eaten anything yet.

"Do you think I can get some steak tacos over here?"

"Sure thing, handsome."

The honorific makes me stiffen, but I banish it without a second thought.

Reese is on his phone, tapping away. Occasionally, his gaze will drift to the mirror where he can get a good gander at Aria. I won't let him get to her. Not tonight.

"So . . . are you a local?" she asks with a flirty smile.

Leave me alone. "I'm a native. Left for the Marine Corps for a bit, but now I'm home."

She grins and her gray eyes sparkle. She's seen something she likes. "I love a man in a uniform." She sighs dreamily.

"So does my girlfriend."

She stiffens and her face falls. "It seems like all the hot ones are taken." She sighs.

Yeah, well. Who knows after tonight.

The thought stops me in my tracks. Two weeks ago, I uncovered a secret she was a part of. Though her intentions were pure, and I told her not to tell me the secret, looking at her enrages me. How could she sit on something like that when it involves my mother?

"Steak tacos," she says monotonously, placing the plate down in front of me without any fanfare. Whatever.

Derek Hawthorn: He's getting ready to leave.

I glance up, and for the briefest of moments, our eyes meet. Dominic purses his lips, throws a wad of cash on the table, and strolls away shortly after. I give him a five-minute head start. As soon as I see the silver Audi through the reflection in the mirror, I pay for my food in cash and race to the truck.

If I were him, I'd stay outside of town. He has to know I'd come after him after the stunt he pulled in Richmond.

My phone vibrates, and Tanner's name pops up. I've only met him twice before when Derek first moved to Sage Creek. We aren't the best of friends, but now that I'm an unofficial member of the group, our paths will cross constantly.

"Hey."

"He just turned onto Western. He's heading toward the shelter."

I cradle the phone between my ear and shoulder as I take a shortcut on Walnut Street. It gives me the perfect opportunity to watch him without showing my truck. I park in front of old man Gerald Hanson's front yard. From this vantage point, I can see everything that's happening.

Dominic climbs out of the car and tries the front door. He knocks and says something, but I can't make it out.

"He's trying to get in," I inform Tanner, even though it's not like he can do anything.

"Hold on. Let me see if I can get ahold of the receptionist."

Tanner taps away on his computer.

"I instant messaged her, and she's seen it. She knows not to let him in."

He still tries regardless.

"Hold on. I'm switching to the other line."

I dial in Jared and merge the calls, instructing Tanner not to say a word before Jared answers.

"Jared, there's a guy trying to break into the shelter after the receptionist told him to leave."

"I'm three streets over. Give me a five."

"Make it two."

We wait quietly. I'm sure Tanner has hacked into the video feed, so he probably has a better view of what's going on than I do. If Dominic tries to break in, I can race over there and probably incapacitate him until Jared gets there.

Sirens blare as they head down the street toward the shelter. I watch as Dominic stiffens, abandoning his efforts at the door and then racing to the car.

"I'm going to talk to the receptionist. He ran away," Jared instructs.

"Call me later. Let me know what she says."

Jared hangs up and leaves Tanner and me on the call.

"Do you think you can pull facial recognition on him?" I ask.

"The cameras are good, but only if he looks straight into them. He's smart. He doesn't want to be detected."

"Surely you have more than just the camera outside watching him."

Tanner chuckles. "Smart fish. I have a camera inside pointed at the door, but again, he didn't look at it. There's not enough camera time on his face, and the ball cap doesn't help anything."

I groan in frustration. "Where is he headed?"

"Looks like to the interstate. Stay on his tail. He's probably going to lie low. When he stops somewhere, let me know, and I'll see what I can do."

I end the call and start toward the interstate. The next town over is an hour away. If I were him, that's where I would stay to keep under the radar.

Dominic Reese is an alias. But if he's working with the Dodge's, I'll bet Annie's house he has at least ten other aliases to cover his tracks.

Fifteen minutes later, I find the Audi on the highway. He drives in the center lane, cruising right at the speed limit as to not draw any attention.

He's headed toward Richmond, which is surprising. That's two hours from Sage Creek. I mean, why would you if you're being paid the big bucks and can stay at five-star hotels on the boss's dime?

I stay behind three other cars, following him when he exits into the city. He parks at a Hilton and swings the keys on his finger.

I dial Tanner to let him know. Unfortunately, there isn't any other audio/visual he can tap into now that he's disappeared into the building. *But* I can at least search the car.

I hop out of the truck to fiddle around with the lock on the driver's side door. I slide into the leather driver's seat, keeping a close eye on the rearview mirror to make sure he isn't coming my way.

The center console is empty. A pack of half-used cigarettes lay open on the seat. I flip the visors open and curse when nothing falls out. I reach for the glovebox and rifle around, noting every piece of paper inside and finding nothing. I pop the trunk and get out of the car. There's a black duffel bag that is zipped up. I unzip it and rifle through old gym clothes when a manila folder drops out of it. Taking it out, I open it to find pictures of Aria, Annie, Jackie, Chris, Momma, Zoey, and Betty Lou. Dossiers of Steve and his band of goons are detailed enough to know that somebody else is looking into Steve.

A sheet of paper floats to the ground. I pick it up and find the name "Eve" circled in green. Underneath is a grainy black-and-white picture of a female doctor, mid-thirties, in the ambulance well of a hospital. I take a picture of it for good measure. Big block letters that read "person of interest" grabs my attention. What does she have to do with this?

My phone vibrates violently in my pocket, telling me it's time to get the fuck out. I stuff everything back into the folder and under the clothes. I shut the trunk and jog to the truck.

This is our first lead.

When I get home, I go straight to Aria's house and text Derek to meet me out front. He quietly invites me in and puts on the TV for some background noise. We situate ourselves at the kitchen table while I show him the pictures.

"Who do you think Eve is?"

"Nate's girlfriend. Well, ex-girlfriend. Looks like ditching her didn't matter in the long run after all." He sighs. "Did you find anything else?"

"No. The car was clean. I'm sure he's keeping everything in the hotel room. Though I wonder why he left the folder in the trunk of all places."

Derek shrugs. "This is lesson one in these types of missions: always assume they're onto you. He may have wanted you to find it."

"I don't think he saw me all night, other than at the restaurant. But I was careful. I stayed three cars behind."

Derek winces. "Men like that are trained to observe everything. It may not have looked like he saw you. My money is on he definitely saw you. You're going to need to take extra precautions. Let me talk to Tanner about finding you a different vehicle. From now on, stay close to home. He might come searching for you."

"He had pictures of Annie, Derek."

My stomach churns when I remember our fight from earlier. What got her so angry?

"That's why we stick around and stay close. They taught you in the Corps to be observant. Use those skills and multiply them. If anything seems fishy, tell one of us, and we'll back you up."

We finish up the chat, and I head back home. Annabelle is fast asleep in her bed. I don't want to wake her, so I make myself comfortable on the couch. It won't always be this weird between us. She's used to having space from me. I just . . . need to remember she didn't tell me because Momma didn't give her a choice.

Fuck.

"Jay?" Her sweet voice flits into the room. She stands in the doorway, her shirt skimming the tops of her creamy, white thighs.

I motion for her to come to me. Her pouty bottom lip sticks out as I pull her into me. I gently kiss her forehead. She's in someone's scope, and the safest place for her is right here.

"I'm sorry I was such a raging bitch tonight."

"Don't be sorry. We all have our bad days. I'm sorry I didn't handle it well."

She snorts. "No, you didn't handle it well at all."

I stiffen, though I'm not looking for another fight. Agree to disagree, and then move on. "What got you so upset?"

She sighs heavily. "My dad. We went for a trail ride, and he was being his normal intrusive self. I think he gets a kick out of planting seeds of doubt."

I arch an eyebrow. "Doubt?"

"He pointed something out to me, and I've been thinking about it all night. He says I hide who I truly am away from everyone except you."

She sighs against my chest, her hair tickling my nose.

"Do you?"

She shrugs. "I didn't used to think so, but now . . ." her voice trails off. "You're happy we told everyone, right? You don't regret it?"

"Of course I don't regret it. Do you?"

"No, of course not. It's just . . . I think I always knew that you and I were going to be together. Blame it on the optimistic side of me. It was something that always felt right . . . Something I was so certain of. But what if I lost myself along the way?"

This is starting to feel like a breakup. My grip around her slackens.

"What do you mean?"

"From work to us . . . I don't know if I want to write for the rest of my life—"

"What about *us?*" I bark.

She stiffens. "Where do you see us, Jay? Five years from now? Ten years from now?" She sits up, and I leap off the couch, pacing the length of the house.

"I see us together. And happy—"

"Do we live here? Do we live in an apartment in Greece?"

Um . . . I don't know.

"Where is all of this coming from? You don't like looking into the future. You told me that! I thought we were on the same page, Annie. I thought that whenever those bridges came along, we would cross them when we got there!"

My voice raises, and tears fill her eyes.

"I love you, Jay. Of course we're together. But you were able to find yourself in the Marine Corps—"

"Don't do that," I snap. "You had four years of college. There were eleven years when we weren't together. If you think I know who I am, I'm sorry to disappoint you. I have no fucking clue."

She lowers herself on the sofa again, burying her face in her hands.

"Why are you questioning this? Why now?"

She sniffles and meets my gaze. "Because I've only known one thing my entire life. I wanted to be with you, and you made me chase you. When you finally stopped running, I thought I knew that the distance would only make us stronger—"

"I can't believe this." I scrub my hand over my face.

"We're not breaking up, Jay! But I am having a freak-out, and I need you to be here with me and tell me everything is going to be okay!"

I stare at her in bewilderment. "This feels like you're leaving."

She shakes her head and closes the distance. Her arms wrap around me, placing her ear next to my heart.

"Jay, I've fought so hard for you. I went through years of your indifference and denial. I finally got to tell the world about us. I'm not going anywhere." Her hands unclasp from me and hold my head so we're looking eye to eye. "I'm just telling you that I'm nearing thirty years old, and I still haven't found my life's purpose."

That makes two of us.

"Blondie, do you really think I know *mine?* I've envied you for years. You know exactly what you want and how you want it. You love to travel. You love to write. Maybe you don't have to be a travel writer . . . but maybe you can find something in between."

She sighs against me. "Do you think I formed myself to be the woman you wanted?"

I take a reflexive step back, almost like she's hit me.

"For years, Annabelle, I've loved you because of *who* you are. Your intelligence, your confidence, your humor, your lack of self-preservation . . ." I sigh and kiss her forehead. "You're Annabelle fucking McKenzie. You have always been unapologetically yourself. That's why I love you. I've tried so hard to be more like you."

Her bottom lip wobbles. I kiss her tears away and pull her close to me.

"My dad's a dick," she sobs.

I chuckle. "Yeah. Yeah, he is."

"I love you. I'm sorry I'm so moody."

"I love you too, Blondie. You're human. When people plant seeds of doubt, it's easy to lose yourself for a minute."

"I'm tired," she admits sadly.

"Let's go to bed. I'll even rub your back until you fall asleep."

23

ANNIE

My sister stands on an ottoman in my mother's living room while my mom takes her measurements. Lucky for us, Momma knows how to do alterations. So when Aria's wedding gown comes in just a little too snug, Momma can cut costs and do the alterations herself. She's even fashioned a full-length mirror that leans against the entertainment center for the full bridal shop effect.

Fucking Brandy Hunt. I'll bet when Aria went in for her appointment and ordered her dress, Brandy fudged the numbers. Like mother, like daughter.

With her hair in a messy bun and a crying baby at her feet, she stares at herself in the mirror with a twisted scowl.

"Be careful. Your face might freeze that way," I tease.

When Momma isn't looking, she flips me off in the mirror. She yelps in pain when Momma sticks her with the needle. She forgets Momma sees all.

"Hey, y'all." Jackie arrives in a huff. Her green Sage Creek Animal Hospital polo is rumpled, and the giant bags under her eyes tell me a story of stolen, sexy moments at the office with Dr. Sam.

"Hey, honey. Grab some champagne and take a load off," Momma instructs.

"Sorry I'm late. It was crazy at the office." She pours herself a glass of champagne and sits next to me on the sofa, gazing at Aria with adoration.

"Or you *got* crazy at the office?"

Jackie scowls at me and sighs. "None of your business. Anyway . . . Did I miss anything?"

"Other than I'm a fat cow?" Aria whines.

We all glower at Aria.

"None of that. You just gave birth, so knock it off. I don't appreciate you talking about my best friend like that," Jackie smarts.

"No. You didn't miss anything," Aria glowers.

I scoop Troy up from around the ottoman and place him in my lap. He plays with my bracelets and babbles nonstop.

"So, sweet pea, how are things with Shane?"

We all raise our eyebrows. *Who is Shane?*

"Oh, um. His name is Sam. Everything is great." She drops her gaze to the floor. Aria and I exchange knowing glances in the mirror.

Jackie O'Brien is in love with our idiot brother and is determined to make his life hell. Too bad it's at Sam's expense.

"Sorry. Sam. He seems like a nice man. When are you going to bring him by?"

She shifts uncomfortably, silently begging me in the mirror to change the subject.

"Momma, did you know Jackie is graduating over the summer with her bachelor's?" I ask quickly.

Momma's face lights up. "Is that so? Oh honey, congratulations! That is so exciting! I bet your momma is so proud of you!"

Jackie's pale cheeks redden, and she mouths a "thank you" in the mirror.

"Thank you. Though, I suspect Derek won't be happy to hear that I'm leaving—"

"Don't tell me you're moving away . . ." Momma pleads, straightening and studying Jackie in the mirror.

She licks her lips and meets Aria's worried gaze. "I love Sage Creek. But I think it's time I spread my wings and find my place in the world. There's only so much Bethany Hunt I can take before it gets to be too much."

Momma frowns. "Any idea where you'll go?"

She silently considers the options in her head before speaking up. "Well, my mom is living in Seattle now, so that's always an option. Or I was looking to go New York or Florida . . ."

"Sounds like you're lookin' for an adventure," Momma says, finally dropping the needle and giving Jackie her full attention.

"An adventure would be nice. I want to be reminded I'm still in my twenties and I'm not an old hag just yet."

We giggle because it's so painfully true. Jackie's mom was a teen mom. And of course, sometimes, she had to be the parent in their dynamic. She needs a night out. Or a freakin' month-long vacation away from here.

I don't want her to leave. I know she's my sister's best friend, but while Aria was gone, we had each other to depend on. We became close.

"What am I supposed to do without you?" Aria asks with an exaggerated pout.

"Oh, I think you'll be fine. You have Derek and your family. And you'll have an excuse to drop your kids and hang out with me for a long weekend."

We laugh, but the elephant is still sitting in the room. Nobody wants to bring up the fling between her and Chris in front of Momma.

I turn my attention to Aria's gown and weakly smile. It's an elegant, short-sleeved gown with a lacy detailed back to cover her scars. The skirt is full, and it makes her waist look so tiny. Aria gazes at herself in the mirror, a small smile appearing on her face. She's admiring the way she looks. But I don't think she understands how *strong* she looks.

"All right, baby. Get one last look, and then we'll go into the bedroom and get you out of this."

She grins in the mirror and hops off the ottoman, following Momma upstairs. I turn to Jackie and grin.

"Don't worry, I made sure he had something to do anywhere else. He isn't here," I reassure her.

Relief washes over her. "Good. And thank you."

"So . . . does Sam know you're thinking about moving?"

She scrunches her nose. “I don’t think that’s going anywhere. It was fun for a minute, but we want different things.”

My brother being one of them. “Oh. I’m sorry.”

“I still have to work with him, which is why I suppose I’m dragging it out. I know it isn’t fair but . . .”

Yeah, I know.

“Um . . . So is she still set on getting the two of us together?” she asks timidly.

I giggle. “Yes. Momma loves you, and if she could legally call you her daughter, all would be right in her world.”

Grimacing, she buries her face in her hands and groans. “Oh, god. I blame Jose Cuervo. He’s never a good idea. Honestly, you can tell Chris he has nothing to worry about. I’m not going to bang on his door and beg him to be with me.”

“I think it broke Momma’s heart. We know he’s her favorite, and she was hoping he’d be settled down by now.”

Jackie rolls her eyes. “Believe me, sleeping with your bother has been the biggest mistake of my life. I regret it, no offense.” She sighs. “You know what? You don’t need to be the messenger. I can tell him to get bent myself.”

“You should come by more often. We miss you.”

Her megawatt grin is enough to turn my day around.

“I miss you guys too. I thought staying away was the right thing. I didn’t want him to think I was here for him.”

Christopher is an idiot.

“Anyway, once I graduate, I want to vacation in Paris for about a week, and then it’ll be time to find a job.”

“You really want to leave here?”

She gives me a half shrug. “Come on, Annie. The odds have been stacked against me from day zero. I’m a product of teen pregnancy. I’ve had to become somebody I’m not to prove a point that I’m not my mom. I’m tired. I want to start over fresh somewhere.”

“You have nothing to prove to anybody. You work harder than anyone I know.”

“My best friend is getting married and has two kids. You’re practically married to Jay, and you're either going to drop everything and go on epic adventures around the world, too busy to make time for me, or you're going to come to your senses and start a family with Jay and will be too busy to make time for me." Her eyes well with tears.

My stomach somersaults. I only want the best for her, but I get where she's coming from.

"Are you breaking up with us?" I ask with a teasing smile.

She groans and pinches the bridge of her nose. "Let me tell you something. You may not be blood, but you are my sister, and I'd be a shitty one if I didn't tell you that cutting us off before we can hurt you is only hurting yourself. Of course we're going to make time for you, Jackie. You're family, and we love you. We don't know what we'd do without you."

She rolls her eyes and giggles. "That's hard to believe. But . . . I suppose I believe you."

"Don't worry about Christopher. He's an asshole and isn't worth your time anyway. One day, things won't be so awkward and you can put it behind you."

Momma and Aria waltz back in the room, and Aria can sense Jackie's discomfort right away. "Oh no. Chris didn't come in here, did he?"

I burst into a fit of giggles as Jackie groans loudly.

"No. She's just emotional. You look beautiful, Peanut."

Aria's cheeks blush. "Should we do lunch, then? Rhonda's set aside a few pies for us, and I could dive into some chocolate."

RHONDA'S IS our home away from home. Our booth is untouched, and when we sit down, Nicole greets us warmly and fills our glasses up with sweet tea. We order food that is so bad for us, but it only tastes good because we can sit around the table and reminisce when things weren't so difficult.

The same people fill the tables. Old Merv from the police station nurses a coffee and a burger while Clay Parker sits across from him with a scowl, watching him devour his lunch. Bethany Hunt and Deb Baker are tucked away in a booth in the corner, scanning the room to silently dig up dirt on everyone around them.

George Hanson sits with his wife who nibbles at a salad while he watches on with quiet admiration. They're both getting up in age. They're the nicest elderly couple in town, yet they'll put Bethany Hunt in her place when she gets too loud.

These are people we've spent decades going to church with. We've gone trick-or-treating at their houses. Some of these people even taught us in school.

But there's one person who doesn't belong. A person who makes my blood boil and recalls unpleasant memories of a homeless man dying at my feet.

Dominic Reese sits at the bar eating a salad and sipping on a coke. He scrolls through his phone, oblivious to the people around him. Aria catches my eye and casually glances over her shoulder. She stiffens and turns to face Jackie.

I quickly text Jay to let him know that he's here. We pretend Dominic doesn't exist and talk wedding plans. Jackie will be doing our hair, and we're hiring someone to do our makeup.

"Nate's going to officiate. I sort of forced him," Aria admits with a guilty smile.

"I doubt it. The guy worships the ground you walk on," Jackie replies darkly with a hint of a smile.

"Henry and Logan will be ushers, leaving the two of you to walk down the aisle with Joey and Tanner."

"Here ya go, ladies. I've got some chocolate peanut butter pie on deck when you're done," Nicole says, gently dropping our plates in front of us.

The bell on the front door jingles, and Jay approaches us. He swoops in next to Jackie so he has a full, unobstructed view of Dominic.

"I'm still mad at you," Jackie smarts.

Jay arches an eyebrow, failing miserably to hide his amused smile. "I apologized like four hundred times, little one."

Jackie scowls at the dig about her height when I meet his gaze.

He's exhausted. And it's the first time we've been in the same room without one of us feeling awkward or guilty.

"Why did you throw me under the bus? I didn't need Betty Lou to know about the one bad decision I made with her son!"

Jay chuckles. "I'm sorry. It slipped. I didn't mean to rat you out. My relationship was being attacked! I had to put him in his place."

Aria scrunches her nose. "Why didn't you tell me? I could've softened the blow!"

"Do you know how humiliating it is to have the guy you've crushed on since you were a little kid reject you?" She sighs impatiently, glancing at me for help. Because yes, I totally know what it feels like. "It was months ago. The relationship with Sam wasn't going anywhere, and I slipped up and made a mistake with your brother. He caught me at a low moment, and I allowed myself to hope for a second."

A second was all it took for Chris to take advantage of her and break her heart.

She huffs and rearranges her silverware. "Anyway, it's done. I've already chased him out of the office, and I'm not interested in hearing his regrets. I'm graduating and will be off on a new adventure soon enough. Jackie O'Brien will be living her best life in a matter of months."

I meet Jay's concerned gaze while Aria stares at her best friend in disbelief.

"That bad, huh?" Jay finally breaks the silence.

"Oh my god," she groans.

"Miss McKenzie."

We all freeze at Dominic's voice. She glances up expectantly. We're all at the ready. We just need him to make his move first.

"Mr. Reese," she replies.

"I was wondering if you thought more about—"

"Reese, I'm glad you're here. Let's take a walk," Jay cuts him off.

Dominic's eyes snap to Jay's and narrow. "Careful, Parker. The cops are here. I wouldn't be too hasty if I were you."

Jay's jaw tics. Dominic smirks. It's a pissing match between good and evil.

"That would be a shame too. I've heard a lot about the police here. Low crime stats. Great neighborhood."

"I'm sure you have. But again, let's take a walk."

"I want to hear it from her," he smarts, turning to Aria. "Or perhaps Annie? The last time we met, things got . . . messy."

I'm so fucking proud of her when Aria doesn't shy away. She clenches her jaw and narrows her eyes. She doesn't lose her cool. As for me, I have no problem telling him to take a hike.

"Like JJ said, I'm not interested. I have a lawyer who's been on the case from the beginning. I'm not looking to speak with anyone from Dodge Enterprises. But you are ruining a lunch with my sister and best friend, so I'd appreciate it if you would get lost."

He chuckles. "Fair enough. Good day to you, Mr. Parker."

My eyes widen as Jay watches him walk out the front door.

What was Reese trying to pull? Especially after what he did in Richmond. Why would he come here to taunt us? In front of the cops, no less!

"Is there something else going on?" I ask when Jackie and Aria return to the wedding dress conversation.

"No, Blondie. I promise."

I nod in agreement, but for the first time ever, I don't believe a single word that comes out of his mouth.

24

JAY

"There's an access road to your left. I double-checked with county records. It belongs to the Parkers. As long as you're quiet about it, you can get in without raising any eyebrows. Just know I won't be able to keep an eye on you. Be smart. Don't take any chances."

Ever since the diner incident, Tanner has been on top of tracking him everywhere he goes. It just so happens he found William's old house. *My* old house. If this is where Reese is meeting up with his cronies, then I'm right that there's a lot more to this than meets the eye. But I'm not about to let my family's lives be snuffed out. Not when we've worked too damn hard to get back on track.

"I know how to get to my old house," I reply in the earpiece.

Ignoring me, Tanner continues with business as usual. "Tell me what you're armed with."

"Derek's Glock, my KA-BAR, and a handgun strapped to my calf."

Tanner groans. "Are you sure that's enough? I'm calling Bubba. You shouldn't be going in alone. This is stupid."

"Stop being a little bitch. I may not be MARSOC, but I know a thing or two about sneaking up on enemy lines. You've already confirmed he isn't there, right?"

MARSOC, or Marine Corps Forces Special Operations Command, is the super-secret unit within the Marine Corps that only marines, sailors, and a very select few civilians who are in MARSOC know what they do.

They're terrifying—and I'm fucking stoked I'm being trained by a group of them.

"His *car* isn't there. We have to assume he knows we're onto him, Parker. Don't underestimate him. He may look like a *Jersey Shore* idiot, but he's working some high-profile case with an unknown. MARSOC 101—don't underestimate the enemy. We already know you're on his radar because of Richmond."

Right. Get in, get out. Assume they're watching. "Tell me about all the entry and exit points in the house."

"Obviously, there are the front and back doors. Four windows in the front, two in the back at ground level, and four windows in the back on the second story. There's a crawl space that is exposed to the outdoors, but unless they're looking for it, they won't find it."

"Is that your plan, Parker? Do you plan on going through the crawl space?"

I chuckle. "Maybe. Depends on what I see when I get there."

Tanner sighs. "This is incredibly stupid. Do you know that? You need a fall man. You need someone with you."

"Are you offering?"

Tanner barks out a laugh. "No, but Derek knows what he's doing."

I immediately push that suggestion aside. I'm capable enough to handle this on my own. "You're on the earpiece with me, right? Just shut your cake-hole and let me do my thing."

Tanner grumbles and obliges.

I start up the gravel driveway on foot. My steps are precise and calculated as to not make any noise.

The colonial house stands eerily quiet. It's the place of nightmares, a place where I almost lost my life. I'm flooded with memories of my mother crying and shouting at my father to stop beating me. The shutters are hanging off their hinges. The place should be condemned. There's too much bad juju here. Nobody should be subject to live on this land. The front window is broken. It gives me the perfect opportunity to crouch down below it and listen around me.

"Talk to me, Parker."

"Shh. I'm trying to listen," I whisper back.

I'm confident nobody is here. There are no lanterns glowing or flickering of candles. I turn slowly and peek through the crack. My old living room is completely empty, save for the card table and two folding chairs in the center of the room. The hardwood floors are dusty and dirty. The sliver of the stairs that are visible are broken through as if the wood is rotting through.

"I'm going around back. There's nobody up front."

"Okay. Stay quiet. Make sure you're looking for any cars that might be passing by. The last thing we need are the cops getting called."

I hop over the picket fence. My old tricycle sits broken in pieces in the middle of the overgrown grass. The outside light is broken. The sliding glass door has a baseball-sized hole in the center of it.

I creep closer, simultaneously keeping an eye out for snakes or old bear traps because that was something William was into back in the day. It was a precaution in case we tried to escape. He never mowed the lawn back then, either. One false step and you'd be on the ground in agony until he came home. Momma learned that the hard way.

The kitchen is home to vermin. Cabinet doors are nonexistent. The refrigerator remains open, though the light isn't on.

"Are you sure about this? There's nobody here."

"I'm positive. His car's GPS shows him coming here every day for hours at a time."

"All right. I'm going in. Don't panic if I don't answer right away."

"You'll have a five-second delay, Parker. Tap your earpiece three times if you're all right. Tap twice if you need backup. Understood?"

"Affirmative."

I gently pull the sliding glass door open. The track is so dirty that the door gets caught. The hole I make is just wide enough for me to slip through.

Stepping into my old dining room is a sickening feeling. Family dinners where my momma played the perfect hostess while my father and uncles berated her. Cousins who threw food at her for the fun of it. Weeknights of the three of us sitting down together. Momma and I sharing terrified looks and staying silent as to not set him off.

Focus.

I clear downstairs, the Glock at the ready. My heart hammers in my chest to the point I can hear the beat in my ears.

"Downstairs is clear," I whisper.

"Head upstairs, then," Tanner instructs.

I skip the steps where there isn't anything to stand on. They groan under my weight, and I pray that I'm not the sucker who falls through the rotted wood. What's left of the carpeted landing is filled with scat and food wrappers. I propel myself up the rest of the way, going through each room and each closet.

"It's clear. Nobody's here."

"Right. But they might come back. You can use your flashlight. Just fasten on the red lens."

I follow his instructions and plod into my old room. None of my furniture is here anymore. The posters of Troy Aikman and Dan Marino that used to don on my walls are no longer here. Graffiti instead takes its place—all in the name of Parker.

I slink back into my parents' room and find exactly what we're looking for.

"It's a murder board," I say softly.

"You did not just call it a murder board," Tanner chastises me.

I place the flashlight in my mouth and snap pictures. It makes me sick. There are hundreds of pictures—of the McKenzies, of Jackie, of Momma—that plaster the wall. There are a few of me and Chris too. I take photos to send back to Tanner once I get out of here.

My heart stops in my chest when I revisit pictures of Annie and Jackie. Betty Lou, Momma . . . *Zoey.* All when I was around. All when we thought we were safe.

"They're of all of us," I say softly under my breath.

Tanner curses. "Take as many pictures as you can. Do *not* send them until I give you the all clear. Do you hear me?"

"Understood."

I snap more pictures until I'm confident this is enough. Every single picture is documented. Every single detail about them is written down. There is no way I'm leaving the rest up to chance.

"You have time to get out, but don't linger. He just left the hotel in Rightsville."

25

ANNIE

When I crack my eyes open, Jay isn't lying next to me. Darkness still hangs over the property. The alarm clock reads two in the morning. Another night of him being anywhere else. Sighing, I kick the covers off and trudge into the living room. My stomach churns when I look out the window and find his truck is missing.

What is going on with him?

I start a pot of coffee and park myself at the dining room table. Autumn has already sent me ten emails from the last time I talked to her eight hours ago. I want to gouge my eyes out with a spoon. All of this "Call me ASAP, this is important" is not what I want to wake up to.

But there is one that makes my heart stop for a moment. Isaac Venney. Elliot's friend. I quickly open the email and scan its contents three times.

He wants to meet!

A broad smile spreads across my lips. This is a step in the right direction!

Giddiness rushes through me. There's no way I'm going back to sleep tonight. I open my article and finish it within the hour. Sending it off to

Autumn is something I can scratch off my to-do list. More free time for me tomorrow!

My ideas flow out of my head like a faucet. I can't sleep, and if I tried, I'd be fidgeting all night. A new Word document is something that gets me going. I open one up and transfer my ideas from my head to paper, my fingers effortlessly dancing along the keys. Once that's done and there aren't any more ideas at the ready, why not make a PowerPoint? That would impress Isaac.

Anything to get out from Autumn's thumb. Hell, I'd even write the pilot episode if he wanted me to. I feel like I'm in high school again. Although, this time, I'm excited about what I'll be presenting.

Before I know it, I have the next five years planned out in a forty-five-slide presentation, an Excel spreadsheet of potential costs, and a detailed outline written for the pilot episode.

I stare at the screen in disbelief. I'm not a planner. I go where the wind takes me. But staring at this plan in front of me invigorates me. My cells yearn for sunlight. Or somebody to practice presenting this to.

Who the fuck needs another person! I can do this myself!

I connect my laptop to the TV and get my slides ready. Headlights illuminate the living room. I peek out the window to see Jay get out of the truck. His shoulders slump, and the exhaustion clings to him. What's a few more minutes? I meet him at the door as he shrugs off his coat and takes his boots off at the door.

"I have to show you something. Sit on the couch, and don't interrupt me."

He stares at me in bewilderment.

"Elliot's contact got back to me. He wants to meet."

He doesn't have the grand reaction I'm looking for, but the fact his face lights up is a good sign.

"I couldn't sleep, so I started doing some research, and that sent me down a rabbit hole which sent me down a different rabbit hole. I made a PowerPoint, Jay. I have a spreadsheet of costs and an outline for a pilot episode."

I know he's tired. But I can't keep this to myself.

"The first location would be Greece. The economy isn't great, which would be beneficial for us. Accommodations would be on the cheaper side.

The euro is pretty damn close to the dollar. This isn't a place Americans are going to be flocking to. We would spend a full six months there. But it isn't like I'm going to spend the entire time lounging around on a beach. I'd be putting myself in the people's shoes working at restaurants, learning how to make wine, working at the museums—basically being dropped in the middle of civilization and having to figure everything out for myself."

"Meaning you become a Greek exchange student for half a year and assimilate to their culture."

"Yes! Exactly! See, when we think of Greece, we think of cruises. We see what the Greek government wants us to see. Sure, Mykonos is great to get lost in for a week, but I want to work in the docks or in the kitchen at a restaurant learning family recipes and things like that. I could shadow a travel guide and have them show me a day in the life of a Greek or something like that."

"So what's your plan? How long are you staying on the mainland? Do you think you'll go to an island or two?"

"I'm glad you asked!" I grin and change the slide. There's a reason why he's my soulmate. He hangs on to my crazy and makes sure I'm at least being responsible. "The mainland would be ideally a two-month stay. Athens, specifically, is covered in graffiti. This is where Ancient Greece was in its prime. There's the Parthenon, the museums, the Plaka . . . but I think we need to take a closer look at the citizens who live in Athens. The buildings are old. They're working against a government that is too busy being cocky about the old days and how they were the leaders of the new world. How are these citizens making ends meet?"

"Do you think these people are going to allow you to be up in their business?"

"Probably not right away. I mean, we have to look at the realities of it. I'm a white woman with a thick southern accent. To them, I'm some airhead American who doesn't give a rat's ass about their culture."

"Okay . . . So tell me about the islands."

"The three I've narrowed down are Mykonos, Santorini, and Crete. Santorini is a major tourist trap, but obviously there are Greek natives there. Where and how do they live? Where are they eating when they get home from busing around a group of rowdy tourists around? Where do they shop? What sort of food are they cooking on a Wednesday night?"

Jay nods as he takes this all in. "And this will all be filmed, so you'll have to start making connections with people who wouldn't mind you disrupting business for a day or two."

"I think that's where the funding could come in. The camera crew *will* be disruptive. There's no way around it. But I think we can donate a good chunk of money to replace the income that would otherwise be lost. In the same breath, the camera crews could attract new people. I think people are curious by nature. If a camera crew is there, it must be something good."

"Right. So then after Greece, are you going to continue to film? Do you plan on taking a break?"

I fiddle with my fingers and take a deep breath. "Well . . . I sort of have the next five years planned out."

He straightens and searches my eyes. "You planned the next five years of your career?" he asks in shock.

"I know how that sounds—"

"When your father asked about your future, you couldn't give him an answer."

I swallow the lump in my throat and gently lower myself onto the coffee table.

"Where am I in these next five years, Annie?"

The reality of it is . . . I didn't think about him.

"Jay . . ."

I want him to interrupt me, to give me more time to think about it. But I'm coming up empty here. *How did I forget that detail?*

"Am I traveling with you?"

"Do you want to?"

My question takes him off guard. I've opened a can of worms I'm not sure we were ready to open just yet.

Jay is the love of my life, my best friend. Of course we'd still be together. Though . . . I'm not sure how he would do with the distance now that he isn't distracted by the Marine Corps.

"Explain this to me, Annabelle, because this sounds like you're taking some time away from . . . *us.*"

I jump off the coffee table and pace the length of the house as I gather my thoughts. I'm not wishy-washy. I'm annoyingly direct and blunt, and for whatever reason, when my soulmate asks me where he is in the next five years I've planned . . . I mistakenly left him out.

"It wouldn't be much different from the Marine Corps."

He laughs without humor and joins me in my pacing. He's drowning in his own thoughts. We pace in silence. My heart splinters little by little with every growing moment of silence.

"That's bullshit. You're not in the line of fire. Your life isn't going to be in jeopardy every time you open your eyes in the morning," he snaps. He rakes his hand through his hair and swears under his breath. "The plan was Sage Creek," he bellows.

I stop in my tracks. For the first time ever, he's putting his foot down. We've had disagreements, but this one is different.

"I don't get it. You were so adamant about us being together. We spent the last two and half years *happy*—"

"Of course I was happy. I still *am* happy with you, Jay." I rake a hand through my loose waves and drop my gaze to the floor. "I can't see myself here," I whimper. When I meet those pools of jade who stare at me with a mixture of disbelief, sadness, and heartbreak, I question if we're going to stay together.

"What are you saying?"

"I love you, Jay. We've spent so much time keeping us a secret. I knew we were going to be together, but I don't think Sage Creek is the place to be."

His Adam's apple bobs with emotion.

"I don't want to talk about this anymore," he grumbles.

"We need to—"

"Am I holding you back?"

I stiffen. "What?"

"You've been talking about a web series for as long as we've been together. Then Elliot magically conjures up some guy that's interested in your idea, and then what? I'm not good enough to have around anymore?"

"You know that's not true," I snap. "I waited for you," I whisper. "After prom. After boot camp graduation. And then there was MCT and schools. There was you going to the fleet and maybe a week or two of leave you've saved up. Every single one of those times I planned a future in my head. You were with me in every single one of them."

Marine Combat Training, or MCT, was essentially another month of boot camp after graduating boot camp. Then he went away for schools—his job training—where we didn't hear from his as often.

He scoffs. "And now? I'm supposed to just be okay with you gallivanting around the world without me? This is a big fucking deal, Annabelle! Five years is a long ass time!"

"Do you want to come with me?" I shriek. "Because having you as a cohost would be awesome. It would be a sweet spin—"

"You can't be serious," he growls.

My heart hammers in my ears as the animosity between us grows.

"I don't want to be the guy who carries your sandals. Come on! You *know* my dream was to turn this place around. This town deserves a reliable police force!"

Tears fill my eyes. For so long, we were on the same page. I don't even think we're in the same book.

"When do I get to live my dreams?" I sound like an ungrateful child. "You joined the Marine Corps to do what, Jay? Get out of Sage Creek? And then what?"

"I fell in love with you."

The breath in my lungs is stolen from me. I'm a guppy gasping for air.

"I fell in love with you, and I saw our future. I saw a reality in which I didn't have to hide myself or my feelings from you. I know we said no kids, but there are times when I see a couple of kids running around that are *ours.*"

There's a proverbial line drawn in the sand. My career has always been there for me. It's always been the escape I needed to lose myself when things were going to shit. Jay . . . He's been here for me. But at the same time, I don't know where his head is at. He's gone most of the time and doesn't talk to me about what he's doing when he's not here.

"You're never here," I spit out.

"Annabelle, I know it hasn't always been easy. But I swear to God, I love you, and I want to spend the rest of my life with you. But having you leave for five years . . . I don't know if I can deal with it. I'm still getting used to the fact that I gave up my military career to come back home!"

This isn't happening. I've put too much into this relationship for him to give up now.

"You promised me happiness," I snap.

"So did you."

That's the reality, isn't it? We promised each other happiness. But when push comes to shove, only one of us can be happy at a time. I suppose that's our punishment for keeping this a secret for so long. *For lying about us for so long.*

"I'm going to go. I can't be here right now," he says, turning on his heel and wrenching the front door open.

"Don't leave," I plead with a sob.

His hands cup my shoulders tightly. "I need space, Annabelle."

26

JAY

The last thing I needed tonight was for my relationship to come into question from the only person I was certain I was on the same page with. I don't believe in fate. I don't believe in a lot of things, actually. But after seeing photos of the people I love hanging on my parents' old bedroom wall, the *only* thing I want to do is protect her.

Her being away from me is the most dangerous position she could be in. If I tell her what's really going on, I risk her running into the line of fire because she thinks she's the big, bad sister who can cut anyone down.

But fuck me. She didn't even *think* about me! Where was I in these plans? Have I not made my feelings crystal clear to her? I gave up my mother fucking military career for her! And now she's just going to travel the world without a second glance? Was she going to shack up with other guys to scratch the itch?

My ringtone rips through my internal rant, and when I see that it's Tanner, I want to chuck my phone out the window. But I answer anyway. This is my job now.

"Where are you?" the voice barks. Though it's not Tanner. It's Nate.

"I'm finding a hotel. Why?"

"I've been trying to reach you for the last hour, Parker," he barks.

"Calm down, Nate," Tanner scolds. "Wherever you are, I need you to pull over and send the photos."

I do as I'm told and pull over just outside of Steve's property line. I send Tanner the photos. Once I get the all clear they've been received, I continue into town.

"I'm running the unknown faces through facial recognition," Nate announces. "Parker, was there anything in that house that gave up any identification of these two idiots?"

"None. It looks like they're using the house as a rendezvous point since their hotel is in Rightsville."

"All right. At least now we know where they're meeting. I'll be down tomorrow morning to see if I can catch them."

On these old country roads, you can pick up speed without the cops pulling you over. I'm hitting sixty to get into town quicker.

"Let me know when you get in. I can take you there."

"Sure thing," Nate says.

We end the call, and I continue down the road toward town. Someone at one of those chain hotels is bound to give me a room for the night. As I accelerate down the road, something hits my truck. I recoil from the hit and try to regain my composure.

What the fuck?

I slow down, but another hit has my truck careening into the ditch to my right. The truck rolls, and my head slams against the window, the glass spidering. My head sings, and I struggle to keep my eyes open.

"I love you, Jay," Annie's sweet voice rings in my head.

The song *Strange Magic* blares through the other car's stereo. I try to reach for my seatbelt, but my arm is pinned behind me. My vision blurs in and out. For a moment, I see Annie walking toward me.

"I love you too, Blondie," I say out loud.

But it isn't Annie who crouches down at the window. It's Dominic Reese.

"Breaking and entering is a crime, Parker." He takes a gun out of his holster and cocks it. "You know, I'll admit I've been waiting for this day for a long, long time. You're in the way, you see." He takes a handkerchief from his breast pocket and dabs the trickle of blood from his forehead.

I hope he dies of a concussion.

"Surprise, bitch," I bite off as I try to unpin my arm.

He chuckles darkly. "When you're in my line of work, I get told to get fucked all day every day by whoever's in charge. I may be at the bottom of the totem pole, but at least I have leverage." He takes out a stack of photos of Annie and Aria. I'm going to kill him. If he fucking kills me right here, right now, I'll come back and haunt him. I'll drive him into insanity.

I can't move. I can't feel my legs.

"Ms. Banks will be so grateful for your cooperation. But I suppose you won't ever get to hear her gratitude. I suppose you know what happens next."

"Yeah? You really think you're tough shit?"

That's right, Jay. Keep pissing him off.

"Beauty's in the eye of the beholder and all that shit." He stands up and aims the gun at me. Shit. I'm dead. All because I couldn't stand being around her. All I want right now is to spend the last few moments of my life with her. "Anyway, I appreciate the memories. You've made it fun these last couple of months. Banks will pick your family off one by one until your father figure doesn't have anyone left. It's poetic, really."

I growl in frustration. This is it. I can kiss my life with Annie goodbye. I'll die knowing I couldn't protect her.

"What do you have against Steve?"

"Everything," he snarls. "Our entire organization is gunning for Stephen McKenzie. It's been a pleasure, Mr. Parker. You'll see your family soon enough. That is, if you go to the right place," he winks.

At the mention of my family, my heart stops long before the shot rings out.

It doesn't matter. The gun fires, and my ears ring from the shot.

Blinding light makes me squeeze my eyes shut. I pray to whoever's listening to be with me until the end and that Annie will forgive me for all of this.

27

DOMINIC REESE

When Jay Parker entered my life, I often wondered about the best way to cease his existence. The man was not stealthy in the least bit, constantly making his presence known, especially when the female McKenzies were concerned. I have to hand it to him, though. He fought to the bitter end.

In my line of work, everyone is fueled by revenge. Whether it's petty or not. My revenge is justified, and at the moment, it's in line with Banks' revenge.

As I walk down the street, I don't spare the wreckage a second glance. Jay Parker's death not only makes the destruction of the McKenzies easier, but it will send Stephen scrambling. Just like he did to me.

I pull out the small burner that was given to me when I was recruited into Banks' ranks and dial the only number in the phone: Wren Ramirez.

"What?" he barks into the phone.

"It's done."

"Good. Get back up here. Banks would like to speak with you." And with that, he hangs up.

I may be at the bottom of the totem pole, but I'm not dumb. I know what happens next. I've seen too much. I've heard too much. I've killed one too many people on my quest for justice.

Killing Parker didn't bring my father back. However, Stephen McKenzie losing everyone he's ever loved will be something I'll bask in for the rest of my days.

My death is not in the cards, whether Banks likes it or not. I haven't even met her.

They may know my true identity, but this isn't the first time I've changed who I am, and it certainly won't be the last.

28

ANNIE

Jay walking out of the house last night made me physically ill. I threw my guts up at least a dozen times. I at least hoped he'd text me when he got to wherever he is, but he never did. I don't want to leave him, but I want the freedom to live my dreams too. Am I being too selfish?

It seems like the entire family is dragging their feet today. I'm the only one up, and if I wait any longer for help, I'm going to have a steed-driven mutiny on my hands. None of which I have the energy to deal with today.

I've called Jay's phone a few times, but it goes straight to voicemail. Sighing, I load up the golf cart with grain and hay and start feeding the pasture horses.

It was only two months ago when Jay came home to spend our life together. Everything was fine. We were happy. We were nervous, but we were happy.

What happened? How did we derail so quickly?

After I feed the last set of pasture horses, I turn the golf cart to the direction of barn number one. Derek appears on the hill between our houses and waves his arms like a crazy person trying to get my attention.

"Annie!" he shouts, his voice echoing in the nothingness around us.

I pull up next to him, the golf cart coming to a screeching stop.

"I'll finish this. You need to go."

I arch an eyebrow. "Where?"

"The hospital! Jo's at your house waiting for you. Run!"

My heart sinks from my chest to the fiery pit of my stomach. My legs have a mind of their own. They send me at the speed of light, sprinting through the pasture, up the hill, and up the front porch steps of my house.

Jo sits on my sofa, her pale face glazed in tears. When her jade eyes meet mine, her sobs turn into full-on wails of pain.

"What happened?" I demand.

"We need to go, Annabelle. Right now. They don't think he'll make it through the day."

My world stops turning. "What?"

"Jay was in a car accident, and somebody shot him."

My voice is stolen from me. The fifteen-year-old girl inside of me wants to fall apart. But I don't have time for that.

I race into the bedroom and grab what I need out of the safe. *I'm* his number one. I'm making the decisions and nobody's going to stop me.

Jo drives like a bat out of hell out of the property. A long line of trucks follows us.

The scenarios race through my head. Who shot him? Has William finally lost his mind? Was it some crazy crackhead he accidentally ran into when trying to find a place to stay? Did Dominic Reese find him and take him out of the picture? What if he doesn't want me in the room?

I can barely speak. Jo can barely hold it together. I text Graves to let him know what's going on, not that he can do anything. But if I have someone outside of my family who knows, maybe he can spread the word and have good vibes sent our way.

"How did this happen, Jo?"

"I don't know, baby. I just got a call from Jeremy. He told me to get down to the hospital."

Has she seen him? Why didn't anyone call me?

I close my eyes, allowing the traitorous tears to escape. This isn't it. Not when we've worked too fucking hard to get here. I won't do the show. It's not worth living a life without him.

You're not leaving me, Jacob Parker. Over my dead body.

When we reach the hospital, I launch myself out of Jo's truck before she can even park. I grasp the manila folder close to my chest and make a run for it, scaring the shit out of the security guard on the other side of the automatic double doors.

"Ma'am, please slow down—"

"I can't slow down! My husband is here!"

His elderly face softens. "Okay. Let's get you a visitor's pass. Stand in front of the camera."

I swear to God if he tells me to smile, I will not hesitate to drop-kick his old ass.

The sticker prints, and he points me toward the ER. My legs carry me where I need to go without me having to think twice. Where my family is, I don't know, and at the moment, I don't really give a shit.

The nurse's desk comes into view, and I approach it. I'm sure I look like an insane person.

"My name is Annabelle McKenzie. I'm here for Jay Parker."

The nurse glances up at me and winces. She looks familiar. "Annie?"

I nod. Though I don't need to stroke her ego. I need information yesterday. *Tell me what I need to know!*

"I'm sorry. I know y'all are close, but you're not family. I can't give you any information—"

"I'm his wife!"

She stares at me blankly. I'm sure people say this all the time.

"What?" Jo's voice comes from behind me.

"Annie, come on. I know you're upset, but I'm not losing my job because you're hot for him—"

I open the manila folder and slap a piece of paper on the desk.

"I'm his *wife.* This is our marriage license, and this—" I reach in for the other legal document and slam it next to the marriage license. "—is his living will showing that I have medical and financial power of attorney. So I need to know where my husband is, and I need to see him. Right now."

She sighs after reviewing the paperwork and reluctantly hands the papers back over. "He's in surgery. Let me see if I can get you an update. Follow me. I'll bring you into the waiting room."

Jo is hot on my heels, and at the moment, I'm sure I just sent her for a ride with one of the biggest secrets I've kept for the last two years.

Yes. Jay and I got married. All of our paperwork is legit. We were together throughout his last deployment. Things move fast in the military, at least that's what Jay told me. We wanted to be married in case he didn't come back.

As the nurse brings me to the waiting room, the memory of our decision flashes before my eyes.

With Jay's deployment looming ahead of us like an approaching tsunami, we lie naked in a giant king-sized bed in a hotel room that doesn't mean anything to us after our latest round of lovemaking. Tomorrow, I go home and pretend everything is okay. But in this moment, I sit here with my stomach in knots because, in a few hours, he's deploying again.

His fingers trail up my arm, and he places a tender kiss on my spine. I could melt here in this moment. With my eyes closed, I could pretend we've been doing this forever, that this is just a speed bump.

Afghanistan is nine time zones away. Our relationship is barely off the ground. I'm not ready to say goodbye. We've only had six months together.

"Your brainwaves could power Texas," he murmurs softly.

I giggle because I'm sure he's right. But I can't stop thinking about it. All we've ever done is say goodbye over and over again. When does it stop?

"They wish they could run on my brainpower."

"Everything is going to be okay, you know. This isn't my first rodeo."

I turn to face him. His full lips quirk into a smile when he meets my gaze. He weaves his fingers through my hair in an attempt to comfort me. God, I wish I could just stop crying about it now.

"I don't even know how long you'll be gone."

"Seven months, maybe. It'll be over before you know it."

I lick my lips nervously, taking in the small tattoo over his heart of the letter A. He got that for me a few weeks ago. He said it was to remind everyone that it's real.

"Hey, Blondie, can we real talk for a minute?"

The "real talk" is new. He said he'd heard Hilderbrand say it to his wife once, and to keep his memory alive, he started using it. It means to talk without holding back.

"Yeah. Always. What's on your mind?"

His eyes rake over my body and settle on my eyes. He cradles my head in his hand and gently brushes my bottom lip with the pad of his thumb. I can faintly taste myself on him, which sends me back to just a few minutes ago when I was writhing on this bed.

"Do you remember prom night when I found you at the creek?"

How could I not? It's what got me to sleep all through college. Jay Parker was afraid of the way I made him feel.

"I told you our age gap mattered."

I roll my eyes. "Yes, you were very high and mighty back then."

He chuckles and pushes the stray hair out of my face. "You told me you were honest about your feelings for me. I think I held onto that sentence since then because you were right. God, you were fifteen, and you were always right."

"What can I say? It's a gift."

He smirks and rolls his eyes. "I love you, Annabelle. I've loved you for a very long time, and when I'm with you, I feel at home."

My heart flutters at his pretty words. If he's trying to get one more round out of me, it's working.

"Anyway. I know you're dreaming of some grand wedding with a trellis, a string quartet, and your dad walking you down the aisle, but that's going to cost money I don't have right now and time I don't want to waste. I want to know what it's like to be married to you, Annabelle. Because in my gut, I know we're each other's destiny."

Tears fill my eyes. I can't believe what I'm hearing. This heals my soul in so many ways and he doesn't even know it.

"I promise we'll do it right one day. I'll give you the string quartet and the outdoor wedding. But please, will you marry me, Annabelle? Today?"

"Yes," I whisper.

In that moment, I knew that was the truest word I'd ever spoken.

"ANNIE," Jo says gently, lowering down next to me, "you got married?"

I nod, the tears flowing out of my eyes. Only this time, it's not happiness leaking from my eyes. It's a pain I can't even begin to explain.

Even though it was secret, with only Graves and his girlfriend as our witnesses, it was a beautiful ceremony. It was a long time coming. And in that moment, I was Mrs. Jacob Parker. I married the love of my life, and I kept my mouth shut about it.

"He was worried before that last deployment. He wanted to know what it was like to be married to me in case he didn't come home."

The anticipation is killing me. That nurse sure is taking her sweet time, and I'm fresh out of patience. I need one more person to cross me, and then I can take out two and a half years of frustration on them.

"Why didn't you tell us?"

"Because!" I wail. "We were going to do it the right way, and then time slipped away from us. It got harder to tell you. We were going to go through the spiel again when everyone knew about us. But then we got into a stupid fight . . ." I collapse into tears.

My family is shuffled into the same waiting room. At this point, I don't care if they find out. I mean, I'd rather they didn't. Not until I have Jay home and on the mend.

Aria sits on my other side and reaches for my hand. She's become such the mother. My head falls onto her shoulder, and she envelopes me in a tight hug, the armrest of the chair digging into my ribs.

"He's going to be okay," she coos.

She doesn't know that. Nobody here does, except for Jay and perhaps the doctor that's operating on him.

My parents talk in hushed tones to Jo, and Chris and Derek herd the children to the play area of the waiting room. The nurse walks in. This time, I read her name tag: Megan. That's right! Megan Rourke! I remember her now. She was the class president in high school. It looks like she's aged a few years from when she greeted us just moments ago.

"Jay's lost a lot of blood. He was in a car accident. Broken clavicle and three broken ribs. He has significant lacerations on his face from the broken windshield. The airbag broke his nose. There are also a few broken toes. On a more serious note . . . he was shot. The doctors are currently performing a peritoneal lavage, which is a washing of the abdominal cavity. I can't give you specifics on that because the doctor would like to speak with you about it. They are searching for the bullet, but you should know, it nicked his spleen."

Vomit rises up my throat. "What does that mean?"

She sighs. "There are a lot of smaller arteries in the spleen. They're taking a close look at the damage. But again . . . he's lost a lot of blood. Look, Annie, this is all I can give you right now. The surgery will take a few hours, and until then, I can't bother the doctor anymore. I'll try to get you an update in a little bit. But until then, you're more than welcome to stay here."

Somebody shot Jay.

I stare at the floor, wondering just who could hate him that much to take his life away. Who would pull the trigger without remorse? Who would have the gall to open fire in a small town where everyone has their nose pressed up against the window as to not miss a thing?

Flashes of the shooting in Richmond cross my mind. Dominic Reese shot a man in broad daylight with witnesses. He's made it a point to get to me and my sister. Jay was the one to run interference every time.

Was this his way of taking him out of the picture?

Jo weeps next to me. I should be the dutiful daughter-in-law and help her through this, but if I lose him . . . and then her . . . What then?

It'll almost be like Jay and Jo Parker were a dream—one that was happy, devastating, earth-shattering, and fantastical, all at the same time.

"Honey? Do you want some coffee?" Momma asks, crouching down beside me and stroking my cheek.

I don't think I can stomach anything. It's six o'clock in the morning—around this time, I'm usually having breakfast, but I can't get myself to eat anything.

"No, thank you," I whimper.

Where was he last night? Why did he come in at three thirty in the morning?

As the day progresses, Jeremy and Jared arrive to take our statements.

Jeremy is convinced I was the one to run him off the road, but that was immediately shot down when I showed him my email log to Autumn.

Derek and my dad sit close together. Daddy holds Troy as they speak, but something about it makes my hackles rise. Do they know anything about this?

At nine o'clock, Tanner and Nate arrive for moral support. Though I didn't think Tanner knew Jay very well. Regardless, they huddle close to Aria and barely speak.

"Annabelle McKenzie?"

The deep voice has me shooting up. Jo follows suit, and we meet the doctor at the doorway.

"Jay is in recovery. He's stable, but he isn't out of the woods yet."

Stable is good.

"We had to remove his spleen. We went through a whole washing of the abdominal cavity and successfully removed the bullet. His intestines were lacerated, but we were able to repair that damage as well. He has a concussion, and with him being asleep right now, you won't be able to see him awake. But we are treating it, along with his other injuries."

"Can I see him?" I plead.

He glances at Jo and weakly smiles.

"It's nice to see you again, Ms. Josephine. I understand you're Jay's mother?"

She nods eagerly. "We'd both like to see him, Dr. Probst. As soon as possible."

He nods. "Okay. We're going to do two at a time," he announces to the others, not that I care.

We follow him down the hallway into a pair of double doors. The recovery room is a tight squeeze, and the only privacy he gets are the curtains around his bed.

When Dr. Probst opens the curtains, the sight before me tears my soul apart.

He's unrecognizable. His face is cut up and swollen. A breathing tube hangs out of his mouth and is attached to machines that make annoying beeping sounds. Most of his body is bandaged up. And that's not even the worst of it.

His left arm is cast and in a sling. I want to hug him and tell him it's going to be okay, but I don't want to hurt him. God, that last thing I want to do is hurt him.

"Hi, baby," Jo coos. She gently strokes his cheek, avoiding the cuts that mar his skin.

His eyes won't open, I know that. But I still hope for those pools of jade, ones that light up whenever I walk into the room.

God, I'm sorry I'm so selfish!

I shakily place my hand in his right hand. The tears trickle out more when he doesn't squeeze back.

"I'm here with Annabelle, sweetheart. We love you so much."

Why won't my words work? Why can't I say anything?

"He's in a medically induced coma. He might hear you, so talking to him or playing music while he's here will help. We're going to keep him here until he wakes up, but the next few days are crucial. We're looking for infections."

"When do you think he'll wake up?" Jo asks.

"It's hard to tell. Until the swelling in the brain goes down, he'll be on a sedative. After he's been taken off the sedative, it'll be up to him when he opens his eyes."

A million things race through my mind. Scenarios of him not waking up or him dying on this table petrify me.

"When will he be moved to his own room?" Jo asks.

"In the next few hours. We'll keep you updated. I promise."

Dr. Probst leaves the room, and now I'm stuck with two Parkers. One is unconscious, while the other I'm sure is livid with the two of us. But I don't think it matters much. She's hurting as much as I am—in more ways than one.

"I'm going to give you a moment alone with him. I know your brother wants to see him," she says gently.

I nod my acknowledgment and lower into the chair, my eyes never leaving his face.

When I'm sure she's gone, I open the floodgates. I sob openly, and if he hears me, I'm sure he'd tell me to stop.

"Jacob, you *promised* me forever," I murmur. "In sickness and in health, through good times and the bad. I promised you my life."

My pleas go unanswered. Not even a muscle twitches in his face.

"I'm sorry we fought. But I need you to know I love you. With every fiber of my being, I love you, and I need you to s-stay. Please don't leave me. We were j-just getting to the good part. Everyone knows about us, and I . . . I can't live this life without you."

I sniffle and kiss his hand.

"I'm so sorry, Jay."

29

ANNIE

We've gone two weeks without an infection. I want to breathe a sigh of relief, but the swelling in his brain is still a major concern. I practically live in this room with him. Between this hospital room and Jo's for her chemotherapy, I don't have to go very far.

He's never alone. I think if he were conscious, he'd be both happy to know the McKenzies would bring the town to its knees to make sure he was being taken care of and a little annoyed to not have a moment alone.

I've brought pictures from home: one of his unit, because I know he misses them; one of Jones, because I know it still hurts him—I think he would like to know that he has someone on the other side looking out for him; there's the iconic one of the lake house with me, Jay, Chris, Aria, and Jackie; one of him and Jo; and my phone that stays on Aria's docking station.

I play music until the nursing staff begs me to stop. They don't like my country music. To be fair, neither does Jay. But I was hoping to annoy him until it forced him to wake up and tell me to turn the shit off.

But still, I sit here and wonder if it truly was me who brought him here.

Was he so upset with me that he had to pick a fight with some guy off the street?

"Hey," Aria's soft voice filters into the room.

"Hey," I respond, my voice hoarse and raspy.

"I brought you some comfort food. I figured you were getting tired of the cafeteria." She enters the room with long strides and, surprisingly, with no children attached to her. She sets the tote bag on the side table, the soup inside still warm as if it just came off the stove.

"Thank you."

Her amber eyes sweep over him. She gently touches his knee, her way of telling him she's here.

"So . . . any progress today?"

"No signs of infection. But other than that, there hasn't been any significant changes."

Aria frowns. "Have you heard from Jeremy? Does he have any leads?"

I shake my head and meet her eyes. "No. They haven't seen a vehicle matching the paint description from the scrapings on the truck."

"How are you?"

Why does that question automatically rev me up? It infuriates me. It doesn't matter how I am! I did this! I drove him so crazy he had to get away from me!

"It doesn't matter—"

"It does, Annie." She sighs. "I don't know when this family started keeping secrets from each other. You and Jay dating, me hiding who Charlie was, Jo keeping her diagnosis to herself . . ."

Yeah, I know. We're just a hodgepodge of dysfunctional people who are too afraid to talk to each other.

"You pretending Charlie didn't destroy your body."

Aria frowns. "That's a low blow." She blows out an impatient huff. "You're not alone, Annie, okay? Whatever you need, I'm here for you."

My bottom lip wobbles, and my eyes fill with tears. God, the last words he said to me was that he needed space.

"We fought that night," I whisper. "I pushed that stupid web series and made a whole five-year plan, and you know what the kicker was? I forgot to include him."

It sounds so harsh saying it out loud. I forgot the one person who has been there for me through thick and thin.

"We're married, Aria." I ignore the gasp that comes out of her mouth. "I forgot to include my *husband* in my five-year plan. Who does that?"

"You've been without each other for so long . . ."

"Regardless. I went on a selfish tangent on living my stupid dreams, and you should've seen how *hurt* he was when he realized he wasn't in the picture."

"Annie—"

"I don't deserve to feel okay. Or fine. Or happy. God! I spent a third of my life chasing him, and it was like as soon as he gave it up, I threw everything in the air and let the universe decide what to do with it."

"Okay, now I know you're talking crazy. He didn't give up the chase, Annie. He fell in love with you. You changed your dynamics so many times that you guys didn't give each other the time to catch up and take a breather. You made a five-year career plan, so what? Guess what? I have one too, and it doesn't involve Derek in any way, shape, or form."

"Your five-year plan doesn't have you traipsing the world for five straight years."

"You're right. It doesn't. But then again, I'm not you, and you're not me. Jay has known your hunger to travel the world since you were a kid. He knew what he was getting into. There wasn't a reality where you were just going to sit at home and become Momma."

She quickly looks over her shoulder to make sure Momma isn't standing behind her. Bless her heart. I love my momma, but I don't want to be the farmer's wife. I don't want to make jams and jellies and be the social queen of the town. That's not who *I* am.

"You know that he loves this place, even though there are a lot of horrible and traumatic memories for him here. He wants to make this town a better place, and there's nothing wrong with that."

"There isn't a reality where this could work."

She shrugs. "Why not? It worked when he was in the Marine Corps. You went days on end not being able to talk to him. At least with you, you're not crossing into enemy lines or handling a rifle."

"It's not that easy."

"Maybe not. But you love him, Annie. And he loves you. You both are pigheaded and stubborn, so I know that it seems like the sky is falling. But let me remind you of this: you and Jay were always meant to be. From you sneaking boys in to get his attention to him calling you every second he got when he was in the fleet. You love each other. And apparently, you're married, which we're not glossing over by the way. You made a commitment to each other. Now you have to compromise. This fight isn't worth ending everything over."

I'm awoken by Jay's monitors going haywire. His eyelids are squeezed tightly shut. His chest bounces, almost like he's a fish out of water. A flurry of nurses flood the room, soon followed by Dr. Probst.

"Get her out of here," he barks.

"No!" I shout. "I'm not leaving!"

A nurse grabs hold of my arm and practically drags me out of the room. "Ma'am, I'm sorry. He needs us, and you can't get in the way."

"What's wrong with him?" I demand.

She shrugs. "I'm not sure. But we need time—"

"He's not dying alone!" I snap.

"Annabelle," my father growls behind me.

Great.

"As soon as we get him stable, we can figure out what's going on," the nurse assures me and then disappears back into the room.

"Let's take a walk," Daddy suggests.

Why? So you can tell me I'm being desperate waiting around here?

"I need to be here, Dad. He's coding or something." My medical degree from *Grey's Anatomy* is telling me to stick around.

"Come on," he insists, starting down the hallway.

We head toward the cafeteria. All the while, I'm listening to the voices on the PA system. I swear . . . If I hear "code blue," I'm going to lose my shit. We walk in silence. My only true friend is the racing thoughts running through my head.

Is he okay? Does he need me? When will he wake up?

We head through a set of automatic double doors that lead to the garden. Other patients sit out here with their families. Others look so horribly sick that a minute in the sun will cook them to a crisp. Then there's the two of us.

Daddy looks like he just ventured out of the grain silos, his long-sleeved, flannel shirt dusty and his dark blue jeans marked with dirt and white dust. And me? Well, I haven't been home since I found out about Jay. Aria has been kind enough to bring clothes. My hair hasn't been brushed and sits in an unattractive, messy knot at the top of my head. My bun barely contains my wild, wavy hair.

"What are we doing?" I demand.

"Sitting in the sunshine."

I swear . . . Sometimes I think he thinks I'm an airhead. No shit, we're sitting out in the sun! *Why?*

"Jay's coding, Dad. I need to get back to his room—"

"He's in the best hands possible," he cuts me off and cups my shoulders, forcing me to sink to the stone bench just behind me.

I don't have to sit down, damn it! But . . . the sun feels nice on my face. I had almost forgotten what fresh air smelled like or how the cool breeze felt on my naked arms.

I give my father a sidelong glance, wondering what the hell he's even doing here, anyway.

"Sometimes, I wonder if I've failed you."

Oh, here we go.

"Please don't start." He's startled by my clipped words. I feel my word vomit bubbling in my stomach. One more prod and it's all going to come out. Every thought I've kept to myself, the things I've wanted to say to him for so long but never had the guts to.

"He wouldn't want you hanging around here."

I swallow the lump in my throat and pray to whoever is listening to give me the strength to handle the aftermath. "You're failing me right now." I whimper.

He snaps his eyes to mine in surprise.

"Dad, he's fighting for his life in there. I'm barely keeping it together. The last thing I need is to hear how much I've disappointed you by placing all of my eggs in one basket, okay? If you love me or care for me at all, then you'll be my dad for a minute and not big, bad, Stephen McKenzie, who intimidates everyone who crosses his path."

Is he angry? Is he going to put me in my place in front of all these people?

He surprises me by wrapping his right arm around my shoulders and pulling me closer to him. He smells of sweat and cattle, something that reminds me of simpler times and *home.*

A sob racks my body. But my dad holds me like I'm the one who got shot. How will we ever move on from this?

"Annie?"

Dr. Probst's worried voice sounds off above us. Daddy's hold slackens as I try to brace myself for whatever he's about to drop on me.

"I'm sorry about the scare. Jay's okay."

I arch an eyebrow. Somebody doesn't just flop around like a fish if they're okay.

"I don't understand . . ."

"It was a mild seizure, which isn't uncommon. We're going to bring him up for another MRI, but I wanted to let you know he was okay."

That didn't look mild. That was the most terrifying thing I'd ever witnessed.

"Go home, Annie. Take a shower. Change your clothes, and then come back. You being here twenty-four seven is going to drive you to insanity," Daddy murmurs.

But he doesn't know that I'm already past insanity. A hot shower or new clothes isn't going to fix that.

30

JAY

Rhythmic beeps filter through my consciousness. Muted pain radiates through my limbs. My face feels like I ran through a forest of razor blades. I can't open my eyes. No matter how hard I try, I can't crack them open.

"It's about time, Gunny. I was getting lonely here." He chuckles. "I can't believe they promoted you to Gunny. What were they thinking?"

I turn to face the voice. Sure enough, Corporal Jones stands before me. He isn't in uniform but in street clothes. He's comfortable on the ground under the oak tree near the creek.

He waves me over. *Is this real?*

"Come on, Jay, I'm not gonna bite. I want to talk to you."

"I'm sorry, Jay," a voice filters through my consciousness. It sounds like somebody over the PA system in a grocery store. It sounds like Annie.

"Where are we, Jones?"

He arches an eyebrow in challenge. "You and I are way past the Corps, Jay. Call me Dean."

I approach *Dean* and sink beside him. The rushing waters of the creek have my suspicions calmed. I haven't seen Jones—sorry—*Dean* since he died.

He just sits so casually. The sun shines on his face and he smiles like nothing bothers him.

"You've gotten yourself in a pickle."

"Sounds like me, doesn't it?"

Dean shrugs. "I don't know about that. I'm the one who got myself blown up. Sounds like something *I'd* do."

Oh my god. He grins and leans against the tree. Should I be doing the same? Do I need to relax for him to talk to me?

"You don't belong here," he tells me.

"Where's *here?*"

"In your head. Don't you hear your girl talking to you?"

"Please don't leave me."

I'm not leaving, Blondie!

Flashes of the accident play in the sky like a bad movie. There's Dominic Reese, and then there's a bang.

"Are you putting two and two together yet?" Dean asks.

Why isn't he making any sense?

"What are you talking about?"

"Watch again, Gunny. Pay attention."

But the show never begins. It all fades to black.

"PARKER, now is not the time to kick the bucket. Wake up. We have shit to do," Derek's voice filters through.

Wherever I am, the sun rises again, but Jones is gone.

"You can't leave yet," he says again, though this time it sounds desperate.

I get sent down that rabbit hole again. The sleep pulls me into unconsciousness. I'm too weak to fight.

"HI, JJ. IT'S PEANUT," Aria's voice filters in. Her rock music fills my brain. The Beatles, The Rolling Stones, Led Zeppelin. If I think hard enough, I'm in the barn. I could be mucking stalls or dropping feed. That's where I'm at. I'm in the barn.

This time, it's Hilderbrand who's here. He leans casually against a stall with his signature shit-eating grin.

"Hiya, Gunny."

I want to say something to her, to let her know I'm okay.

"I know about you and Annie . . . That you're married."

Oh no. Is Steve pissed? Is he going to kill me?

"Dude, you got married?" he exclaims, laughing behind his hand. Despite the urgency of Aria's voice, I laugh at Hilderbrand. God, I've missed him. "Tell me it's the hot one. The one with the blonde hair and big tits . . ."

"I'm going to kill you, idiot."

He guffaws, making me laugh harder. "I'm already dead. I doubt you could do anything to make it worse."

He's dead, and I'm . . .

"And I know you fought before your accident."

That's right. She made a plan to globe trot for the next five years without me.

"She loves you, Jay. Sometimes when she hyper-fixates on something, she gets carried away. She's been at your side since you got here."

Hilderbrand's smile fades, and he approaches me hesitantly. "Don't hold this against her, Parker. She loves what she does."

"Please wake up. She blames herself."

Annabelle . . . God, I wish I can see her.

But she's in danger. They all are. Does Reese know he didn't kill me?

"How do I go back?"

And then he's gone.

Annie without me is dangerous. But . . . Annie with me is even more dangerous. If Reese is keeping watch on the girls, that means it's only a matter of time for him to figure out he failed and come back to finish the job.

I need to disappear. I need to meet up with Tanner, hide until I can catch the fucker, and end his life.

31

ANNIE

"Good morning, Annie," Dr. Probst greets with a hesitant smile.

I want to tell him to kick rocks, but at the moment, he holds all the answers. The fate of Jay's life lies in this man's brain, and the only thing I can do is sit here and shut up.

"Good morning, Dr. Probst."

It's been a month. We're in September. Zoey and Chris are back in school now, not that the weather has gotten the memo.

Jo is in this room about as much as I am. Though with every passing day, she becomes more pessimistic. She doesn't want to say goodbye to her only child. I get that.

He crosses the room and takes a look at Jay's vitals. He checks the dressing on his wounds and redresses the sutures on his face.

"I wanted to give you the rundown for today. In about an hour, he'll be taken for an MRI. We want to check the swelling in the brain. If things look good, then it'll be up to him when he wakes up. If not . . . Well, we might need to surgically release the pressure."

They're going to drill into his skull. I've watched enough *Grey's Anatomy* to know that's not a good sign.

"And if that's the case?"

He sighs. "Then we'll pull you into the conference room and go over next steps." He glances at Jay and then back at me. "He's a strong man, Annie. He's only thirty-three years old. He's in the best shape of his life, and he's healthy. I have faith he's going to get through this. We're not jumping to the worst-case scenarios just yet."

I nod, more stray tears escaping my eyes.

It seems that all I ever do nowadays is cry. I can't stop. I cry for Jay. He's the only one who knows what happened, and I want to get him justice. I cry for Jo, who has had the hardest life. They were two peas in a pod, best friends. She shouldn't have to bury her son. Mostly, I cry for *us.* Our last words were awful. If he's in there cursing my name, I wouldn't blame him. I wouldn't blame him for telling me to fuck off and never talk to him again. We were meant to be. I feel that in my bones. I won't be able to take it if he decides to call it quits.

"So when we bring him back, that would be an opportune time to go home and change . . . take a nap maybe?"

I snort. "I can sleep in the chair. But . . . I think I'll go into town and grab a bite to eat."

He nods and lingers in the doorway. "I'll update you when we have time to review the results."

I sigh and lean back in the chair. I study his body. Most of the lacerations are healed. He has about two more weeks in the cast, though I don't think he's going to be too happy about not being able to use it much.

And when he finds out he won't be able to run for a long time . . . his world is going to crumble beneath his feet. It was the one thing he had control over. His last tie to the Marine Corps.

"It's going to be okay," I say out loud, though I'm not entirely sure who I'm trying to convince. "We're going to find who did this to you and force Jeremy to lock him up. Even if it means I go to the cop shop myself and start making demands."

I giggle to myself. I can see it now. Jeremy will be too scared to say anything, and Clay will try to hold me back. I'm not afraid to knock a Parker out.

My phone has been incessantly buzzing. I know it isn't Autumn trying to get a hold of me, but after looking at the screen, I see it's actually Nick and Geoffrey. They heard about Jay's accident and gave me a sabbatical until I knew more about what was happening. But it's been a month. *A Fish Out of Water* isn't my only source of income, but it is the biggest. I don't want to leave my job, but I will for however long Jay needs me.

I send the call to voicemail. I don't have the energy to talk to them, to wear a charming smile and pretend everything is okay. Nothing about this is okay.

"B-Blondie . . ."

I snap my neck to see him. His eyes aren't open. His voice is so raspy.

"Jay?"

He doesn't respond. I squeeze his hand to let him know I'm here.

"It's okay, baby. I miss you," I murmur into his hair. "I love you."

32

JAY

When I open my eyes, a beige cage is over my face, and the sounds of banging and clanging sends my anxiety through the roof. I attempt to move my arm, but it's pinned down by something. *Am I still in the truck?*

"Help," I manage to choke out. My throat is sore, like I haven't had anything to drink in months.

I try moving my head side to side, but the cage restricts my movement. I can't figure out where I am. My heart races in my chest. I can't get out.

"Mr. Parker?" a female voice says through an intercom above my head, one I don't recognize. "Mr. Parker, please try to keep still. You're having an MRI. You're okay."

I don't *feel* okay. My collarbone sings and sends a wave of pain straight to my stomach. My intestines are on fire, I'm sure of it.

"I need to get out," I raise my voice, not exactly yelling.

My anxiety is coursing through me. My hands shake. The cool air that wafts up between my legs is disorienting. I'm about to headbutt this cage—

"Mr. Parker, I know this is disorienting, but I need you to calm down.

You're okay. Cole is coming in the room now to take you out of the machine, okay? Can you answer me?"

"Yes." It comes out shaky. The banging stops, and suddenly, the bed I'm on moves out of the tube.

The man in the green scrubs takes the cage off my head and shines a flashlight in my eyes. I squeeze my eyes shut and move my head out of the way.

"Page Dr. Probst," he says calmly.

Who the fuck is Dr. Probst?

"How are you feeling, Mr. Parker? Are you nauseous? Dizzy?"

"Where's Annie?"

Cole frowns. "She went to get a bite to eat, but she should be back in your room by the time we wheel you back in there."

Do I want to see her? Do I want her to see me like this?

"Tell me how you're feeling, Mr. Parker."

I don't fucking know! "Fine," I snap.

"I'm going to need you to be more specific. Do you know what happened to you?"

What happened? I was driving. And then the truck flipped. What happened after that? "I . . . I was driving and somebody crashed into me."

He presses his lips in a hard line. He wants to say more, but I don't think he's allowed to. Suddenly, an older man sweeps into the room and shines another flashlight into my eyes.

"If you keep fucking doing that, I'm going to go blind," I snap. The flashlight is removed, and I get a good look at the man who stands above me.

"You've been asleep a long time, Mr. Parker. How are you feeling?"

"Like I'm going to lose my goddamned mind if somebody doesn't tell me what's going on."

He nods, an amused grin on his rounded face.

"Jay, you were in an accident. Your truck flipped twice. Police found you in a ditch. There were three gunshot wounds to your abdomen."

He drones on while everything comes back to me. I was driving into town when somebody crashed into me. My arm was pinned behind me.

Glass was stuck in my face. And then . . . somebody came up to the window. Who was at the window?

"Do you know who shot you, Jay?"

I wish he'd stop saying my name like we're old pals.

"Breaking and entering is a crime . . ."

Dominic Reese. He found me and shot me.

"I need to speak with Derek Hawthorn. Right now."

Dr. Probst opens his mouth to say something, but when I try to sit up, he holds my shoulder down, and my intestines remind me somebody shot me in the fucking gut.

"One thing at a time, son. Right now, we have what we need from the MRI. We're going to wheel you back into your room. We have a lot to talk about."

Two other stronger nurses wheel me back to the room, lift me up, and place me back in the hospital bed. I bite back my curse and growl instead. I'm never going to get used to this. I should just die now.

The hospital is cold. I don't enjoy being here. In these halls, I was treated by hospital staff—that is, the family that works here so my father wouldn't get put in jail. Every part of my body ignites with unwanted memories.

The room I'm wheeled into is decked in photos. Annie's old iPod sits on the dock playing her annoying country music.

"I convinced your wife to leave the hospital for a bit. She's been by your side every second of every day."

My stomach twists. What about work? What about the farm?

"I don't have a wife," I snap.

We haven't told anyone. It would only piss everyone off even more.

Dr. Probst smirks. "She was ready with your living will and power of attorney. She wasn't ready to let anyone else have decisions when it came to you."

Annabelle. I miss her so much. I want to smell her, to kiss her.

Flashes of photos blur my vision. She's shopping. She's traveling. She's working on the farm. There was even one of her getting into the shower.

They're watching them for something. But *what?* I thought Aria was the only one being targeted because she survived Charlie. But what about the others?"

"Jay . . .? Do you understand?"

I wildly glance up at Dr. Probst. I didn't hear a single word he said.

"I'm sorry, what?"

He frowns. "You'll be here until further notice. We need to keep you for observation. This will be invasive. We'll need to run several tests and schedule you for rehab. In the meantime, relax. Watch some TV. I'm going to review your MRI results. Then we'll come up with a plan. Together."

When Dr. Probst leaves, there's a sense of dread that falls over the room. I'm stuck here. Literally. I think if I got up my body would give up, and my organs would shut down one by one.

I need to talk to Derek. More importantly, I need to get to Tanner and Nate. Right now, time is on my side. Reese doesn't know I'm not dead. We have the upper hand.

The door flies open. My blonde bombshell deteriorates into tears when her eyes lock onto mine. She races over to me and gently throws her arms around me. She kisses my cheek and murmurs her apologies.

"Oh, God. You had me so scared. I'm sorry—"

"Shh, Blondie. I'm okay."

She shakes her head. "No, Jay. You're not." She sobs and lets go of me. Her cool hands caress my cheeks.

She's different. Exhaustion is etched into her features. Her bags under her eyes have bags. Her hair is thrown carelessly into a ponytail, the hair from the elastic sticking out in all different directions. "You were shot."

"I know," I murmur. My uncasted hand holds hers and squeezes in reassurance.

"Who shot you?" Right here is where I *should* tell her the truth. But I can't do that until I talk to Derek.

"I don't know."

It's the first time I've lied to her. I mean, I lied about my feelings for years, but this is different. This is earth-shattering. This could change the very fabric of her soul. I don't want her to change. I love her just the way she is.

"I'm sorry," she whispers. "It was so selfish of me to make that plan—"

"No."

She stares at me in bewilderment, pursing her lips.

"We've spent most of our relationship apart. I know me being home has sort of thrown a wrench into your plans. I want you to live your dream, Annabelle. I want you to follow your passion."

"But I don't want you to think you'd be the guy holding my sandals," she whimpers. "You're more than that. I should've thought about you. I don't know why I didn't. I won't do the show. You're too important."

"Blondie, there's one thing I've known about us for as long as I could remember. When it comes to you and me, no matter what life throws at us, we're going to be okay. I love you. I love you more than life itself. If this gets picked up by a network, then we'll cross that bridge when we get there."

She sighs. "I'm so sorry."

"I'm sorry too." She leans over and brushes her lips against mine. Her tears soak my face, but it's the sweetest gift I've ever been given. Right now, we're Annabelle and Jay. The two who were meant to be.

But if I'm following the strong feeling in my gut, we won't be this way for long.

SLEEP IS something I never used to hate. Now I wish I could stay awake for longer than ten minutes at a time. I drift in and out of consciousness, dreams coming to me in snippets of memories.

When Annie left for the night, I barely ate dinner. I was given clear chicken broth and a container of orange Jell-O. A glass of water goes untouched, and the nurse who came by to check on me after an hour tried her hardest to convince me that it's edible.

Hard pass.

"Hey, buddy." Three taps on the door yank me awake.

Derek, Nate, and Tanner enter through the door, tightly closing it behind them. Nate locks the door and settles in the chair across the room.

"You had us worried there for a second," Derek says, occupying Annie's seat.

"Yeah, well, I was impossible to kill in Afghanistan. I'm impossible to kill here too." Derek chuckles and his eyes sweep over me. "It was Reese who shot me." The men in the room sit up a little straighter.

"You're sure?" Nate asks, his Disney Princess green eyes shining in the darkness.

"I haven't been more positive about anything in my life. They're going after the women. He said something about Steve losing everything."

"Steve? He's the target then?" Derek asks.

"I don't know," I respond.

"Charlie had ties. He was in touch with someone the night he kidnapped Aria. We still don't know who that was," Nate reasons.

I'm lost. They're talking in circles about things I only know a little about.

"Regardless, they've left town," Tanner announces. "Dominic Reese is actually Dominic Worthington. He's from a small town in the UK."

"He said he was the bottom of the totem pole," I offer. They all consider this.

"Who is he working for? Because it can't be the Dodge's," Nate smarts.

"He couldn't have been the one working for Dodge that night. Zoey said it was a woman on the phone," Derek adds.

When Aria was held captive by Charlie, Zoey's mother, Emily, stole Zoey in the dead of night. It turned out she was the one sheltering Charlie so that she could have Zoey to herself without all the judicial red tape.

Zoey recalled a woman calling Emily on their way out of the state. They had met up with a woman at a gas station before Zoey ran for her life to a nearby police station.

"That night in Richmond, his partner confirmed they said something about 'Banks.' "

"So then he's working for the woman?" Tanner asks.

The room grows quiet.

"Did you pull phone records from when Emily called her?"

"It was a burner," Nate and Tanner answer in unison.

"What can I do? Does Reese know I'm alive?"

Derek sighs. "Jay, I don't think you should be involved anymore. I'm sorry I got you into this. Look where it's got you . . ."

"No, you don't get to do that," I snap. "I walked into my parents' old bedroom and found pictures of everyone I love. I'm capable, and I'm not backing down."

"Dude, you're strapped to a hospital bed," Tanner unhelpfully points out.

"They'll have to let me out eventually."

"We don't know what we're looking for," Derek warns me.

"My *wife* was one of those pictures, Derek. She's about to meet with networks in Hollywood to start a five-year trek around the world where our laws don't apply to these people. I don't give a shit if I can't walk or if I have to crawl using my fingernails to get to these assholes. You're not kicking me out. I've already seen too much."

Our eyes meet, and I hold them for as long as my body will allow me to.

"Okay," Nate speaks for Derek. "This is as much as your problem as it is ours. You're not allowed to go into the field, though. Not until you're medically cleared."

"If I stay here, he's going to know I'm alive. I'm better off disappearing and working behind the scenes."

Tanner arches an eyebrow, a cocky smile twitching at his lips. "You have a wife."

"Yeah, I do. And you know what? There's not a thing I can do to satisfy her at the moment. The only thing I *can* do is keep her safe."

Derek curses. "Jay, you can't be that much of an idiot."

"Wanna bet? I'm not being stupid. I'm looking out for her."

"Nate left his girlfriend to handle this case, and he's a miserable fuck," he roars.

Nate grimaces and crosses his arms.

"When are you idiots going to realize that leaving the people you love is never the answer? She's safer *with* you, dumbass!"

"If she's so safe with me, Derek, then why were their pictures of her getting into the fucking shower? Hmm? Because I was in one of them and I had no idea someone was peeping! I have the upper hand! Tanner found out who he is. I can stalk him and end him."

"And then what? What's your next move after that?"

I don't know. The threat would be neutralized, and Annie would be safe.

"If you kill him, then we are nowhere close to finding out who the ringleader is. People like this work for creatures like the Hydra. Cut off one head, and another appears. You can't even get out of bed right now," Derek snaps.

"He's right, Bubba," Nate says quietly to Derek. "We have the upper hand. He can corner him and get answers out of him."

"Then I'm the asshole who knew all along where Jay was! I can't lie to Aria. No. I won't do it."

"Then what do you suggest we do?" Nate barks.

Derek doesn't have an answer, and neither do the rest of us.

"We search for him. I'll put in a search for all of the aliases we know about. But until then, he's with the wind."

That doesn't make me feel any better. Regardless, Dominic Reese will pay for what he did. And I will be the fucker leading the charge to bring down *whatever this is*. For Annabelle.

33

ANNIE

After two weeks of observation and all of Jay's physical therapy and rehab scheduled, he's discharged from the hospital. Jo arrives bright and early with me while Jay blankly watches the TV, like he isn't looking forward to leaving at all.

"Good morning, sweetheart," Jo greets quietly.

He doesn't say a word. He trains his eyes on the early morning news and presses his lips in a hard line.

For the last fourteen days, his pain has gotten worse. He refuses the pain medication because he doesn't want to find out if he has an addictive personality like his father. And with that pain comes anger that would scorch the earth if he had the ability.

The pain is too much. He's dealing with it the best he can, but in doing that, he turned into this angry shell of himself. He's distancing himself. For what? I'm not sure. But he's made it crystal clear he doesn't appreciate our presence at all.

She kisses him on the forehead and starts cleaning up his trash from last night. I cross the room and open the curtains, allowing the sunlight to illuminate the dark, dank room.

Jay growls and pulls the pillow over his eyes in protest.

The last two weeks have been . . . difficult.

For a man who prided himself on being able to do anything, his injuries from the accident tell him otherwise. His cast is on for one more week. Getting out of bed to use the bathroom is an entire event that tires him out in less than three seconds. We've done some rehab for his legs, but walking remains a challenge.

He's angry. He doesn't remember anything about that night, except for our fight, and he's holding onto that anger with a death grip.

"Hey, you get to be sprung from this place and be in your own bed. How does that sound?" Jo asks, dropping in the chair next to his bed and offering him a cheerful smile.

Unfortunately for her, he isn't having it. If it were up to him, we'd leave him alone until he started feeling like himself again. I feel like an intruder. Not once has his eyes met mine. His eyes are cool and angry, almost like it's the world's fault he's tied to a hospital bed.

His silence breaks my heart. I'd give anything for him to speak to us. I just have to let him be and be supportive.

"Good morning, everyone," Tilly, Jay's nurse, greets brightly, her bleached blonde hair swinging in behind her.

"Good morning," Jo replies, just as sunny.

"How are we feeling today?" she asks Jay, approaching his bed and fiddling with his IV.

"Fine."

One word. That's all we get.

"Okay . . . Well, I'm just here to take out your IV. We'll get you some breakfast, and Dr. Probst will be in soon to talk about your next steps. You should be discharged in the next hour and a half."

"I already know my next steps," Jay says through gritted teeth.

"Hospital policy, babe. Take it up with Dr. Probst."

The "babe" comment sends a rippling shock through me. What the actual fuck? I glance at him, but he refuses to meet my gaze. What goes on behind the scenes when I'm not here?

This next part will be fun. Food service arrives, and he's presented with some scrambled eggs and fruit. Nothing too hard on his stomach.

"Can I at least have some salt and pepper?" he growls at the woman.

"Sorry, Mr. Parker. No added sodium. Enjoy your breakfast." She sashays out, rolling her cart with her.

When the door closes, we're three different people. I'm "Annie" all of a sudden, and for the first time in my life, I'm too afraid to say anything. I don't want to set him off. Jo isn't just the mom anymore. She's taken the role of caregiver, making me totally obsolete. And Jay . . . Well, I've never seen him like this.

"I think I'm going to take you up on your offer, baby," Jo directs at me. "I think for the first week or two, I'll move into the guest room. Then I can at least help out with cooking and showering—"

"No."

I swallow the anxiety that rises in my throat. We turn to Jay, who *finally* gives us the time of day.

"Baby, you can't be cooking. Let me help . . ."

"Annie can warm up a bowl of chicken broth. It's not that hard."

Tears prick my eyes. I don't think he means to push my shortcomings in my face, but I get it. If I was coming home from the hospital, I wouldn't want Momma moving in either. I wish he'd stop calling me Annie.

Jo shifts her gaze to me, worry etched into her exhausted features.

"I'm sure the company every day would be nice," I offer, desperate for some lighthearted conversation.

"No, it wouldn't. I want to rehab alone."

Jo's eyes well up with tears. She excuses herself, citing she needed a cup of coffee.

"Jay . . ."

"Don't start," he warns.

I lick my lips nervously. He doesn't get to talk to people like that. I don't care how much he's hurting. "She's worried about you."

He chuckles darkly. "Not that much if she's still hanging around William."

I suck in a deep breath. "Is that your goal, then? You're going to push away everyone who loves you? Then what?"

"I don't know why you care so much. You're about to gallivant the world for five years and forget all about us."

My stomach bottoms out, and I'm stuck looking like a guppy gasping for air.

"I already canceled with Isaac, Jay, so you can stop the pouting."

His eyes bore into the side of my skull. I want to smack him for being so callous.

"Pouting?" he seethes. "This isn't pouting, Annie. This is me losing *everything.*"

"I never pegged you to be such a drama queen," I hiss. "You're not losing anything, idiot. You have your family who loves you. You have your wife who would do anything for you—"

"Yeah, let's not forget you opened your mouth about that."

I take a few hesitant steps forward and lower myself so I'm in his eyeline. "You got into an accident, and then someone shot you. I understand your hesitation with the pain medication. I know this is your pain talking. I get you're angry. I'd be angry too. Especially if I couldn't remember who did it. Your life was altered, but not to the degree where you're some vegetable sitting in a La-Z-Boy in front of a TV watching reruns of *The Price is Right.* If your marines could see you right now, they'd be disappointed."

"Don't talk about shit you don't understand," he snarls, his jade eyes darkening.

"I've been talking to Graves. They're working out a schedule so they can all visit you. So let's test your theory, hmm? I'm not telling you to get over it, Jacob. I'm telling you to stop pushing us away because we love you and we want to help you."

This shuts him up.

"Eat your breakfast. The sooner you get home, the better you'll feel."

I don't think he believes me. He picks at his eggs and doesn't touch the fruit. Jo eventually meanders back this way, albeit silent as a church mouse, and Dr. Probst strolls in with a big smile on his face.

"Who's ready to go home?"

None of us say a word. I think the tension in the room is palpable enough for him to figure out he needs to get the show on the road.

"Right . . . Okay. If you feel any sharp pain or notice any bleeding in your urine or if you cough up blood, get back here ASAP. Your physical therapy is all scheduled. Your prescriptions are waiting for you at the pharmacy when you're ready to pick them up. You're in good hands with Ms. Josephine and your wife." He turns to me and weakly smiles. "Any problems, feel free to give my office a call, and we'll see him right away." He places a stack of papers on the rollaway table with a pen. "You're a free man, Mr. Parker."

GETTING Jay up my front porch steps was another challenge. One I should've foreseen coming. He growled in agony with each step, and by the time we reached the deck, he was sweating profusely and exhausted.

He wanted to sleep, so we acted as his crutch to my room and tucked him in as he protested the entire time that he isn't a child and can do it himself.

"I don't think he wants me here," Jo says quietly when we enter the kitchen. She gets out my big stockpot and a tote bag full of stock ingredients to make her own stock.

"I think he's just exhausted, and he takes it out on the people around him. He's used to doing everything on his own."

She shrugs and starts doing her thing. Bones of chicken are pulled out of Tupperware, onion and garlic peels, celery, and carrots. I don't know how she does it, but she can make magic out of everything.

"I cut William off again. It was only going to hurt Jay and . . . I don't know. It was stupid of me to go to him."

I think at this point, it's too little too late, though I'm not going to be the one to tell her that.

"That's good. You didn't need him anyway. He can go rot with the rest of the Parkers."

She cracks a small smile and stirs the ingredients. "I spent so much time living in fear after William left. I worried Jay would be angry like him. When he turned out to be even-tempered, I worried if he was okay. I think I worried so much about him that I may have smothered him."

That's not the case. "He's out of your life for good now. The only thing we have to do now is get you and Jay on the mend."

"Speaking of . . . I shouldn't have made you keep my secret."

Resentment crackles within me, though I don't have a leg to stand on. She kept mine first. And now I'm asking her to keep a bigger secret from my parents—that I got married and left them out of it.

"Jo . . ."

"I can't remember the last time I've felt like myself," she admits with a sniffle. "This disease makes me into somebody I don't like. It hurts people, and I can't live with that."

"Well . . . for what it's worth, I'm sorry I made you keep our secret. There has to come a time when I can't fear my parents anymore."

"I've known your parents a long time. I knew them as kids, as teenagers, as young adults . . ." She sighs dreamily. "I think you, your brother, and your sister put them on such a high pedestal that you forget they aren't perfect. Your momma was once the social pariah of this town. Your grandparents weren't exactly welcoming of her either."

I stare at her in shock. I always knew my grandparents were on the Parker train and didn't like Daddy. But I didn't know Momma was in any hot water with Daddy's parents. Sure when they were alive, we didn't see each other often, but I always thought it was because she and Momma were the ones who didn't get along. I know she was promised to a Parker. But this isn't something we talk about. And if I can get Jo to talk about it . . .

"Seriously?"

"Mm-hmm. It's not my story to tell, so I'm not going to get into specifics. Your Daddy wasn't always the calm, cool, collected man he is now. Your momma wasn't always able to advocate for herself. That all comes out with age and experience. Anyway, what I'm trying to tell you is they probably understand better than what you give them credit for. Give them a chance."

God, I can't even imagine what that's supposed to mean.

"You and your mother are so similar it isn't even funny. After everything that happened, she put a plan together. After high school, she took every penny she ever made working around town and used it to travel Europe for a year. She walked for graduation. After that, I drove her to the airport before your grandmother could even get a picture with her. You see, baby, she pissed off her parents to no end. But in the end, she did what she thought was right for *her*. Look what it's gotten her."

I need to tell them we're married. I've seen what secrets can do to people. It's not worth tearing my family apart.

We reach a comfortable silence. When the broth is done an hour later, Jo packs up her things and leaves. My place isn't messy, but I pick up the clutter and throw shit away. I know Jay would appreciate it. I think that's his biggest gripe about me. I'm a hot mess express. I don't know what to do with myself knowing Jay is probably wide awake and hating my guts.

I gently pad to our room and gently open the door. He stares at the ceiling fan like it holds all the answers. I'm not even sure if he's slept.

"Hey," I murmur quietly.

He doesn't answer me—or even acknowledge me for that matter.

"Are you getting hungry? I can warm up some broth for you if you're feeling up to it."

"No, thank you."

Does he plan on starving himself?

"When I was sixteen, my momma threw me this obnoxious sweet sixteen party. Do you remember that?"

Silence.

"I remember sulking most of the night because I knew you couldn't be there. And when it was time for cake, I wished that I could see you, even if it was for five minutes."

"I'm not in the mood, Annie," he growls.

"I still think you and I have this superpower where we can read each other's minds. Because that night, you came home. You got in around midnight and you climbed up the window."

His lava eyes narrow at me. I'm waiting for him to explode.

"I was a lovesick teenager who was naïve when it came to a boy who would rather pretend I didn't exist than be honest with his feelings for me. I always hoped the best from you because I knew you were capable of it."

"So what? Are you disappointed at this turn of events? I can no longer fuck you into submission or I'm too angry, is that it?"

I take a deep breath.

"You're angry, and I understand that. I fucked up big time, and I'll spend the rest of my life apologizing for it. But I know you're not this person, Jay. You've spent your entire adult life working overtime to not become your father."

He stills at my words, and the realization washes over him.

"Anyway. I'm sorry for the part I played in your accident. I'm around if you need anything. Text me or something. I'll be in the living room."

I close the door behind me, and the traitorous tears escape me. He's a good man. I know this in my heart, and I can feel it in my bones.

I won't let him turn into William.

34

JAY

I wish there were some way to justify the anger rushing through me. Everything *hurts.* Where the surgical scar is, my broken ribs, my broken clavicle. Getting up to go to the bathroom is fucking torture, and I can't stand the doe-eyed looks from Annie when she sweeps in here to help me.

I'm not an invalid. I can run three miles in the blink of an eye. I can make love to my wife and have her beg for more. *This* is pathetic.

My muscles ache everywhere. I've refused the painkillers because William was addicted to alcohol, and I don't want to test to see if I'm the same way.

This morning, I vomited all over the nightstand and mattress because I couldn't move to the bathroom quick enough and the pain radiating through me made me physically ill. Annie ended up stripping the bed and is now running me a bath to help with some of the pain. I don't like having simple things done for me. It enrages me.

She sweeps in from the bathroom with a towel slung over her shoulder. Her wild blonde hair is in a bun that reminds me of Mrs. Trunchbull from *Matilda.* She hasn't slept in the same room as me. And I haven't left this room since I got out of the hospital a few days ago. I don't know if she's sleeping, but judging by the swollen, purple bags under her eyes, I'm confident she isn't.

"Okay, the tub is filling up. Do you want help getting undressed?"

Jay from a month ago would wriggle his eyebrows suggestively and ask her to help. I'm not that Jay. Part of me is still so angry that she easily left me out of her plans when she didn't want to talk about the next five years of our relationship.

The thought of having to lift my shirt over my head sends my stomach swirling with nausea. As much as I don't like her right now, I need her help.

"I need help."

The fact she crosses the room and hides her gaze from me, reminds me that she truly is sorry. She's trying to not rock the boat. I wish she'd make it adorably awkward. She undoes my sling and supports my cast with her hand while she reaches for the hem of my shirt and pulls it over my head.

Her breath catches in her throat as her eyes sweep over my torso. She catalogs every angry cut, the long surgery scar, and the bruising on my ribs.

She's a fucking trooper. Still, she doesn't say a thing. She swallows her tears, and as soon as the shirt is free, she reassembles the sling and helps me with my sweatpants.

My dick stands at attention, though if she notices it, she doesn't let on. Despite the fact I'm still angry with her, she's still the only person I'd ever want to be with—the most beautiful person on the planet.

When we get to the bathroom, she guides me to the toilet and sits me down so she can move the shower curtain all the way back. When she returns, I swing my arm around her neck and hold my breath as I attempt to stand up again. Searing pain from my ribs brings tears to my eyes.

"Okay, take your time. Don't rush it," she instructs softly.

I swing my left foot over the tub, and the hot water is cleansing in a way that makes me stop clenching my jaw.

Her hands move to my hips as I lower down. She's inflated the bath pillow so the porcelain tub isn't frigid against my back.

"Can I get you anything to drink?"

"No."

She sighs. "Okay. I'm going to get started on lunch, then. Any requests?"

Yes. A big burger from Rhonda's with extra bacon.

"Whatever you have is fine."

She purses her lips and nods without a word. Her presence is missed terribly the second she leaves.

I manage to scoot back so I can rest my head against the wall behind me. The hot water soothes my aching muscles. Annie's lavender soap has always had a calming effect in the bathroom, and now that I'm looking at it, I'm kicking myself for not inviting her in with me.

Soft music plays from the kitchen. Knowing Annabelle, she can't sit in the silence. She needs something on in the background. I wish her taste in music was broader, but the sounds of Tim McGraw crooning about the stars turning blue is oddly calming.

Exhaustion has been a friend of mine. If I don't want to deal with something, I fall asleep. If I don't want to think about Annie, I fall asleep. When I inevitably think about Annie, I fall asleep.

Perhaps it's the lavender that brings the exhaustion out in me. My eyelids droop, and soon I'm dreaming of that night she was talking about a few days ago. I climbed up her window and nearly killed myself because there was a nail sticking out of the siding from when the Christmas lights were hung, and I accidentally scraped my leg on the way up.

I sat on Annie's bedroom floor while she snuck away to get Betty Lou's first aid kit to patch me up. I remember watching her take care of me and wanting to rake my hand through her wild, blonde waves. She fired a string of questions I barely had time to answer before the next question was spit out.

But mostly, I remember staring at her, knowing how insanely stupid I was to be in love with her. Yet there I was, sneaking into her room to wish her a happy birthday.

We spent two hours together before I had to leave. She gave me Chris's last energy drink and a kiss on the cheek that I was so tempted to turn into something more meaningful.

Nobody knew I was there except for her.

I love you, Jay. She whispered that when she thought I couldn't hear her, as

I was climbing down the side of the house. The stupid part is, I was in love with her too. It was inappropriate. But damn it, I'm not sorry for it.

When I open my eyes, she's at my side, dutifully and gently washing my body with a washcloth, wiping away the dried blood and the little dirt the nurses weren't able to get to. The washcloth is just behind my ear, and she narrows her eyes in concentration. She's so beautiful.

"I remember that night," I say quietly.

She's right, though. She and I have this uncanny ability to know what the other is thinking. She doesn't have to ask me what I'm talking about.

"Yeah?"

"I scratched the hell out of my leg."

A smile tugs at the corners of her lips, but she doesn't betray herself. "Yeah, you nearly had me caught by Momma. I told her I nicked my leg when I was shaving. She didn't even question me about it." She washes my chest with precision, doing her best to avoid the scars.

"I heard you."

"Hmm?" she asks without meeting my eyes.

"When I was climbing down, you whispered you loved me."

A melancholy smile touches her lips, but it doesn't take long for the tears to burn her eyes.

"Annabelle . . ."

"I'm sorry. I'm just tired. Are you ready to come out? The bathwater is cooling."

I sigh. "Ah, no. You can finish up in the kitchen if you want. I'm not ready to get out yet."

She doesn't need to be told twice. You'd think there was a fire in the kitchen or something. I gently rock myself up. With my unbroken hand, I grip the side of the tub tight and pull myself up. I bite back my curses as the fiery streaks of pain strike me like lightning.

I manage to step out of the tub on my own. But now I'm stuck doing my towel one-handed. She races into the bathroom, stunned.

"You shouldn't be doing that yourself," she scolds as she wraps the towel around my waist. "You're going to hurt yourself if you aren't careful."

I'm fine, Blondie.

"I'm hungry."

She sighs impatiently. "Okay. I can make you something after I get you dressed."

I don't want her to dress me, and I sigh in impatience.

"I know you want to do it yourself, okay?" She straightens up and pinches the bridge of her nose. "You're not a weak man if you ask for help, Jay. I'm happy to help you."

Just her saying the word *weak* fuels me with rage. I'm not weak. But this *situation* has me depending on everyone else to help me. I needed her help to take a stupid bath!

"I know I'm not weak," I snap. "Do you have any idea how much pain I'm in?"

"No, I really don't, because you won't talk to me." She storms out of the bathroom and slams the dresser drawers around before coming back in to make sure I don't slip and knock myself unconscious. "I laid your clothes out for you. So if you want to try to dress yourself, be my guest."

She storms out of the room and slams the door behind her.

God, I have to stop being an asshole.

35

ANNIE

When Aria, Derek, and the kids enter without knocking, I could kiss them. I'm drowning. I need a break. Aria takes over kitchen duty, and before I know it, I'm heading to the one place I haven't gone to get away since I was a teenager.

Daddy is in Peoria picking up a herd of goats, and I know Momma will be cleaning up the house or helping with some admin work for the shelter Jo and Aria run. Color me surprised when I find her on the couch watching a Hallmark movie.

Her kind blue eyes, the ones we share, snap to me. I don't have to say anything. She already knows I'm a blubbering mess. I burst into tears the second she rises from the couch.

"Shh, baby. Come talk to me."

I collapse on the couch, stretching my legs out and resting my head on her lap. She strokes my hair and allows me to bawl my eyes out.

"Annie, baby? Do you want to talk about it?"

Who else am I going to talk to?

"I messed up, Momma. He's hurt because I'm selfish."

"That's not true."

I shouldn't feel so angry around her. We're so alike it isn't funny. Maybe she wants me to learn from her mistakes, but crying on her lap like this, I know I've been unfair to her.

"We got into a major fight that night. He left because he was angry with me."

I'm glad she isn't looking at my face. Or if she is, she's not making it obvious.

"Couples fight all the time, baby."

"Elliot has a friend in television. He loves my idea of turning my column into a TV series. When he emailed me the info, I got so excited that I drafted up a five-year plan."

"*That's* what he's upset over?"

"No. He's upset because I forgot to think about him."

"I don't think I understand . . ."

"I would've been working for five years straight overseas. Jay wasn't a part of the plan."

"Ahh."

If everyone knew the truth, they'd side with him, not that I blame them.

"Honey, I know you think that him being hurt is your fault, but you weren't the one who ran him off the road or shot him in the gut."

But he left the house because of me.

"Jay left the house on his own cognition. He could've gone to another room. He could've crossed the street and went to your brother's house. It was his own choice to leave that night. Not yours."

My eyes are on fire from all the sobbing.

"He's in pain and he's angry. You're the unfortunate person who happens to live with him. He doesn't mean to take it out on you."

"There was a moment today I thought we turned a corner. But it was short-lived. He barely talks to me, Momma. And when he does, he's short and cutting."

She sighs. "Your father was a lot older than me, you know. It took him years to put the age difference to bed. And of course, we fought a lot. He was gone a lot when we first got married. We were different people for a long time."

"It's not the same, Momma."

"I know, baby."

"I don't know how to fix it. I don't even know if he still loves me."

"He does. If he didn't, he'd be looking for any and every excuse to get out of that house." She sighs. "The two of you have been dancing around the fact the two of you are meant to be for over a decade. It's going to take more than a car accident to tear you apart."

But it *was* more than a car accident.

"I'm scared to go back home, Momma."

"Then stay here a bit. Let your sister take care of him. You can rest your heart here for a while. Are you hungry? I made a chocolate chip Bundt cake . . ."

I sniffle. "Tell me about Paris."

She sighs. She's told these stories over million times, but they never get old.

"There's a little bistro near the Louvre. When I would wake up in the morning, I'd pack my backpack and walk there. I'd have coffee, a croissant, and fresh fruit, and I'd watch the Parisians start their day. I'd sit there and wish I could be more like them."

"How so?"

She bites her bottom lip in concentration. "Posh. Fabulous. Confident."

I snort. "You're the most confident person I know, Momma. Come on. Tell the real stories."

"You need to hear a story, baby. So hush up and listen." She wiggles in her seat, situating herself until she's comfortable. Her fingers weave through my hair. I close my eyes in relaxation. "I was running out of money, and I knew I'd have to go home soon. In my last two weeks in Paris, I happened to sit down at this bistro one morning and this man sits across from me.

"I thought it so strange, as this never happened before. But when I lifted my gaze to meet his eyes, I couldn't stop smiling."

"Are you telling me that Chris might not be Daddy's son?"

We both fall into easy laughter.

"The man was your father. He was a familiar face, and honestly, I was just so happy to see someone from home."

"Is this the story then? Daddy stalked you until you settled down in Paris and asked for your hand?"

"You know, Annabelle, all this snark building up in your head must be so painful."

I giggle. "That's why I'm getting it out with you."

She groans and takes a deep breath. "My sister was getting married, and I didn't know. Your father was the one to break the news to me. I avoided calling my parents, but I wrote once a week to let them know I was still alive. When he told me that, I sat there shocked. They never mentioned it in any of their letters. Hell, I didn't even know she was dating anyone."

"Jo mentioned Gran wasn't crazy about you . . ."

"I knew Stephen from him helping out around town, but we weren't close. My parents were committed to the Parkers. Michael was better than the others, but I didn't want to be tied down by a man. I wasn't even sure I wanted children."

I gasp in mock horror. "And you call yourself our loving mother? For shame."

Momma giggles, and it transports me back to my childhood when she would lay with me in bed and tell me her stories.

"But when your daddy told me that your aunt was getting married, something changed in me. I wanted to come back home to Sage Creek, but I wanted to live my own life. I wanted to rent the apartment above Rhonda's, work out of Sarah Beth Reynolds' bakery, and learn how to bake cakes and pastries. I wanted it all without taking anything from my parents. I knew that if I was going to live a happy life, I'd have to cut my parents off."

I'm not entirely sure what lesson she wants me to learn from this.

"Why are you telling me this, Momma?"

"Because, baby. I think you and I are more alike than you think. I left home at eighteen because I didn't know who *I* was. I left to find myself. I didn't leave to pass the time. I can honestly say I did that. You left home at eighteen to get your education in journalism so you can get paid to do what I did. Can you honestly say that you discovered yourself?"

I'm glad I'm not facing her. I came here to be coddled a little bit. When I close my eyes and think about me, the one person I see is Jay.

Did I lose myself to him? Did I go through all of this bullshit because I loved him so fucking much that I forgot my dream mattered too?

36

JAY

When Annabelle leaves the house, my heart plummets to the fiery depths of my stomach. I think I took it too far. But the banging and clanging in the kitchen, Troy's baby babbles, and Derek speaking in a low, rumbling tone to Aria assures me there's been a change in guard.

Good. She deserves a break.

A light tap on the door has my nerves running on overdrive. The doorknob twists, much to my dismay, and Dr. I-Think-I'm-So-Pretty strides in, tightly closing the door behind him.

"I heard you're a prick."

Is that what she said?

"What do you want?" I growl.

"What are you doing?"

I glare at him, hoping he gets the hint that I don't want to talk about this with him. "I don't know what you're talking about."

"I know Annie. She doesn't take shit from anyone. But when we got here, she couldn't get out of the house fast enough."

I guess the apple doesn't fall too far from the tree. I'm just like William. I may not have physically hurt her, but I hurt her heart.

"Don't pretend you know what you're talking about."

Drive the point home. Get him the fuck out of here. I'm done.

"Hey, idiot. Annie's my family. So is Aria who took over heating broth up for your crabby ass."

When I don't say anything, he drags one of Annie's decorative chairs over to the side of the bed and lowers himself onto it.

"When Nate left Evangeline because he thought he was protecting her, he was wrong. Eve's miserable. He's miserable. And all the while, they could've still been together and *happy* if they just talked. You're making a big mistake by pushing her away."

Fire rages through me. He doesn't know anything.

"Where exactly am I going to go?" I snap. I can't even go to the bathroom by myself. How does he expect me to hunt down the asshole who tried to kill me?

"Jay—"

"Tell me! Because I can't take my own fucking clothes off by myself. I might piss myself if I have to aim a gun at someone. So tell me, *Hawthorn,* what do you expect me to do?"

Derek's jaw ticks in anger. His crystal blue eyes narrow, and if I didn't look or feel like I was shoved through a meat grinder, I'm sure he'd give me a black eye.

"Is this how you would talk to your CO if you were blown up in Afghanistan?"

"You're not my CO," I hiss.

"No, idiot. I'm your friend."

That one shakes me to my core. I've forgotten the most basic human needs and have been playing this woe-is-me game for weeks.

"As your friend, I'm telling you to knock it off. You're going to ruin everything good in your life if you keep this shit up. Guess what, asshole? Your injuries heal. This broken collar bone you have? It'll be sore. But it's nothing like losing your wife to your shitty attitude."

I swallow and blink back tears. He's right. I'm being a little bitch.

"Fix it with her. Because I'm telling you, she's at the end of her rope."

Derek leaves without another word, and all that's left for me is the bed I've messed up and a world of horrible decisions I've made in the last two weeks.

I watch the numbers on her alarm clock slowly blink away. It's been two hours, and she hasn't come home.

Aria sits with me for a while. She tells me all about the progress the shelter has made, but hearing about it still makes my stomach churn. Troy waddles in after a bit and stares at me like I'm a monster.

Which . . . I don't think he's too far off. I've only known one person to act like this, and I know this is child's play compared to what my father put us through.

Zoey reads me a chapter of *Harry Potter and the Prisoner of Azkaban* because she knows it's my favorite, and soon they're all ready to call it a night.

The front door opens and closes, and the silence around me is too uncomfortable. I need something. I need Annie.

Dr. Probst told me not to overdo it. I should be careful about overexerting myself and cut myself some slack. I'm not going to let Dominic Fucking Reese—or whatever his real name is—keep me down. Annie needs me.

Bravely, I slowly swing my legs over the bed until my feet touch the plush, fuzzy carpet. I'm working with one arm, and even when I put the slightest pressure on it, the vomit in my stomach threatens to projectile from my mouth.

Deep breaths, Parker.

I gently stand up. My legs cry in agony. My stomach somersaults with a fury. I stumble over to the dresser, using it as my crutch. Where am I going?

The front door swings open, and like a kid caught red-handed from trying to witness Santa Claus, I freeze in place. The bedroom door swings open and I'm met staring at a beautiful, but sad, princess. Her mouth hangs open in a perfect O like I've surprised her.

"What are you doing? You shouldn't be up." She rushes over to me and slowly leads me back to the bed. When she deems me comfortable, she slides off her flip-flops, crosses the room, and climbs into bed.

Her face is swollen and glazed with tears. She stares at the ceiling as if it's the most interesting thing in the universe.

"Where'd you go?" I ask because I'm genuinely curious. Who'd she run to?

"I went to Momma's house. I let her feed me cake."

Her eyes fill with tears. The unspoken truths sit between us like rotten garbage. We're in a stalemate. None of us wants to open the can of worms.

"Blondie?"

"I think it might be best if I move into the guest room for a little while."

I wish she'd look at me. Is this really what she wants? "Annabelle."

She sniffles, the tears rolling off her cheeks and onto the bedspread. "I think you and I could do with a little space. Don't you think?"

The truth is . . . *yes.* She needs to live her life while I try to get mine back together. But I don't want to. We've spent too long dancing around our feelings—*I* spent too much time dancing around my feelings for her. I don't want this to end.

"Anyway, you stay here since the bathroom is attached. Just text me whenever you need something."

"Is this what you want?"

She swallows the lump in her throat and turns to me. "I don't know what I want."

That sentence cuts me deep. Annabelle *always* knows what she wants. I nod and keep my trap shut.

"I'm going to go get your meds set up and bring you in a glass of water. Is there anything else you think you might need overnight?"

You. "No. I think I should be okay."

She slowly gets out of bed and crosses the room. Her absence is noticeable. What's more noticeable is the gaping hole in my chest. She took that with her. This is spiraling. If I don't do something quick, I'm afraid we might not find our way back to each other.

37

ANNIE

When I was a teenager, Aria, Jackie and I would have a sleepover twice a month. So when Aria insists we're due for another one, I reluctantly agree. She even goes as far as driving us off the property all the way into town to Jackie's apartment.

When we reach the landing, the door is pulled open, and Jackie beams at us, already in her jammies with two glasses of rosé in hand.

"Yay! You're here! Come on in. I've had a few glasses already, so you need to catch up."

She shoves the glass in my hand and leads us in. We drop our stuff in the small living room and settle on the couch.

Derek is on kid duty; Chris is on Jay duty. I just wish that made me feel a little bit better. I can already see how Chris is going to react to Jay's shitty behavior. Whatever. As long as I'm not on the receiving end for once.

"So . . . dealer's choice. We can order in and put on a movie? Or we can talk shit about everyone in town?"

"That seemed to be more fun when we were in high school," Aria grumbles.

She isn't wrong.

"Wedding plans?" Jackie asks.

Pass.

Please don't get me wrong. I'm over the moon for her. But my own marriage is falling apart at the seams, and I don't know how I'm going to survive without him.

There it is. I've become so dependent on this idea of us together that I've hung onto it like a life raft.

"Annie . . .?" Peanut quickly places her glass down on the coffee table and wraps me up in her arms.

All I ever do is cry, and I'm so tired of it. I'm not this person! I'm badass. I'm a badass bitch!

But . . . my heart is being held together by the thinnest of threads. It's going to take more than one night of hanging out with my baby sister and our friend to completely sever it. I don't think I'm ready for it.

"Did you pregame too? Are we into emotional Annie already?" Jackie cries.

Despite my sour mood, I giggle. "No pregaming. Just wallowing."

"Okay . . . so takeout and movie it is."

We order an ungodly amount of food. There is no way the three of us are possibly going to finish this. We ordered Chinese, Italian, Rhonda's, Rico's—hell, even McDonald's!

Jackie flips on a movie—some Netflix Christmas movie—and I'm lost in it. I envy those fictional characters. Their lives fall apart so easily. A bakery that goes out of business, a boyfriend breaks up with her, a friend moves out of town . . .

None of these scenarios apply to me.

And yet, it comforts my heart. As we build a mattress out of couch cushions and snuggle in to watch these dumb movies, a part of me revives. I might not be normal, bubbly Annie. But for a minute, I feel like I can breathe.

Jackie is drifting off to sleep when the credits roll. Food sits on every surface of her tiny apartment, and it's nearing midnight. My family will figure out what to do about morning feed, and maybe for the first time since

Boston, I can sleep in until my body tells me to get up. I could use all the sleep I can get.

"What are you thinking about so hard over there?" Aria asks softly.

"Stuff and things," I tease, my lips quirking into a small smile.

She sighs. "Things aren't good between you two."

I shake my head sadly. Maybe it's been like that for a while, and I ignored it because I wanted to be with him so desperately.

"The accident took a lot out of him."

"Is that all?"

Smart Peanut. "What do you think you know, Peanut?"

She shrugs. "I don't know. I know Jo's secret was a bombshell. Then William came into the picture again. It just seems like things kind of blew up the second he decided he was ready to come home."

"It's funny because I was thinking along those same lines." I weakly smile at my sister who watches me with concern. "He wanted to live life with me, and the second he steps back into Sage Creek, fights burst out left and right."

Aria snorts. "You *knew* that was coming. You hid your relationship for two years!"

I giggle. I sort of miss those days when he came home and the most scandalous thing was that we were secretly together.

"I've been wondering if he was better off staying in the Marine Corps."

"Don't do that," she murmurs. "You can't play the what-if game, Annie. It will only destroy you."

"He's so angry," I whimper.

"You can't hold that against him," Jackie says sleepily, turning to face us with her eyes closed. "I'd be pissed too if someone ran me off the road and shot me in the gut."

"But *I'm* the reason he was out in the first place."

"It sounds like you're looking for an excuse for this to end," Aria smarts.

"I've spent the majority of my life chasing him, Peanut. I took the gig with Nick and Geoffrey because it meant I would be kept busy while Jay was in Afghanistan."

"You *love* him."

"Yeah. I do." *I married him, for God's sake!* "But when I think about who *I* am, I've molded my life with him in mind. I had it set in my mind we'd be together and I forgot about me."

Aria frowns. Jackie falls into a deep sleep, her soft snores softening our silence.

"You don't know who you are?"

"I don't know who I am when you take him out of the picture."

There it is. The truth bomb fifteen-year-old me would absolutely go on a killing spree to keep hidden. In one conversation, I detonated it and didn't care who was around.

"There's counseling . . ."

I admire her for her optimism. That ship has sailed.

"Jay's going to go through his life resenting me for the part I played in his accident."

"That's reaching and you know it."

Maybe it is. But Momma and Daddy are right. I lost myself along the way.

"He's angry with me too, Peanut. I kept a big secret from him. And then when it really counted, I forgot him."

"But . . . forgiveness . . ."

"There were times when I would visit Jay and I'd listen to him and the boys talk. That Jay was different. He left home Jay Parker. He was built into somebody else, Peanut. As much as he doesn't want to admit it, he doesn't know who he is without the Marine Corps."

She sighs. "What are you saying?"

"I think we might need to spend some time apart."

38

JAY

When Chris comes over, he plugs in the Xbox into the TV in our room and crashes next to me on the bed. He realizes his mistake when he hands me the controller. You can't play one-handed. And if you can, I sure as hell haven't figured it out yet.

I watch him play, though. We barely speak a word. He's my brother, but we may as well be strangers who met at a church youth group as plus ones. It's awkward.

Annie's been distant. I know her. I know she's drifting away from me, but it might be for the best. I can't keep worrying about her if I'm going to go after this guy. She shouldn't have to wait in limbo for a grumpy idiot who isn't fun to be around. She could do that five-year thing. In Greece. With Greek guys who could show her the time of her life.

"Do you need to use the bathroom?" Chris asks, breaking me out of my trance.

"What?"

"You look like you're shitting yourself. I agreed to babysit, not change diapers."

I playfully shove him with my good arm and chuckle. "No, asshole. I don't need to use the bathroom."

"Do you want to watch a movie?"

No. I'd really appreciate it if he left, though.

"You don't have to stay here. I can take care of myself."

He gives me that *"riiiight"* look and returns his attention to the TV.

My phone buzzes on the nightstand. I reach over for it, and a rush of adrenaline washes over me when I see Tanner's name on the screen.

"Yes?" I answer. I don't want Chris knowing I'm talking to one of Derek's goons. Part of me thinks he won't take that well.

"You, my friend, are dead in the eyes of Dominic Reese."

The knot in my stomach releases.

"I know Chris is in the room with you, so I'll make this quick. He's coming back into town, so you're going to need to lie low. Lower than low."

"How do you mean?"

"I mean, I can set you up in a cabin somewhere with a grocery delivery service. You can still make your dumb PT appointments, but we have a ghost, Parker. Do you know what ghosts do?"

"They're able to see things you can't."

"Exactly. So this is what we're going to do. We're going to set you up. You don't leave the house until I say so."

Chris gets the hint and walks out of the room when I sit up uncomfortably.

"That sounds a lot like house arrest."

He chuckles. "It sort of is. But in order for this to work, you have to stay out of sight."

Which means I need to end it with Annie. I can't lie low with her around. A bowling ball hits my gut hard. I'm not ready to say goodbye.

"When do we get started?"

"Patience, grasshopper. Let me get in touch with Nate, and then we'll start getting the ball rolling. Okay?"

"Yeah. Fine."

I hang up the phone. Chris awkwardly enters the doorway.

"You're leaving her," he says, almost disappointed.

"What?"

"Don't be dumb, Jay. House arrest? With who? Because I know it isn't with Jeremy."

I swallow nervously. *Do I spill my guts and be honest with him? Or do I shut the fuck up and play dumb?*

"Derek's friend found who shot me."

Realization washes over his face. "So you're going to kill him?"

I shake my head. Honestly, no. That's not what I'm going to do. He's too valuable to end his life right then and there. "There's a lot you don't understand—"

"Don't give me that bullshit, man! Since when are you and Derek besties for the restie, huh? You're my brother. Be fucking honest with me!"

My temper rises, and I don't think I can hold it in any longer. "There're still people after your sister, Chris. They're after all of us."

This sobers him.

"I found out where they're hiding. There were pictures of Aria, Annie. Of your mom, *my* mom. Of *Zoey*. Of us. I'm not letting anyone touch them, and if he's dead, that means there's going to be somebody else looking for them too."

Chris takes a reflexive step back. His face is hard and untrusting.

"So yeah, Chris. I'm leaving her because I need to make sure she stays safe. In the eyes of the fucker who shot me, I'm dead. If he sees me hanging around your sister, he's going to finish the job, and I'm not exactly keen on dying. I have the upper hand, and you can bet your ass I'm not going to squander that chance!"

We stare at each other for a long moment. I wonder if he'll pounce at the chance to punch me out. He's no longer the skinny kid who you could take down by a sweep of the legs. He's my height. My build. And when it comes to his sisters, he's reluctantly their protector.

"I can't believe you," he seethes.

Yeah, I know. I'm not too crazy about myself either.

"Even you know I'm right."

"If she finds someone else, you don't get to ruin her life. I don't care if you think you're going on a gallant mission to keep her safe. Do you want to know why the three of us are so tight? Because even though we grate on each other's nerves a thousand percent of the time, the three of us can lean on each other without second-guessing."

"Well, bully for you, Chris! I'm an only child—"

"You had *us!*"

His face slowly changes to a tomato red. The veins in his neck stick out and his pulse is visible.

Of course I had them. But I can't tell them about the secret vigilante group their father is heading up! He wanted them out of that for a reason.

"You're an asshole. Here I thought she was going to be the one to drive you away, but it turns out it's your own stupidity that's doing it."

"You wouldn't understand."

"That's a cop-out. Derek has been with Aria this entire time and she's fine."

"Derek's training and my training are totally different!"

He crosses his arms, his anger oozing from every pore on his body.

"Look. I don't expect you to understand. But her happiness and safety mean more to me than anything else. I'm going to hunt down the people who are trying to take her away and exterminate the threat. If I lose her in the process . . ."

Well, at least she'll be safe. She can still live a life of happiness.

He doesn't say a word to me the rest of the night. He ends up sleeping on the couch. Meanwhile, I can't sleep a wink.

We're at a crossroads. But she means more to me than anything. And if I *have* to do this to keep her safe, then so be it. She'll thank me in the long run."

In the morning, I manage to get out of bed and shuffle into the bathroom to take a leak. It's painful, and every time I take a step, it feels like a bunch of jagged rocks are rolling around in my belly, cutting it up for good measure.

But I don't throw up, so that's progress.

When I'm done, I shuffle out of the bathroom and out into the living room.

Chris is long gone. Instead, my beautiful, blonde bombshell stands at the stove, stirring something in a frying pan with pursed lips and sad eyes.

"How was your night?" I ask quietly.

"Fine. We ended up ordering in and watching movies."

She's hiding something. My girl will *always* look me in the eye when she talks to me. She says it's so we feel more connected.

"Annabelle."

She slowly lifts her gaze and swallows. "I'm making some eggs. And before you start complaining, yes, I can scramble some eggs. Go ahead and get comfortable. I'll make you a plate."

"Talk to me, Blondie."

She sets the silicone spatula down and slowly turns so she's facing me. Her bottom lip wobbles.

I can see the end in her eyes. Maybe I can take away the pain if I don't make her say it.

"I don't know who I am," she admits with a sob.

She can't see it, but my heart is shattered. I know exactly how she feels. I'm lost without the Marine Corps. I'm treading water as it is. I can't be who she needs me to be when my body is broken. When my mind is barely functioning without structure.

What the hell am I going to do now that my body is broken? I can't actually track down Dominic Reese and eviscerate him. I can barely walk to the bathroom without help! My police dreams are dead in the water. The Parkers will continue their negligence of the home I love so much. And even if I were to reenlist with the Marine Corps, they'd take one look at my medical records and send me on my way.

What's left? After everything, after losing my guys, SCPD, my mobility, *Annabelle*—what's left for me?

I want to wrap her up in my arms and tell her it's okay, but I don't think I can move from this spot. My breathing quickens. My heart spasms in my chest.

"I've spent every waking moment living my life with you in mind. And it was always okay because I know you and I are supposed to be together.

We're built for each other. But . . ." She takes a deep breath. "I think I lost myself along the way. I've gotten so dependent on you . . ."

And I've gotten so fucking dependent on her!

"Come here."

She shakes her head. "God, I feel like such an idiot. I chased you for years. And when I finally landed you, it was like I was someone else."

I swallow the lump of tears in my throat.

"Please, Annabelle, come here." I need to hold her. Because I don't know when I'll get the chance to hold her again. She deserves someone who can be who she needs.

She holds my gaze as she turns off the burner. She hesitantly crosses the room, and when she's close enough to where I can wrap my one good arm around her, I pull her close and bury my nose in her hair. I'm committing her floral scent to memory. My beautiful, amazing wife.

"I love you so much," I murmur in her hair, loose strands tickling my nose. I'm not a man who cries. But the tears escape my eyes so easily. "And because I love you, you and I need to take a step back."

Her grip around my torso tightens. The urge to vomit returns, but I tamp it down. I refuse to ruin this moment.

"I love you too," she whimpers. "You have no idea how much."

"I think I have an idea. Go find yourself. You and me? We're tied together for life. I promise you we'll find our way back to each other." *Whether it's two weeks from now or sixty years.*

We stand in the middle of the room for what feels like hours. We're both sobbing idiots. But this is for the best. She needs to know who she is before we start our life together—properly. I need to know who I am if we're truly not meant to be. I need to know how to live a life without her.

Knowing her, she'll follow her wild spirit across the globe without looking back. No regrets.

But for me, she's imprinted on my soul. I'll wipe out any threat. With Reese on the loose, he threatens her existence. I don't know how I'll do it, but he will die at my hands.

I just wish this didn't hurt so goddamn much.

COMING SOON

OUT OF MY MIND

THE SAGE CREEK SERIES - BOOK THREE

DILLON BANCROFT

OUT OF MY MIND - A SNIPPET

JAY

In the city that never sleeps, it's impossible to be singled out by the people searching for you. Most people don't have the resources I've been generously lent. Said resource assured me he would be here. He'd be lying low, paying cash, and only leaving his hidey-hole if it was absolutely necessary.

Tanner Novak is a computer genius and a fucking great Marine. It's truly their loss that he decided he was done. I'm grateful he was willing to help me and keep it on the down-low from Derek and Steve.

At the moment, I run on retribution. Dominic Reese sunk three bullets in my gut and left me for dead with the intention of killing everyone I love. I'm a ghost in the night to him and his organization, which is why ending his life will give me the *best* satisfaction.

In the underbelly of Harlem is a dilapidated apartment building where bad things happen and nobody even blinks. With the untraceable Sig Sauer weighing heavy in my pocket, I know that when I cross the threshold of that apartment, I go in as the good ol' boy from Sage Creek, Virginia, but I'll come out a murderer.

What becomes of my soul? That's for whoever's waiting for me in the great beyond to decide.

I lost everything. And I won't stop until he loses everything too.

My intel tells me he's left the building to replenish his food supply. For hired muscle, he's an idiot for keeping his routine predictable. The exterior door is propped open by a large rock. *Thank you, hoodlums.* Reese's apartment is on the top floor, not that it will resemble anything like the penthouses he's used to shacking up in.

I race up the stairs, skipping a step with my ascension. When I reach the fifth floor, I reach for the handle and roll my eyes when the doorknob doesn't give. It's nothing a credit card can't fix.

I have to give it to the guy. He's resourceful. He's rigged up an alarm that won't notify the police. It's a simple trip wire that will send a full-sized dresser toppling to the ground. I step over it and limp over to the lone red recliner in the middle of his living room. The dusty, hardwood floors aren't there for decoration, and if he ends up falling through the rotten wood, I wouldn't rush to help him.

The earpiece in my ear crackles.

"He's on his way back, Parker. Sit tight."

Tanner is the only one who knows where I am. He figured I deserved some justice after the hand I was dealt.

"Do what you need to do and get out. My contact is waiting in the alleyway. *Do not* draw this out. Do you hear me?"

"Loud and clear," I reply, though I have every intention of dragging it out. The door opens. The little bit of light from the flickering hallway sconces bathe the room in a dim glow. Our eyes meet, and when I'm certain it's him, I pull the Sig Sauer out of my pocket and fire a shot into his leg.

He hits the ground like a sack of potatoes, and I'm disappointed he didn't fall through the floor.

"Fuck!" he shouts. I race across the room and lock the door. Everything inside of me is on fire. It's been a month since I left Annie's house. I haven't been to any of my PT appointments, and the kickback from the gun has me hissing in pain from my healing collarbone.

I crouch down beside him, ignoring the pain. His eyes widen in surprise.

"Hello, Reese," I greet, even-toned. "I'm surprised to see you alive."

He growls through the pain, putting pressure on the bullet hole. Crimson leaks from between his fingers. He won't have long.

"Right back at you, Parker."

Grinning, I stand up and place the gun on the bar. "I need some information."

"You fucked up your leverage, idiot. You shot me, and I'm losing a fuck ton of blood. I'll be dead in mere minutes. You're not getting a morsel out of me."

I shrug indifferently. "See, I know a guy. He can bring you back from the brink of death." He's a veterinarian, and he has no idea I'm here. Here's to hoping he doesn't call my bluff. When Reese doesn't say anything, I take that as my cue to continue spewing my bullshit. "You said you were going after Steve. Why?"

"The man you consider a father is no saint. He's left bodies that could wrap around the Earth at least twice."

He shifts so that he's sitting up, and his agonizing scream fills the apartment. Blood covers the floor.

I don't buy what he's selling. Steve is a farmer. He's the leader of the little vigilante group, but they only go after the people that wronged them.

"Explain."

He struggles to catch his breath. Sweat gushes out of his pores. *Suffer like I did, bitch.*

"He killed my parents." He rests his head against the wall behind him. "London. 1985."

"Steve would never go to London."

"He killed them right in front of me, dickwad. I know what I saw." He takes a deep breath and starts to shake. "Why did you join the military, Parker?"

I don't answer.

"People join to serve their country and whatever patriotic bullshit they spew. It's easy to command people who have the same agenda."

"What is he talking about?" Tanner barks in my ear. "Keep him talking, Parker," he growls.

"What are you saying? You're part of someone's war?"

He coughs. "Like I said. He's no saint. His body count is larger than you could ever imagine."

I don't believe a word he's saying, yet something in my gut is telling me to hear him out.

"Banks has an army. Hundreds, maybe thousands, of people who have a grievance against that man."

"Who is Banks?" I demand.

"Ever heard the saying, 'Hell hath no fury like a woman scorned'?" With a sinister grin, he takes his hand off the wound and blood gushes out.

"Get out of there, Parker. *Now!*" I slide the window open, grab the Sig Sauer off the bar, and race down the fire escape.

The streets are empty. Sirens sound off from every direction, though none will come this way. Tanner guides me out of the maze of the worst part of Harlem to a convenience store in a better part of town.

He has me buy a pack of cigarettes, a lighter, and a can of sweet tea. I stand in front of the store and wait for whatever contact he has in the area.

A silver Honda crawls to stop in front of me. I don't waste any time throwing myself into the passenger seat.

The driver is none other than Tanner himself, and he's beyond pissed. He grips the steering wheel so tight that his knuckles turn white.

"Nobody hears about this; do you understand me?" he barks.

"I shot and killed a guy, Novak. *No shit* nobody hears about this!"

Tanner nods once and stays quiet while he navigates the streets of the city. An hour later, we're in the heart of Brooklyn.

"What did he mean by that quote?" I ask.

Tanner's jaw ticks. "I don't even know if it's true. He confirmed Banks is a woman. It sounds like Steve did Banks wrong."

"Steve's been with Betty Lou forever. There's no way there's another woman." Tanner street parks and leaves the car running. His chocolate-brown eyes meet mine.

"There is a huge chunk of time between the time he left high school and got married that nobody knows anything about. Don't be naïve."

He can't be right. Steve doesn't socialize. He's the king of being annoyingly antisocial.

"Are you going to look into him?"

The silence in the car speaks volumes.

"I need to talk to everyone else first."

AUTHOR'S NOTE

Okay, okay, put your pitchforks down. I know you're probably livid with me, and you probably want to explode on me. I've anticipated this.

But I desperately, desperately need you to know that too much happens in Book Three that I couldn't fit it into one book. Trust the process, y'all. That's all I'm asking.

I truly never meant for this series to become autobiographical, but here we are. I'm not saying this is what happened with my husband and me, but there are some elements that remain very true.

My husband separated from the Marine Corps in 2013. We had these grand plans on how we thought our lives would go, but the one thing we never took into account was the excruciating and inevitable identity crisis he would go through.

Now, I'm not going to completely vomit his story for you, but it's true what they say: They tear you down, to bring you back up, but they never teach you how to come home. He knew how to be part of a brotherhood. He completely understood and took to heart the "honor, integrity, justice." How do you go back to being a civilian after all of the early morning formations? The company runs, the camaraderie you've grown accustomed to for so long?

It wasn't easy. A lot of the time I prayed to whoever was out there listening that he would go and talk to someone. Anyone. But needless to say, he's grown. It wasn't pretty or romantic. It was raw and real and sometimes really fucking painful for everyone in our family.

Healing is not a quick process. And while it's been almost a decade since he's left, the Bancroft household still holds on to so many memories. His Staff Sergeant has retired and lives an hour away from us. A fellow Sergeant lives on the other side of the state. But still, we've made somewhat of a dysfunctional family with them. Life isn't the same, but we continue pushing forward.

WHAT DID YOU THINK?

Did you love it? Like it? Hate it?

Let me know by leaving a review!

Did you know I also have a reader group? Whether you want to gush about the characters or talk about the future of the Sage Creek Series, feel free to join me on the Boulevard! We'd love to have you!

Bancroft Boulevard Reader Group!

ACKNOWLEDGMENTS

It took me WAY too long to write this book. I finished the first draft in November 2021 and I pretty much took a wrecking ball to it and started over. This version is so much better—in my totally *unbiased* opinion. As always, there are so many people who have had a hand in this book—and I'm not just talking about the writing either. So let's get into it, shall we?

To the Bancrofts that reside in the same house as me - Thanks for being cool about me playing the same music on a loop for hours on end. Thanks for being cool about me breaking my "no working on weekends" rule and being patient. You guys are the apples of my eye, the chaos I love so much, and my reason for living.

Jessica - I don't think thank you begins to cover what you do for me. I'm sure you roll your eyes when my name pops up on your phone, asking the same question every single time, "What's that thing I'm thinking of?" when I have absolutely no idea what I'm even thinking about. Also, when I found out the gut punching twist to the series and I texted you in the dead of night to tell you, even though it came out of no where—basically, thank you for being my sounding board. You are the bomb dot com and I love you so much!

My beta readers, Jessica, Scarlette, Andrea, Lauren, Amy, and Jackie - First and foremost, THANK YOU for reading this twice. I know you guys are busy, but I truly value your opinions and feedback. (I also apologize that you had to read it twice!)

My editor, Kimberly Steinke - Holy moly, lady! We did it! This book was the thorn in my side and this couldn't have been done without you. Thank you so much for your brutal honesty, your thorough notes, and your friendship through all of this!

My proofreader, Jackie: Thank you so for offering your help on this! Your initial comments during the beta read helped make this an easier read for those who haven't read the first book. I really appreciate the time you took (especially during your VACATION!) to read this through again.

Laura Mowery - My best friend, the sister to my soul, my work wife—thank you so much for letting me vent and complain to you! You've been the rock I've so needed—otherwise I would've quit by now! Thank you for being my release buddy and I can't wait to read Code name: Grizzly!

Last, but never least, to my friends and family - I'm sure you're all tired of me by now, but your constant and unwavering support has been felt. The phone calls, the prayers, the text messages, the messages through messenger, the comments—everything is appreciated more than you could ever know. Thank you for sticking with me through all of this. I love you all so much!

ABOUT THE AUTHOR

Dillon Bancroft is a Contemporary Romance Author based in Tampa, Florida. She was always considered a dreamer, and was constantly scolded as a student to get her head out of the clouds and pay attention.

She is a mother to two crazy girls and wife to a former marine who has enhanced her vocabulary in the worst ways, but has supported her through all of her hare-brained ideas.

She is a sucker for second chance romances, puppies, and cheesy Christmas movies on the Hallmark Channel. She watches entirely too much TV and quotes very obscure lines in popular TV shows.

LOOKING TO CONNECT?

Do you want to stay in the know and receive behind the scenes musings, deleted scenes, and upcoming project updates? Signing up for my newsletter is the best way to do that!

Email: dillon@dillonbancroft.com

Social Media Profiles: https://linktr.ee/dillon.bancroft

Website: www.dillonbancroft.com

Bancroft Boulevard Facebook Group: https://www.facebook.com/groups/bancroftblvd

ALSO BY DILLON BANCROFT

Standalones

Back and Forth

The Sage Creek Series

Make Me Dream

Out of My Head

Out of My Mind

Give You Hell

One and Only

Made in the USA
Middletown, DE
16 September 2024